I0582504

A Dose of Discovery

Book 2

Big Pharma Series

By Lotus James

Lotus James

A Dose of Discovery – Big Pharma Series
Copyright © 2022 Lotus James

ISBN: 978-1-7359745-6-9 (Paperback)

Library of Congress TX0009190034

First Paperback Edition October 2022

This is a work of fiction. Names, characters, places, incidents, and events are either the product of the author's imagination or are used fictitiously for entertainment. Any resemblance to actual persons, living or dead, is coincidental.

Inquiries/Permissions:
Life Garden Publishing Inc.
P.O. Box 333
Borden, IN 47106 USA
Lifegardenpublishing.com

Table of Contents

Chapter 1 ~ Reunited

Christmas Eve, 2019

Jack Foster followed the resort manager down the hall from the reception check-in area. The man had been gracious to trust that his father had money and would pay for his accommodations. Exhausted and limping with his leg, he struggled to keep up the pace with the man's quick strides.

They finally reached the room and Jack stood back, leaning his arm against the opposite wall as the manager opened the door of room 1224. He flipped on a light switch and motioned for Jack to enter. Once inside, the manager left the door ajar as he made a quick walk through, pointing out amenities. The best one Jack had noticed so far was air conditioning. This was something he had really missed in the sweltering heat of the jungle.

"Is there anything else I can get you?" he asked.

Jack thought for a few seconds. "No, this is very nice. Thank you."

"Let us know if you need anything. Here is the phone with instructions should you need room service or the front desk."

"Yes, of course. Thanks again," he said, walking with the manager toward the door. He shut the heavy wooden door and ran his fingers through his hair. Filthy, that's how he felt. Never had a bathroom looked so inviting.

He entered the tiled room and could not wait to get the clothes he had been wearing for a long time off his body. How long, he wasn't sure. His mind was still fuzzy about so many things. But he had not forgotten how great it was to have a hot shower.

Hot water pulsated from the shower head as he stood a long time letting it run down his back. Headaches were still a daily occurrence. Carefully, he shampooed noting there was a large area that still felt tender. Reaching up, he massaged his shoulders and upper back muscles to relieve some of the tight pressure he felt.

The room was steamy as he stepped out. He dried off, wrapping a towel around his waistline which was a tad slimmer. The clothes he wore to the hotel appeared too soiled to wear, possibly ever -- even if washed. *What now?* He took his hand and cleared the fogged mirror above the sink. While the hotel had provided soap, shampoo, conditioner, and a small comb, there was no razor. He combed through his hair when he heard a knock at the door. Assuming it was hotel staff, he stood behind the door as he asked, "Who is it?"

"Jack, it's me Jason." Hurriedly, Jack swung the door open almost losing the towel at his waist.

"Jason that was fast, you must have been close."

"I was. We've had a team looking for you. Myself and another guy were only 15 minutes away from here. Small world, huh?"

Jack laughed. "Brother, it's so good to see you. Thank God you're here."

"You're looking a little shaggier than the last time I saw you," Jason chided. "Honestly, I am so damn happy to see you!"

"Someone tried to kill us in that plane. What do you know about Sercy, Ethan, and Lance?"

Jason realized Jack knew little of what had occurred. "They're gone, Jack. I'm so sorry!"

"And the pilot?"

"Yes, he died also."

A solemn expression came over Jack's face. He sat on the edge of the bed and stared at the floor. "I can't fucking believe they would do this to us!" Jack raged.

"Jack, you need to share some information with us, at least with me. We need to solve this crime. First, you need some clothing."

Jason sat a large duffel bag on the dresser and unzipped it. "Let's get you a new outfit. Have you been wearing the same clothes all this time?"

"Yes, I have," Jack responded, almost apathetically.

"There's another guy traveling with me. His name is Lucas. He's been a tremendous help in navigating things here in Brazil. He's picking up food for us and will be here soon."

"Sounds good. I'm starving."

"I see you're wearing the green heart stone. Must have brought you some good luck."

Jack felt for the stone around his neck with his fingers. "I'm not sure where I got this. Maybe one of the women at the village gave it to me, or an elder there. The strange thing is I know I'm not supposed to take it off."

Jason knew who had given him the stone. It was from Haley, the wife back home in the United States that Jack could not remember.

Jason handed a pair of cargo pants, underwear, socks, and a shirt to his brother. Jack began dressing, walking back toward the bathroom to hang up the towel when he was finished. He returned and propped pillows up on the bed and reclined against them. Jason sat down in a chair opposite the bed beside the window.

"Who would want to get rid of you and your team, Jack? It has to be someone up high at Chadwell."

Jack leaned back further, relaxing more and put his arms behind his head.

"Well, they didn't succeed in getting me. But I am hit hard about my team members and the pilot being killed. I suspect this is the work of Tellinger and others above him that we don't see or hear from often."

"Why would he do that, Jack? You've made them a lot of money with your work."

"It's a story that still has pieces missing. Many of the projects we worked on were compartmentalized, similar to how the government works within their various agencies. No one knew every piece of the puzzle. In my position, I had many of the pieces collected and could roughly decipher what was going down in the near future."

Jason listened as his brother continued, "Let's just say I didn't like their plans. I let Tellinger know this. Since that time, I've been careful to keep my mouth shut and do my work as requested and do it well. But I felt a huge resistance from Tellinger after that."

Jason shifted in his chair leaning closer to Jack. "I know you have always been tight-lipped, but what were you working on?"

"A parasitic plant that grows almost like Spanish moss does back home. I isolated its anti-viral properties and started testing it in several mediums. We found that when it was combined with another element, it was an antidote for many viruses. It showed tremendous promise in that way."

"Why would that make anyone want to eliminate you and your team?" Jason asked.

"There is something coming. Something that they don't want a treatment for except the protocol they have planned. It will be a huge moneymaker not only for Chadwell, but other pharmaceutical companies around the world. That's all I can tell you right now."

"Is that because you're having trouble remembering what's coming?"

"No. I remember."

"What's coming, Jack?"

"I'm not sure exactly. Something that will affect everyone worldwide or at least that's how it's been described to me. We're talking a plague of some sort."

Jason looked perplexed. "How can they know that?"

Jack chuckled sarcastically. "They pay people a lot of money to predict these things. I'd say there's an agenda behind all of it and that's why it's highly probable it's going to happen. The drug my team and I were working on may have not been ready as a remedy fast enough. There are so many trials it would have to go through first. We also had a difficult time propagating the plant outside its natural environment. We did get a successful animal study with it. The first one was sabotaged."

"It sounds like you've been fighting a battle to make this drug happen. "

"Let's just say they wanted me to pull off that project. But, I don't work like that — never have. If I see promise in something, I follow it. I suspect that pissed Tellinger off."

"But couldn't they have made money from the drug you were developing?"

"Oh yes, they could have patented it and made a lot of money until it went generic later. There's something else going on here though with what they're planning. As I said, think compartmentalized. I'm not privy to all of the pieces of this puzzle. I know just a little more, but it's technical stuff that I'll leave for later, if necessary."

A knock at the door interrupted the conversation. "Let's keep this only between you and me for now," Jack requested. Jason nodded in agreement and answered the door, finding Lucas with their dinner.

"Christmas Eve dinner is delivered or the closest thing I could find," he said smiling.

Chapter 2 ~ Video Call

Christmas Day, 2019

Haley and Sonya began gathering the used dessert plates and silverware from the dining room table where they anticipated Sarah would set up her laptop. The announcement by her in-laws of Jack's survival was beyond a wish come true. Expectation filled the air as an instrumental of *The Christmas Song* played softly in the background. The entire family anxiously anticipated finally seeing Jack alive.

Despite the heightened feeling of celebration, Haley detected some fear inside of her too. The length of time her husband had been gone seemed extended into months, instead of weeks. Gone since early December, Jack was alive and it was almost as if it was too good to be true. A deep, nagging worry felt stuck in her chest, a feeling that something could snatch this new reality away from her in an instant.

Papa Foster broke the news gently to her. Jack did not remember her right now or that he was married. She wondered what else he had forgotten. Familiar with various forms of memory loss from her training as a nurse, she hoped he would regain everything and soon. But her husband was alive, and this was a miracle, one they had prayed for.

Haley smiled as big Uncle Mike sat on the floor putting together the race car set given to Sarah and Jason's children. She watched as Sonya picked up stray ribbons and bows on the living room floor and placed them in a small box. Jack being alive was the best gift they could hope for. A stray tear slid down her face and she did not bother hiding her emotional state.

Sarah slid beside her as she stood in the kitchen doorway. "It's going to be okay, Haley. You have been through so much emotionally, but this is going to come to an end. Soon, you will see Jack and I know his memory will come back. There's no way he could forget you for long."

"I know. I believe he will remember. All this time, I struggled with staying as positive as I could about him being alive. It was very difficult, but not impossible. With this memory loss situation, I will stay positive too. He probably needs to see an actual doctor and have some tests."

"We'll ask about that when they come online in a few minutes. I'm going to make sure everything is ready to go."

"Thank you, Sarah," Haley said, grabbing her sister-in-law in a tight embrace before letting her go.

Joe Foster paced the floor as the time was nearing for the video call. Overall, he was all smiles today, something Haley had not seen from her father-in-law since this nightmare began. Sharon sat in a chair in the dining room, patiently waiting to see both of her sons.

As the time neared for the call, everyone stopped their activities and began gathering. Uncle Mike and Aunt Molly stood in one corner of the dining room wanting to allow more immediate family members their choice of chairs first. Sonya joined and stood by their side. One by one, they were all in their own way waiting with stifled excitement for the big Christmas gift — seeing Jack alive.

Sarah and Haley sat close to the computer. Each held one of Sarah's and Jason's children on their laps. The room was quiet now as Sarah waited for the call to connect. And then, he was there. Right beside Jason and wearing the malachite stone on the leather cord around his neck. Haley squeezed her fingernails into the palms of her hands hard. She wanted to yell at Jack, declare her love, or do something significant. But she sat there with fists clinched feeling anxiety combined with relief at the sight of him.

Haley's eyes scanned the image of both her husband and his twin, Jason, on the screen. No longer did they look alike. Instead, Jack's hair had grown considerably. Her eyes began watering, but she vowed to hold herself together emotionally.

Sharon's eyes began tearing as she saw both of her sons. The entire Christmas clan gathered around the dining room table where the laptop came alive with the image of the two brothers. In an unusual move, Jack looked to his brother to begin the conversation.

"Can you guys hear me?" Jason asked.

Sarah spoke up quickly, "Your voice is coming through fine. Can you hear me?"

"Yes, and I miss you and those two munchkins I'm seeing right now. I miss you all! Merry Christmas everyone."

In unison, everyone called out, "Merry Christmas!"

Jack smiled and said, "Merry Christmas!"

Other than the Christmas wish, Haley stayed quiet. Papa Joe initiated the conversation. "Jack, seeing you and being able to speak with you is the best gift any of us could ask for. We are so glad you are alive and you found a way to reach out to us. Do you recognize where we are right now?"

"No, I can't see much detail, only people," he replied.

"Okay, do you recognize anyone?"

"Yes, I see you and mom. I also see Sarah, Allison and little Eli."

"Anyone else?" his father asked.

"No, not right now, but I'm having some trouble."

"That's why it might be a good idea to have you seen by a doctor or hospital in Brazil before the trip back here to the United States. What do you think?"

Jack looked at Jason and scowled. Jason spoke up. "Dad, right now might not be good. Jack is convinced there are those who want him gone. I feel his reasoning is sound on this. He's limping a bit. His leg appears to have been injured. Some indigenous people in a remote village have been caring for him. Jack told me today how they were able to get him walking again. If Jack goes anywhere for medical treatment, his name could slip into the computer networks. He would be discovered as being alive. Right now, he wants Chadwell or whoever is behind this to believe he's dead."

Jack got closer to the screen and appeared a little larger. "Dad, listen. I am breathing and getting around okay. It bothers me that I cannot remember everything, but I don't want to be noticed by anyone right now or they may kill me."

Sarah spoke next, "Jack, we understand and do not want anything to happen to you. I cannot tell you how we have all cried and prayed for your life. Jason, how can we get him back to the United States without them knowing?"

"I've been thinking about that. The only idea I have come up with is to let him fly back impersonating me with my passport."

"Well, how will you get home?" she asked.

"I would have to risk waiting for Jack to arrive and then reporting my passport as lost to the embassy here."

Joe Foster looked frustrated, "There must be someone who could at least examine him. Could we bring a private doctor to the hotel, Jason?"

Jack spoke up again. "Dad, I'm getting around fine. One thing I want to do before I leave here is go back to the people who helped me. I want to make an offering to them for the care they gave me. I might not have made it alive otherwise. Jason can go with me."

"Okay, how far away is the place you have to travel to?"

"It's a couple of hours, at least."

"I understand, Jack." Papa Foster hesitated and then felt compelled to ask the looming question, "How did you survive that crash, Jack?"

Everyone fell silent.

"By the grace of God, I suppose. I am struggling to remember. Why am I alive and everyone else didn't make it? I suppose I have as many questions surrounding it as you do."

Chapter 3 ~ Aftermath

Haley glanced once more at the Christmas tree Jack had purchased and helped her decorate weeks ago. She clicked the lights off and made her way toward bed. She could hear Uncle Mike and Aunt Molly talking in their bedroom even though the door was closed. Sonya was probably watching television in her room. She was glad to have her family here during Christmas.

Seeing Jack on the call tonight was exhilarating, but also frustrating. He truly didn't know who she was. She wondered if she looked somewhat familiar to him. She grabbed her cell phone and scrolled through recent photos, searching for one that had the two of them together. There weren't many. Most were only of Jack or places they had been. But there was one she had saved on her phone, a favorite. It was a photograph taken by their waiter on their last night out in Savannah, Georgia.

Haley cued the picture to send to Jason with a message:

Jason, thank you for all you're doing. I know Jack doesn't recognize me, but I wanted to send this to you.

Maybe it will get some response from him. Taken during our last dinner out in Savannah, Georgia when we were dating. Love to you both xoxo

Haley brushed her teeth and changed into a warm pair of pajamas. She normally didn't wear anything so heavy to bed, but tonight, it felt comforting to her body. The soft flannel seemed to create a barrier that made her feel safe and calm.

Why am I not overjoyed right now? My husband is alive. 'Tis the season, she thought.

It was like a big emotional build up before Christmas as a child, only to be disappointed that you did not fully get what you wanted. Like receiving a knockoff brand of the toy you had dreamed about.

Jack did not know who she was. Her husband had been through a damn plane crash and survived. From her medical training, she knew this could be typical for traumatic events. Sometimes severe trauma could cause dissociative memory loss. Hopefully, that would change, but what if it didn't? Haley knew she would still love him anyway. That, she knew. But she needed him loving her back. She wished he could get some immediate medical care to see if anything could be done for his leg and his memory.

Haley slid into the bed she and Jack had made tender memories in. She remembered everything. As she pulled the down comforter and sheet up to her waist, she wondered why Jack's mind would choose to forget her, but remember other people. Did he remember their home or was that memory erased too? What about their friends next door, Jessie and Alex? Had Jack forgotten about what he was working on?

All these questions swirled in her mind until her brain felt like it would split in two. She was angry at herself for being selfish right now. *He's alive! It should not matter to you if he can't remember.*

But if she was honest, it mattered. And that was a truth she had to face about herself. This whole situation revealed to her that while she was terribly concerned about Jack, she was more concerned about herself. She hated that she was like this. Why couldn't she just go with the flow and stop thinking like this?

It's like she felt slighted by Jack not remembering her. There was a feeling of being wiped out, abandoned. It was a familiar emotion that ran in the background consistently during her childhood.

She grabbed the pillow Jack always used, his favorite that still carried his scent. Haley had declared the pillowcase would not be changed — not until he was back in their bed. Seeing him tonight on that screen was wonderful, but it created more questions! When would he be here by her side?

Haley could not hold her feelings inside another fraction of a moment. She pressed her face into Jack's pillow inhaling the last traces of him. She kept her face there, coming up for air periodically as she attempted to muffle her sobs. Significant time passed until she finally stopped crying.

She raised from the bed, reaching for tissues on the night side table. After blowing her nose, she prayed aloud.

"Thank you for keeping him alive somehow. Thank you, God!"

Rolling over on her back, Haley told herself that she needed to stay emotionally steady right now. There was still a lot to work out about Jack's return and going forward. All had agreed tonight that his survival was completely top secret. No one outside the persons in the house tonight could know Jack was alive. That included their best friends next door. It didn't mean it would be secret forever, but at least for now.

Chadwell's insurance company had mailed her a large check for Jack's life insurance policy. She had placed it in the middle drawer of his desk. While it would be wonderful to have that money, she would rather have Jack and at some point, people would know he was alive. Right now, they needed to make sure he stayed that way.

It occurred to her throughout these weeks, she had been forgetting something very important Jack told her before he left. He said there was information on his current project hidden in their home somewhere. When she asked about the location, he told her not to worry about it. If Jack didn't remember Haley, how could he remember the house they bought together — the one where they planned to raise a family? How would he remember where he hid the information? She had to find Jack's hiding place. Tomorrow, the search would begin.

Chapter 4 ~ Confidential

Brazil, Christmas Day, 2019

Jason turned to look at Jack after the call home ended. "What now, brother?"

"She's beautiful. And, you say she's my wife?" Jack asked in a low voice.

"Yes, Haley is your wife and prior to this accident, you lived and breathed her, Jack."

"How did we meet?" Jack asked pausing and then hitting his fist hard on top of the dresser. "No, don't tell me. I've got to remember!" he snarled.

"Give it some more time," Jason said reassuringly. He wondered how difficult it must be for his brother right now. "Listen, you are the bravest, bad-ass scientist on the planet right now. You've been through a lot. I don't even know what all has happened to you. Be easy with yourself. Everyone is so happy you are alive. Besides, we need to worry about getting you back to the states."

"Yep, you're right."

Lucas stood and used his finger to slightly open the drapes. He kept the gap just large enough to peer outside into the courtyard of the hotel. Only lush tropical foliage and a view of three people in the pool area were visible.

"See anything interesting?" Jason asked.

"No, not many people and quiet. But, it is Christmas day."

Jason looked at Jack nervously. "Anyone could be following Lucas and I. Hell, they could already know you're alive, but I doubt it."

"Why are you talking like this, Jason?"

"Because we have to be more cautious than ever. I can't let anything happen."

"Hey, we're invincible together — just like when we were about twelve years old."

"Jack, we are a team and a formidable one. But we almost lost you and three of your coworkers are gone."

As soon as Jason mentioned this, Jack grabbed his head and bent over looking at the floor. He had tried not to think about losing Sercy, his employee and friend who totally missed his calling as a stand-up comedian. He was a hell of a funny guy.

Jack would not forget the dedication he had from Ethan and Lance. It was unparalleled. He would never find people like them again. Whoever was behind this needed to pay dearly for their lives. Loved ones left behind should receive justice and compensation.

"Haley, your wife, met with the spouses of each of them, Jack. There are a lot of people back home and some here working on finding who is behind what happened on that plane. I cannot risk anything happening to you again. That's all I'm saying. We've just got to be as careful as we can."

He was silent and just looked at Jason for a moment. "I understand. Hey Lucas, what do you do when you're not here with us?" Jack asked, changing the subject.

Lucas lightly chuckled. "I serve as private security for various individuals from time to time. When I'm not doing this, I have a small company selling gear for rain forest expeditions."

"Interesting. I had some new gear I was anxious to give a try, but it went down with the plane," Jack replied.

"Do you know where the village is that you want to visit?" Lucas asked.

Jack smiled, "I think I remember how to get back there."

"You think?" Jason asked, smiling broadly.

"Yeah, I'm pretty sure I do. It's a few hours from here toward the west. The roads were actually pretty good. What kind of vehicle do you have, Lucas?"

Lucas spoke up, "A Jeep."

"Ah, that's my style," Jack said. "I've always driven a jeep."

Lucas gave Jack a thumbs up. "It sounds like we should probably plan an overnight stay at the village. By the time we collect food and other things for the trip in the morning, we will probably make it there by late afternoon or early evening."

"They are very gracious people. I'm sure they would allow an overnight stay," Jack replied.

Jason felt bad pushing the subject, but he had to ask. "Are you sure we have to make this visit, Jack? We need to get you back home."

"It would haunt me if I didn't make an offering of goods to their tribe. They really did rescue and heal me back to health."

"Alright. I can understand it's important to you. We'll use my credit card tomorrow to purchase goods to take to them. Might be a good time to get you a shave and a haircut so that you'll look like your regular self. I think we'll let you use my passport to fly back. Then, I'll go to the embassy here and claim my passport is lost or stolen to get a new one."

Lucas spoke up, "I think we need to wait until you're close to boarding a plane before we make you look alike again. Identical twins are something people notice and may talk about if you're both seen together. If the people who are after you have been watching your brother and I, we can't have a third person showing up that looks like Jason also. That would be a real giveaway. We need to make you look even more different."

"You're right. How can we make my brother look even scruffier than he does now?" Jason chuckled.

"If we dyed his hair lighter, that might help, but that puts us in a predicament for the trip home with your passport."

Jack laughed, "Good, I'm glad that option's off the table."

Luke studied Jack for a moment. I think if we tie a bandana around his head that would help. He's going to need a hat also. The faster his facial hair grows, the better. Once we come back from the village, we can get him cleaned up at a barber in town and a flight booked."

"Well, I vote we get some sleep. Sounds like we're going to need to be at peak performance for the next couple of days," Jason said.

Jack nodded in agreement and pointed at the two double beds in the room.

"Lucas, you take the bed closest to the door since you're armed. Jason and I will bunk in the other one."

"Good plan," Lucas replied.

Jack awoke to Lucas coming into the room with coffee, setting the drinks on the dresser. He was not aware the man had left, sleeping through it all. He knew his father must be paying a lot of money for this type of detailed security. Jack needed to get home. Perhaps he could travel to the village during another trip. He was feeling a sense of urgency to get back to the United States now.

His eyes feeling lazy, he watched as Jason and Lucas stood huddled over a map of the area spread out on the opposite bed. They were curious, no doubt, about where Jack had planned to take them. He made a trip to the bathroom and splashed some water on his face. Today felt different. His priorities had changed. He might as well unravel last night's plan and tell Jason.

"Listen you guys, I feel like I should get back home sooner, rather than later."

"Really?" Jason asked, looking surprised. "It seemed so important for you to make the trip to the village."

"It is, but I think I better put it on hold and do it during a future trip here. There's just something nagging at me to get back home. I can't explain it, really. Plus, I know dad's spending a lot of money financing this venture. I don't feel right about extending the time here. You are concerned about someone harming us and rightfully so. Time to get the hell out of here and return under safer conditions."

"Okay, we can make that happen. I think it's a good call," Jason said. "I'll look into flights now. We'll need to figure in travel time to the airport and making you look like me at the barber."

The three men downed their coffee and packed what few belongings they carried.

"I think it would be better if Jack let the front desk know he's leaving. We can wait for him in my jeep. That way, we are not seen with him." Lucas said.

"What about that, Jack?" Jason asked.

"I can do it. You guys just wait for me where you won't be noticed. I'll let them know they can tally up the bill and charge it to the card on file."

The three split up as agreed and Jack hobbled to the desk at the front of the hotel. A small older woman with dark hair pulled back in a chignon smiled at him. "Posso te ajudar, senhor?"

"Voce fala ingles?" Jack asked, hoping she spoke his language.

"Yes, I do," she answered.

"Great! I'm Jack Foster. Room 1224. Just checking out now and wanted to let you know."

"Did you enjoy your stay?"

"Yes, everything was perfect."

"Thank you for your business. Did you want to use the card on file?"

"Yes, please."

"Okay, I will take care of that now and print your receipt."

Jack waited as she charged his father's card and the receipt printed. He thanked her again as she handed it to him along with a customer survey card. He made his way toward the entrance doors and tried to walk as smoothly as he could without limping. The pain in his leg was dull, but sometimes he had sharp pain too if he had been on his leg too long. Overall, his pain was nothing like it was right after the crash.

As he exited the building, the wet humidity in the air hit him immediately. He spotted the jeep Lucas and Jason were in and walked toward it. As he did so, he felt as if something was behind him or someone was watching him. He hesitated and turned, but saw no one. Just being paranoid, he thought.

Jason emerged as he approached the vehicle and directed Jack to sit in the back. They pulled out and made their way down the steep terrain toward the town below. In his rear view and side mirror, Lucas kept an eye out for anyone that could be following them. There was no one — not a single vehicle behind them at all.

Chapter 5 ~ Undercover

Thursday, December 26, 2019

Lucky studied the map and data on her phone's screen which revealed each place Evan Mitchell had traveled to in his car. It hadn't been many days since she placed the tracker on the bottom of his Porsche. It was also the holidays, but she noticed he had gone nowhere on Christmas Eve or day. Maybe he entertained guests for the holiday at his condo.

Besides a large grocery chain store and Chadwell Pharmaceuticals, he had only driven to a bakery and a bar in a rundown area of Atlanta. He must have a sweet tooth or picked up goodies for Christmas. But the bar was a big question. That looked out of character for a guy who dressed to the nines and held his position at Chadwell. The bar definitely peaked Lucky's interest.

Unfortunately, Evan had not signed up for her yoga or Pilates classes at the clubhouse. She had not seen him inside the facility either. She wondered if there was a way to view times the residents came and went. Since they had to use a key card, there must be some digital evidence of them arriving. She placed a call to Ric Hartford, someone she knew might be able to get her that information.

"Hey Ric, how was Christmas?"

"Santa didn't bring what I was hoping for?"

"And, that was?" Lucky asked, chuckling.

"I was hoping for a car like Evan's — a Porsche, you know."

"Ric, I don't want to burst your bubble, but you're a good guy. You're not an ass kisser or dirty deed doer as I suspect Evan Mitchell is. So, you may never own a Porsche."

"Wrong, Lucky. I'll buy it for pennies on the dollar when he needs to put together a legal team for his defense," Ric said, laughing loudly.

Lucky laughed along with him, "Feeling confident today? Got something?"

"Not enough to convict, but collecting and uncovering things people thought were deleted and gone."

"Fantastic! I'm trying to get a "bump into" arranged between myself and Evan, but it's been tough. I was wondering if you could get me data on when the residents use their pass keys to enter the clubhouse so I could get an idea of any pattern he might have of going there."

"Maybe. I'll need to get in there physically to check out the setup first."

"Yeah, well, I can get you in. I teach a class tonight at seven. Come looking like you are there to exercise."

"I'll see you then."

"Can't wait."

Lucky sat looking again at the map on her phone of the bar. *Time to check that place out. What is his business there?*

She decided to dress as a house painter, driving her white van to the bar. Lucky had a ball cap hat which sported a popular paint brand and tennis shoes with numerous paint splatters from painting her own place a year ago. She wore a blue shirt and coveralls which also had unique Picasso-like paint splotches. Lucky finished her disguise with a dark brown, pageboy style wig.

It was easy to park her van across the street from the establishment. The bar didn't look busy, even though they advertised a lunch special. Situated in a two-story brick building which took up an entire city corner, it appeared to have living quarters on the second level. *Was Evan visiting the bar or someone upstairs?*

Lucky's paint splattered tennis shoes hit the old oak wood floors that were probably original to the structure. The place smelled like stale cigarette smoke and spilled drinks that had probably saturated into the wood flooring for many, many years.

Her eyes scanned the long bar and tables for any patrons present. There were only a few. A heavy set man sat at the bar eating what appeared to be a bowl of spaghetti and drinking a beer. Another man sat at the end of the bar talking on his phone. There were two men playing pool toward the back of the old tavern.

"What can I get you?" an older lady from behind the bar asked. She was a friendly sort. Lucky could tell by the lines on her face and the way her skin sagged she was not so much old, but had lived a rough life.

"I'll have what he's having, but with cream soda instead," she said, pointing to the heavy-set man.

The bartender quickly went into motion lifting a soup ladle of spaghetti and sauce from a large pot behind her into a bowl. She garnished it with a piece of garlic toast. Lucky watched as she filled a glass with ice and then poured in red cream soda. She placed it all in front of Lucky. "Pay now or later?"

"How much do I owe you?"

"Seven dollars," she replied.

Lucky pulled out a ten dollar bill and placed it on the counter. "Keep that for you."

"Thank you!" the woman said. "Haven't seen you here before."

"It's my first time. I'm helping rehab a building in the area. Do you have many women come into the bar?"

"We have mostly men, but a few come in, usually with their boyfriend or husband."

"How long have you worked here?"

"Eighteen years."

"Wow, that's quite a while."

"I inherited the place from my husband when he died along with a small life insurance amount. It's how I keep afloat."

"Looks like it could be lucrative," Lucky said, not elaborating. She knew this was the kind of place that stayed afloat with dirty deals and illegal trades.

"Yeah, I sold our house when he died which gave me a little extra after the mortgage was paid off. Now, I live upstairs. It's a short drive to work," she said, throwing her head back laughing.

Lucky laughed, "Short drive down the stairs. Do you have any other space in the building you're not using?"

"No, I guess you could say I take up the entire building. Say, I might want to get some painting done upstairs. How much do you charge?"

"I would need to see the space to know what you require. Then, I could give you a price. I have time to take a look when I get finished eating."

"Great, I'll get Ben here at the end of the bar to watch things for me when you're ready to go up."

The woman scurried toward the end of the bar with a towel wiping things as she went. She eventually landed at the end, speaking with Ben who was still on his phone. The bar owner must have mentioned taking Lucky upstairs, as he looked at her for a moment while she spoke to him. Lucky noticed the lady placed a kiss on

Ben's cheek before she fluttered away, checking to see if the man a few feet away wanted another beer.

With the kiss, it appeared Ben was at least a close friend, maybe a boyfriend. He had some sort of tie to the bar that was more than a usual customer. He took over as Lucky finished her cream soda and followed the lady who had now introduced herself as Alice.

The entrance to the apartment was outside the bar. They left, using a side door, and made their way around the rear of the building which held a set of steps. The two women climbed the wooden stairs which were in good shape, but needed a coat of stain. At the top of the staircase, Alice had a large rooftop deck with outdoor furnishings. Lucky could tell she was quite proud of it.

"This is really nice. You can sit up here and observe the stars."

Alice laughed. "Or, listen to the rowdy neighbors. Seriously though, this outdoor area is my little oasis at times. But, the wooden deck needs to be pressure washed and stained again. Come inside and I'll show you what I would like painted, at least to begin with."

Lucky followed Alice, knowing she would not be doing any painting, but wanted to see the upstairs of any place that Evan had frequented. Alice carried an extensive set of keys and unlocked three different locks in order to open the heavy door to her upstairs apartment.

Once they stepped inside, she flipped on a light switch. The scent of bacon having been fried recently lingered in the air. There was a long hallway that held all the rooms off to the right.

"I think the kitchen and bath need paint the most," Alice said, leading Lucky into the apartment.

"Okay, let me get a look at them and I'll come by again with an actual written estimate. Does that work for you?"

"Yeah, that would be great."

Lucky busied herself with estimating wall space in the rooms without a tape measure. It didn't matter. She would not be bringing the estimate to this lady ... or maybe she would. Who knew where this might lead. She needed to keep all options open. There was something going on at this location, the question was what?

"You have a few drywall repairs that will need to be made first. How soon did you want the painting to happen?" Lucky asked.

"I'm in no rush."

"Are the kitchen and bath the only rooms you need painted?"

"I think so for now. I don't want to get into moving a bunch of furniture. Things are tight in here already."

Lucky nodded her head in agreement. "It's the same way at my place."

"Okay, I'll drop by with an estimate once I get it worked up. Any idea what colors you want to use?"

"I'd like to stay in the same color range for the kitchen. What do you think about a light gray for the bath?"

Lucky walked back toward the bathroom and flipped the light switch on once more. "It would contrast nice in here. Light gray is a good choice."

"I thought so. Now, I do need the deck stained again." Alice walked her back toward the apartment entrance and they stepped outside.

"You have a lot of square footage on this deck. It's huge. I'll work up a separate bid for the pressure washing and staining of this area. Just so you know, it would be better to wait until late spring or early summer for this outdoor work. The stain will adhere better."

"Yes, I've heard that before."

Lucky walked off the deck's measurements and made a note on her phone.

"I'm guessing you want to include the staircase and landing off the deck as well, right?"

"Oh yes, it all needs to be done."

Lucky descended the steps, counting each one and making another note in her phone at the bottom of the staircase. Alice followed her and they walked at the side of the building toward the front of the bar.

"Well, I've taken a pretty long lunch now. I better get going. I'll be in touch," Lucky called making her way across the street toward her van.

"Have a great day. Drop off that estimate whenever you can. Thanks for stopping by," Alice yelled to her.

Lucky climbed into the van and placed her seatbelt on. She started up the engine and began driving away. As she did so, she looked in her left side view mirror and noticed Ben, the man who had been on the phone at the bar earlier, grabbing Alice by her arm in a rough manner. They appeared to have words. *Hmmm, this is interesting.*

Chapter 6 ~ Searching

The video call with Jack and Jason was still fresh on Haley's mind as she awoke. Her husband was alive. This is what counted. If Jack did not remember her, he probably didn't remember their house they bought together or where he hid information about the project he was working on.

Eager to begin the search, Haley wondered where he would put something that he wanted no one to find -- unless something happened to him. His office would be too obvious for a hiding spot. Maybe he put it in the basement somewhere. As daunting as it seemed, Haley decided that is where she would begin her search. She could put most of the Christmas decor away at the same time.

She would wait until Aunt Molly and Uncle Mike left to return to Valdosta. With hurried preparations for Christmas day and hosting the family, she had spent no real one-on-one time with them. She could hear the two of them in the kitchen with Sonya now. Haley quickly dressed and pulled her hair back, making her way out to greet everyone.

"Good morning," she said, smiling.

"Hey, good morning to you," Uncle Mike called back in his deep voice.

"Did you sleep well?" Aunt Molly asked.

"Once I fell asleep, I was out of it. How about you two? Is the bed comfortable in that room?"

"Yes, of course it feels different from home, but that's just because we're old and used to certain things. It's a wonderful bed and room," Aunt Molly added.

"Good, I'm so glad you guys came here for Christmas. I know you've never left home this time of year, but it was all the more special that you were here for the announcement that Jack was found alive."

"Yes, and I am so glad we could see him and his brother, Jason. Thank God for technology!" Uncle Mike said.

"How do you feel this morning about it all, Haley?" Sonya asked.

"Sonya, without you, the Christmas celebration would not have been so special. If I did not thank you before, I am now. To answer your question, I am overjoyed that Jack is walking, talking and …. alive. Did I wish he could remember everything? Yes, hopefully that will come."

Aunt Molly walked toward Haley and took her hand. "I think it will, honey."

"Me too. I must have the same faith he'll remember me that I had while hoping he was alive."

"Haley, do you think this means we can stop the investigation into what happened since he's been found?" Sonya asked.

"No. We have to find out who is behind this and keep the investigation going. Three people died in that crash along with the pilot. They were drugged or poisoned. It's a crime."

Sonya nodded understandably. "Well, I didn't know. But, you're right. It is a shameful, horrific crime."

Haley leaned with her back against the kitchen sink. "They might still want Jack gone. That's another thing to worry about."

Uncle Mike came toward her and held out his arms. "Give me a big bear hug young lady. We're going to head back. But, I want you to remember something important."

"What's that," Haley said, looking up at him.

"So far, everything is working out okay for you. God has a way and you keep your faith in him during this, Haley. Molly and I will be praying for you and Jack daily."

She hugged him tight and smelled his familiar cologne he always wore, probably since high school.

"You're right. Thank you."

"Miss Sonya, enjoy those art classes Haley gave you for Christmas," her father said.

"I will, dad. I really appreciate the gift and I know it's going to be fun," she said, looking at Haley.

They helped Mike and Molly to the car with their bags and stood outside in the frigid morning air until they could no longer stand it. They quickly waved goodbye.

"Inside, inside," Haley called to Sonya. "Burr, it is cold today."

"What would you like to do today?" Sonya asked.

"Well, I know what I'm going to do. You can help if you want."

"I have nothing on my agenda," Sonya replied.

"This is top secret work, truly. Before Jack went to Brazil, he told me there were notes or information on the project he was working on hidden in our house. He would not say where. We have to find them. There could be something in that information that reveals why someone might want him and the team gone."

"Wow, I wasn't expecting this, but it sort of sounds fun."

"It's probably going to be a real scavenger hunt, but without clues," Haley said.

"Do you think we can search everything here in a day?"

"Probably not. I was thinking of beginning with the basement. We could also put away some of the Christmas decor at the same time."

"Sounds like a good plan."

"You hungry?" Haley asked.

"Starving!"

"Okay, let's get something to eat first and then get started"

Haley decided the lights along the walkway outside and the wreaths could stay up for a while, especially with how cold it was. They would go ahead and dismantle the tree, sad as that was. The beautiful live tree had represented so many things to her since the night Jack bought it. But, it was losing more needles and not going to last too much longer.

The two ladies made a trip downstairs to retrieve the plastic tote boxes the tree decor would be stored in.

"Sonya, I'll do the tree ornaments. How about you do all the other decor inside the house?"

"Sure thing."

Haley began carefully removing the ornaments and wrapping each before placing them in the box. She continued this until the tree was empty of everything except the lights. Once full, she carried the tote with the ornaments to the basement and placed it back on the shelf.

She stood momentarily looking around at what they had stored in the vast space. Jack had talked about turning the basement into a large play area for the children they planned on having. Maybe all that could still happen. There were numerous boxes of stored items, such as photographs from the past, books, and albums. She wondered if Jack would have hid his information in one of those.

She pulled the closest one off the shelf and decided to go through it in the basement, rather than carry it upstairs. She really needed some place comfortable to sit and go through things slowly. A portable card table sat against the back of the staircase. She grabbed it, carrying it toward the center of the basement, and popped the legs out. *Now, I just need a chair!* There were no chairs. Haley used the step stool as her seat. She began the search through the first box of memorabilia.

Sonya came down carrying another plastic tote. "This is the last of it."

"Oh good, you can relax now and join me in looking through tons of old stuff. The only problem is you need a chair."

"Do you want me to finish the tree for you upstairs? It still has lights on it?"

"Would you? Honestly, I hate putting lights on or taking them off. Guess that's why I quit at that point," she said.

"No problem. With all my twinkling lights I have in my room back home, I'm very adept with lighting."

Haley smiled at her. "You're adept at a lot of things, Sonya."

An hour later, Haley had discovered nothing that looked like Jack's secret work. But she had come across things she had saved from long ago about her mother. There were old photographs and copies of medical records from her mother's gynecological surgery back in 1999. That is when she became addicted to opiates.

The silence in the basement was both good and bad. As Haley ruffled through documents and more photographs, many memories resurfaced. She pushed them away and tried to focus on the task at hand, finding Jack's secret stash. That was all that mattered right now.

Chapter 7 ~ Boys in Brazil

There was a feeling of anticipation as the three men rode together. This was the rainy season, and it fell in light droplets five minutes into their drive. The hotel was remote from the nearest town, but had boasted beautiful views. The radio was on low, playing what were probably the latest, popular Latin tunes.

Lucas had announced the air conditioning was currently not working. The high humidity and wet rainy season conditions made everything in the jeep feel damp. They passed a hodge-podge of residences that were sparsely littered throughout the drive. Some were very well constructed and large. Many others were meager dwellings.

Having the windows down had provided a cool breeze. They rolled them up as rain started falling in large sheets of water against the vehicle. As they continued downhill toward the town, Lucas pulled off the road, waiting for the heaviest of the rain to die down.

"It's dangerous and stressful trying to drive in this rainy mess," Jason said, looking at Lucas.

"Hopefully, it will let up in a few moments so we can continue. This is common right now. Most of the time, it passes quickly."

"We'll see what happens," Jason replied. "I would imagine there will only be one flight out of this city to San Pau today. If we've missed it, we will need a backup plan or place to stay until he can catch the next flight out tomorrow."

"Do you know of a barber in town?" Jack asked of Lucas.

"No, I've not spent much time in this city, but I'm sure we will find one in the business district."

Jason grabbed three energy bars out of his bag and passed one to each.

"Ah, food of any type is welcome," Lucas said.

"I want to show you something, Jack," Jason said, handing his phone to his brother. "Do you recognize this?"

Jack took the phone from him and stared at a photo of that same beautiful woman who was supposed to be his wife and himself dining at a restaurant. Something felt familiar about it, but it was like knowing the name of something you've seen or heard of but can't remember it. It nagged at him that he could not place it.

Jason waited patiently while Jack gazed at the phone. Finally, he looked at Jason and shook his head. "No, it seems like I vaguely remember, but not really. I just can't place myself being there or who she is."

In a way, Jason wished he had not shown Jack the picture. It certainly put a heavy mood inside the cramped jeep with fogged windows and rain pouring down.

The men sat there for another fifteen minutes while rain poured so heavily it reduced visibility all around them. The sound on the jeep's roof was loud enough to almost make one put their hands over their ears. Waiting like this in the hot jeep made fifteen minutes seem like well over an hour. And then, it began to ease up.

The rain slowed to light drops as quickly as it had changed to a drenching storm. Visibility was hazy and the windows of the jeep were foggy.

"I think we can make it now." Lucas started the jeep and handed Jason a t-shirt he stored behind the console area. "See if you can get these windows wiped down."

Jason grabbed the t-shirt and began clearing the glass on his door's window when his mouth fell open. Two men stood there dressed in black with rifles pointed — one at Jason and one at Jack.

"Holy shit," Jason muttered.

Another man dressed in dark fatigues approached the jeep door on the driver's side and opened it.

"Turn off the vehicle. Everyone out with your arms in the air!" he ordered in English.

Lucas cut the engine. His 9mm was in the right lower pocket of his cargo pants. He debated leaving it in the jeep and then decided against it. As he stepped out, he noticed they were surrounded by the invaders who obviously belonged to the Special Operations Brigade of the Brazilian Army.

Officers patted down each of them, easily finding Lucas' gun which they confiscated. The three men kept quiet, not sure if this was a mistake or something more sinister. Jason's passport, phone, and wallet were taken. They found little to nothing on Jack to take.

The one who had ordered them out of the vehicle appeared to be the leader. After the frisking, there was talk in Portuguese between him and another officer. They took Lucas and inquired of him separately. He answered their questions in the native language, of which Jack could only pick up certain words. They searched his jeep, possibly looking for more weapons. After they turned up nothing of consequence, the leader of the group ordered Jack and Jason into the back of what appeared to be a modified paddy wagon for prisoners.

Jack needed assistance getting into the back with his sore leg. Once inside, both were handcuffed to interior bars hanging from the ceiling.

The brothers watched as the vehicle they were now held in as prisoners drove away, leaving Lucas standing with two guards still surrounding him. They sat across from one another on hard metal bench seats. Jack tried not to let panic set in. He could see it was already threatening his brother. Wanting to distract him, he said, "Watch out the small window if you can, Jason. Watch for number signs on the road so we might know where we are going or how to leave if we somehow escape."

Jason nodded his head and sat tall, trying to see out the tiny window. Jack did the same on his side of the vehicle. Mist hung in the air from the rain, creating a fog that made it difficult to see signs until you were right up on them.

"I can't tell for sure, but I think we're headed south," Jason mentioned.

"I think you're right about that."

"Great, but where are they taking us and why?" Jason added.

"I don't know, brother. I'm so sorry you're in this mess with me. It's got to be about me."

Rain continued to pour, sometimes in heavy downpours and then light again. About forty-five minutes passed and the vehicle made a few turns and then came to a stop. The twin brothers could see they were at some sort of installation for the military.

The back door opened and two armed guards with weapons pointed at the brothers stood guard while another one came inside and released the brothers from the internal bar their handcuffs were hooked to. The leader who spoke English appeared again and said, "Slide toward the door and we will take off the handcuffs."

Both men did as told and it was a relief to have their arms and hands free from the cramped position they had been in. The lead guard now pointed toward a small electric vehicle that was a little larger than a golf cart. "Get in the back," he ordered.

Jack and Jason walked toward the small vehicle, both taking in the sights around them. This was definitely a base of some type with an airfield. Two separate guards flanked each brother as they went to sit in the back of the electric vehicle. They were again handcuffed, this time behind their backs. A driver and another guard entered the front and the vehicle moved quietly toward the airfield until it came to a helicopter.

Jason looked at Jack and shook his head from side to side. "So much for memorizing roads with numbers."

Chapter 8 ~ Moving on Evan

At home, Lucky ditched her brown pageboy wig, placing it on the mannequin head in her walk-in closet. She showered and changed into her exercise instructor attire. As usual, she would drive her z-car to Evan's condominium complex. Ric needed her to be there ahead of time to gain entrance to the community clubhouse.

She arrived about twenty minutes early, plenty of time to spare. There was no sign of Ric so she drove around the parking lot to visually survey Evan's unit. His Porsche was parked in its usual assigned spot. Lucky could have known that from the app on her phone, but she had not looked at it for a while today.

Her preferred parking space was far away from the clubhouse in the outer lot. She liked this spot because it gave her a better view of the entire area between the clubhouse and Evan's condo unit. She grabbed her tote bag and water bottle, and then locked the vehicle, heading inside.

Keeping her sunglasses on, her eyes were peeled, watching the back side of Evan's condo unit for any sign of movement at his windows which were slightly tinted. He would have to be standing close to the glass to view him. There was no sign of him.

Lucky didn't have a plan in her mind of what she would do when she met him. Would she drop something and see if he picked it up for her? *Kind of juvenile,* she thought. Would she simply give him a look of interest and then play coy, taking seductive steps away from him as he watched her? *Don't think about this right now. Just get your key card out and enter the building.* She would get her classroom set up, check her hair and makeup, and wait for Ric to text her when he arrived.

Remembering her identity for the job was crucial. She was Chelsea Roberts, yoga and Pilates instructor — just in case anyone asked. As soon as she entered the building, she gasped slightly, like when you bump into an old friend you haven't seen in years. There Evan stood -- at the door to her exercise room, reading the itinerary. This was too easy. Sometimes she just wished for things and they happened.

Lucky walked up behind him and lightly cleared her throat so he knew she was there. "Excuse me. I'm Chelsea Roberts, the instructor. Interested in classes?"

Evan turned to see who was speaking to him and took one step sideways to put some distance between himself and the gorgeous tall blond in front of him. She wore form fitting yoga pants and sports bra covered with a thin tank top. Her windbreaker jacket hung loosely with the zipper open, barely covering her upper torso. As she removed her sunglasses, he was met with hypnotic green eyes.

"Hello, I was just curious. I've never done yoga. This must be a recent addition here at the club."

"You might love it. Something new, huh?" she replied.

Lucky grabbed the door handle to the room and pushed it open. "Come in if you like and I'll be glad to answer any questions you have."

Evan followed her inside, watching her bend over as she sat her tote bag on the floor in the corner. Questions? The only question he had was her phone number. He stayed silent, and it was an uncomfortable stillness between the two of them in the room. Lucky made her way to the front. She fiddled with her phone and suddenly there was music coming from two speakers in each corner of the exercise area.

She walked toward him now and he watched as her hips swayed with each step. She came within three feet and leaned slightly on one leg. He couldn't tell if she had medium or huge tits. The sports bra pushed them together until they were bulging in the center and evident through the thin tank top. Realizing his eyes were fixated too long at her chest, he quickly looked away at the exercise mats in the room.

"So, did you have any questions?" she asked.

"Uh, yes. What's your name? I haven't seen you here before."

Lucky smiled. I think I told you, but perhaps you didn't hear me. I'm Chelsea Roberts, the new yoga and Pilates instructor. I just started, so classes are still filling up."

Evan's interest in her was obvious, and it was beyond her being a potential exercise instructor. Suddenly, she remembered Ric was on his way. With him working at Chadwell, she did not want him running into Evan. "Excuse me. I need to check my messages."

She walked with her phone to the corner of the room again and sent Ric a message.

He's here with me. Abort mission. Talk later.

Ric messaged back quickly.

Got it. Be safe!

"Sorry about that. I had to let my friend know I won't be dropping by tonight after work. Now, you know my name, what is yours?"

"Evan Mitchell."

"What is your favorite type of exercise?"

Evan gave her a sly smile. He looked at her as if she had asked a loaded question. "To tell you the truth, I don't have a favorite. I don't really enjoy working out initially. I have to talk myself into it. Afterward, it feels good. I mean it's not like other things I do love, things I don't have to talk myself into that also make me feel good afterward."

Lucky took the hint. He was obviously referring to sex. *Damn, watch it! He is a Scorpio. Dangerous, secretive type as well.* She decided to let him know she was the boss in this room and ignored his sexual innuendo. If she appeared easy to him, it would take all the fun out of it. Obviously, he liked games and challenges or he wouldn't be mixed up in this Chadwell thing to the extent she believed he might be.

"Well, if you don't have any questions, I will begin getting ready for my class. My students will arrive soon. Have you decided if you're going to be one of them?"

"I don't know. Would I be the only male in the class?"

"No, you would be the first male in the class. I know we'll have more. Lots of men are doing yoga. It's not just a physical exercise, it's a mind practice. Many use it to increase their spiritual awareness too," she said, looking at him wryly.

"Can I think about it?"

"Sure. Anytime you have more questions, just let me know. Or, if you want to try it out, just come to class."

"Thanks, I'll let you know. Hope to see you again, Chelsea," Evan said, emphasizing her name.

She watched him walk away toward the weight lifting area. He was an attractive man, especially up close. While he wasn't built like the Greek god she noticed her first time here, Evan had broad shoulders and a nice physique. Just before entering the weight room, he turned in her direction and they made eye contact. She smiled and turned around, going back into the studio. *Now, he's seen me staring after him. I don't know if that's good or bad.*

Chapter 9 ~ The Dark Ride

A stream of sweat trickled down Jason's face from his temple to his chin. He cocked his head down, wiping the moisture on his shoulder. The brothers were shaken that they were being taken to yet another location. They both could not wrap their minds around why the military would capture and take them hostage.

With guns held, but pointed downward, Jack and Jason were required to walk toward the helicopter. Each remained handcuffed behind their backs. A beefy guard strode toward them and placed noise canceling headphones on each of their heads. Up close, the helicopter was enormous with a dark painted exterior. An emblem of the Brazilian flag was on the side, along with numbers identifying the vehicle. Jack wondered if he should memorize the numbers.

The brothers were directed to enter and move toward the back of the chopper. Each sat on opposite sides. Seat belts were buckled around them by two additional guards. Jason looked at Jack pensively. Jack took a deep breath in an exaggerated manner to communicate to Jason to stay calm and steady with his emotions.

There was some chatter outside between the pilot and the lone military person they knew spoke English. The conversation was imperceptible from where that sat, especially with the headphones. Finally, the pilot entered the helicopter and began touching controls on the dashboard area. The military chopper fired up, gaining in noise and lifted into the air. Both brothers gazed out the windows, glimpsing the large military installment below.

Soaring now in the chopper, Jack's mind was churning, along with his stomach. As they flew, he felt panic set in. He was smart enough to know it was from the stress of being taken hostage combined with feelings associated with the plane crash he had survived.

The helicopter was ripe with the smell of sweaty men who had been in hot, humid conditions for a while. All of it made him want to heave, but he took two more deep breaths and tried to stay calm. Feeling helpless, there was nothing he could do but see where this ended up.

Jack doubted Chadwell would have the Brazilian military at their disposal. He knew they had facilities in Brazil, but so did just about every other pharmaceutical company. Something about this felt different. Deep down, he felt they wanted him and not his brother.

If Chadwell was involved, wouldn't they have already killed him before going to all this trouble? These guys were taking him somewhere. Unfortunately, Jason was along for the ride too. He looked at his brother who still had great concern in his expression. He glanced at Jack. They had always been good at reading one another and he felt his anxiety and shock. They were dealing with an unknown captor. *Who in the hell was behind this?*

Both men were without a watch or cell phone. Time passed, but Jack had no real sense of how much. Generally, one would think a helicopter ride would be for short distances but they were traveling far. Finally, he noticed the pilot speaking to air control and slowing down. He couldn't hear a damn word. The chopper seemed to make a circle and then hover. Both brothers gazed out the windows below to try and determine what type of place they were landing.

A towering mountain, which appeared to be granite, stood supreme in the background. A stone mansion sat some distance away from it at its base. Secluded, there were no signs of civilization as they approached the area. It looked palatial, but governmental with the Brazilian flag flying in a mezzanine area in the center of the grounds. Two statues flanked its sides.

The landing of the craft on the pad was smooth, yet it could still be felt as a slight physical jolt. Jack noticed tall palm trees and shorter areca palms accenting the perfectly groomed lawn. A short stone retaining wall separated the large mansion from the lower area landing pad where the chopper now sat.

They were about one hundred feet away from the stone mansion with steps leading up to it. The structure was imposing in its size, but nothing compared to the mountain that rose majestically behind it.

The brothers were assisted from the helicopter and their earphones removed. Jason noticed the clothing the soldiers wore appeared highly technical, not the usual issued fatigues one would expect. It was the same as the uniforms of the men who had taken them hostage at Lucas' jeep. He looked at Jack, "They must be a special force branch of their military, don't you think?"

"Or they could be part of some billionaire's private security force," Jack said, smirking.

"Nah, they're in military issued vehicles."

Despite landing at this site in their chopper and the Brazilian flag waving on the grounds, the two-story stone manor looked more like someone's very remote residence. Three tall Spanish arches composed a massive front porch area also made of stone. The steps leading up to the entrance were wide.

Still handcuffed, Jack and Jason were directed to walk up the steps with guards at their side and behind them. Once they reached the top of the stone staircase, they crossed a drive for vehicles to pull up in front of the manor. They climbed a shorter flight of stairs that led to the massive porch and entrance. Once they reached the last step, the guards stopped and held both of the brothers there momentarily.

"What is this place?" Jason asked.

Jack shook his head. "I'm not sure. It looks like part of the government, but then again not."

"Does anyone here speak English?" Jack called out to the group.

"I do," came a reply from a female who had just emerged from the front door.

She was dressed in a gray business suit with dark hair. She was attractive and older, with a bit of gray at her temples. "What is it that you would like to know?" she asked, looking at Jack.

"Where are we and why?" he questioned her.

She looked at both of them. "Two Mr. Fosters brought to an unknown location for unknown reasons. I would imagine you are curious. I promise that you will soon be told the nature of your visit. Please come inside," she said, her arms pointing toward the front door.

Armed military guards accompanied the two men into the manor house. Upon entering, their eyes stretched upward into the two-story open foyer with a wide, curved stairway leading to the second level. They were directed to turn right and asked to sit at a table in a large room that resembled a formal dining room. Each brother was released from the handcuffs.

"My name is Karla," the lady who spoke English said. "Would you like something to drink? We have coffee, tea or bottled water."

They both spoke up simultaneously, "Water, please."

She left the room and the guards stayed in armed position at the door. Karla came back into the room, delivering water bottles to each.

Jack took a swig of his water and watched her take a seat across from them. "Karla, where are we?"

"This is a place of holiday for the President of Brazil. For the purpose of secrecy, it is a preferred location for meeting. You will not be recorded as an official visitor as you would at the Presidential Palace or other government buildings."

Jason nodded and then asked, "Does that mean no one could find a trace of us if something nefarious happens?"

Karla smiled and tapped a finger on the table before replying. "Hopefully, nothing like that occurs."

Jack interjected, "So, why are we here?"

At that moment, a short, balding man entered the room with a wide smile. "Sorry to be running behind," he said in English.

Karla smiled "We know you are very busy. This is Bento Cardoso, Special Counsel to the President of Brazil."

He nodded his head toward each of the men and sat a briefcase upon the table.

"Both men are quite anxious to know why they are here, Mr. Cardoso."

"Yes, I certainly understand. Gentlemen, the President would like to meet with Dr. Jack Foster," he began. "Which one of you is Dr. Jack Foster?" Jack raised his hand slightly. "Then you must be Jason Foster," he said turning his head to him.

"That's right," Jason replied.

"Do you know what this is about?" Jack asked the counsel.

"Yes, but it would be better explained in a secure location. I hope that our special unit was not too forceful with either of you. I see you arrived here safely."

The brothers nodded they were unharmed. Yet, the tension was rising in the room as they wondered why the President of Brazil would want to talk to Jack.

"I know there are many questions and I assure you they will be answered in due time. Before we go further in speaking to one another, it would be best to make our way to the secure location where you will meet with our President. You will still be under guard, so please do not try to do anything stupid or dangerous. I promise you that everything will make more sense soon."

Karla and counsel for the President stood, motioning for the brothers to do so as well. Two guards directed them from the room and back toward the grand foyer. Karla led them to the opposite side of the foyer and pointed to a door. "It would be wise to relieve yourself now if you are inclined to do so. One at a time and the guard will wait outside the door."

Jason felt like they were in elementary school and he didn't like Karla. She was full of secrets and wielded too much control with her armed personnel. Nevertheless, he was first to take advantage of the bathroom facilities, then followed by Jack. Once they were finished, Karla led the two brothers to an enclosure behind the staircase. She placed her entire palm against a glass panel on the wall. They watched as elevator doors opened. Stepping inside, they noticed Karla used her hand again on the interior control panel. The elevator began to descend.

Chapter 10 ~ Following

Everything Evan told Chelsea surrounding his feelings about exercising was true. He had to make himself. And, the discipline of doing so made him feel in control. He was doing this for him, no other person including his father. He made himself work out to stay lean, healthy, and strong.

Evan finished with a mile run around the indoor track. Sweat drizzled down his face. He had made himself do it again, and it felt good to have his heart beating fast. He would shower once inside his condo and get to bed early. While most of the employees at Chadwell had taken today and tomorrow off for a long Christmas holiday, he needed to be at work. Taking over for Jack was proving to be much more complex than he anticipated. He was surprised how efficiently Jack had handled the position. Ultimately, he would outshine Jack Foster.

He grabbed his jacket from the locker that held his wallet, two phones, and keys. Glancing at the burner phone, he noticed a message. It was from Ragland.

Blown all my dough on Christmas. Ready to get into that place sooner than later. Let's talk.

They still needed to find what Jack had hid in his house. What if Haley already had it? He decided to wait until he got back to his place before responding to the text.

As he approached the clubhouse foyer, he noticed the lights were off in the room Chelsea taught her class in. He walked up to the door, looking to see if a phone number was displayed for her. No number was listed, so he noted the nights and hours she would be there again. After all, she was looking at him as he walked away from her earlier. Evan felt this must mean she has an interest in him. He definitely had an interest in her.

Chelsea, the yoga instructor, was downright hot. Typically, he liked long hair on women, but her platinum blond pixie hairstyle was very sexy on her. The bangs around her face accented her hypnotic green eyes. She reminded him of a lioness and he wondered what it would take to make her purr, or roar. Whoever she was, he wanted to get to know her more.

Evan walked the short distance to his condominium unit and entered. Unlike other residents, he didn't decorate for the holidays. Right now, nothing like that was important to him. The only thing that mattered now was advancing ahead with Chadwell. That meant finally getting on the board. He had to make sure Jack Foster was gone for good.

Lucky waited in her car, watching for Evan to leave the facility. Why, she wasn't sure. It was cold as hell and the night after Christmas. She didn't figure anything would happen now that would lead to some kind of break, but you never knew. She pulled her black hoody tighter around her head so as not to be noticed when he emerged from the building. He could glance her way, although she was parked in a direction he probably would not normally look.

She reflected on the class and her students. All women so far, and that was okay with her.

And then came Evan. He walked briskly, probably due to the cold temperatures. He wore sweatpants and had a jacket on. He never looked at her, but proceeded to his condominium. She waited until he was a safe distance away, started her engine, and drove toward her apartment.

Once home, she messaged Ric. Since they began working together, they each promised that when they were going to possibly engage with the enemy in any form, they would report in frequently, letting each other know they were alright. Ric was such a help to her, a pillar for her to lean on at times when things had become sticky or unmanageable.

Hey, letting you know I'm back home now. The bump into was just that and not too much more. He's not into yoga. LOL

Glad to hear you're safe. I need to catch you up on what I've found so far. Coffee or something tomorrow?

Yes. Where and when?

How about the new Thai restaurant for lunch — the one by your place? Noonish

See you at noon. Good night

Sweet dreams

Lucky put her phone down and went to the kitchen for something quick to eat. As soon as she stepped away, the phone signaled a tone, the same one used for tracking Evan's vehicle. She ran over to fetch it and pulled up the app. He was on the move.

Holding her phone with her left hand, she watched in almost real time where he was traveling. She grabbed a banana with her other hand and then set the phone down to peel it. Lucky ate, watching the area Evan was moving toward. She had concluded that it didn't look like he was going out for pizza or something. He was headed toward that bar. *I have to follow him and see what he is doing there.*

She needed to think quick. What should she wear? She couldn't show up as Evan had met her with her pixie hairdo. Nor did she want to be the painter dropping by again at the bar the same night. Or, maybe she could.

Lucky hatched a quick on-the-fly plan to go back to the bar in her paint gear and wig. She might not even go in, but if she did, it would be under the guise of needing to come back with a tape measure for a more accurate estimate. *Damn, I cannot forget a tape measure this time!*

Lucky dressed the same as earlier in the day and grabbed some surveillance equipment while running out of her apartment. With those devices, she might be able to sit in her van and hear part of what Evan was saying. She wondered about filming him. It just depended on the circumstances she found once there.

She jumped in the van and gunned it toward the bar. There was no time to message Ric. She'd try once she was there and could see about setting up some surveillance. She looked in the mirror and realized she had forgotten the painter's ball cap. *Shit! I hope this wig stays on!*

Chapter 11 ~ Hard Choices

Jack's stomach rumbled as the elevator came to a stop. In such close quarters, everyone heard it. Karla smiled with her lips closed. She looked at both of the brothers. "Food will arrive shortly."

Jack nodded. Jason said nothing. The stress he was feeling from this experience was louder in his body than his hunger.

Karla stepped out of the elevator first and turned, waiting for Jack and Jason to follow along with the armed guards. They were in a concrete corridor with low fluorescent lighting coming from small fixtures placed intermittently in the walls. Jason estimated they were following her for at least five hundred feet, maybe a thousand. He had not seen another passageway or door to enter, only this long tunnel.

"Do you know where we are?" she asked each of them, still walking swiftly. This irritated Jason. Of course, they didn't know. Why was she asking this question?

""Somewhere underground would be my best guess," Jason answered. Karla looked at Jack. He hesitated and then answered, "Inside the mountain?"

"Correct! One of the safest places you could be on the planet," she answered, almost in a proud way.

"Then why are we at gunpoint?" Jason asked. "It's stressing the shit out of me and I don't feel safe."

Karla turned her head to look at him, but continued walking forward. "Just standard procedure. It's only precautionary."

Finally, they came to a set of steel doors and Karla held her palm up to the same biometric type scanner. You could hear the locking mechanism release as she did so. The doors automatically opened and they proceeded inside.

Jack and Jason found themselves in what would look like a normal reception area of any office. They could have been inside a doctor's office. The only difference was the uniformed and armed receptionist behind the check-in area. Karla approached the glass window and spoke to the reception guard in Portuguese. A buzzer sounded and double doors unlatched and opened to their left.

"This way, please," Karla said. They continued to follow her down a short hallway toward another door guarded by two more military members. "Line up to be scanned electronically, please," she requested of Jack, Jason and the men guarding them. Jason noticed the counsel for the president did not follow them. He must have stayed in the waiting area.

Karla handed her phone and watch to the person guarding the door on the left. She was then scanned with a device by the guard on the right. "Clear," the guard called. Jack had nothing electronic on him at all. He did not know what happened to his watch. His cell and satellite phones were long gone with the crash, somewhere in the jungle. Jason's watch and cell phone had been confiscated by the same people leading him into this room. The guard scanned each of them and declared they were clear to enter the room.

As they entered, Jason ascertained the walls were about twelve inches thick, based on the size of the trim around the door frame. The room was plush with leather executive style chairs on wheels surrounding a conference table large enough for eighteen people. He noticed the walls were metal, aluminum he believed, with intermittent areas of thick fabric covering them. A large screen took up one entire end wall. Four smaller screens were situated on the opposite wall.

"We should have food and drink arriving any moment," Karla announced. "While we are waiting, let me prepare you for meeting the President of Brazil. You should stand, of course, when he enters and leaves the room. Sit down only when directed by him. Always address him as Senor Presidente or Mr. President."

Karla opened the drawer of a credenza below the wall with the four screens. She pulled out notepads and pens, handing one to each of the brothers.

"Keep your questions on paper or in your head until you are asked something by the President. He will give you an opportunity to ask when it is appropriate."

The door to the secret compartmentalized room opened and a cart on wheels was rolled inside.

"Gracias. Please, select whatever you want as the cart comes to you," Karla said.

Jack chose two sandwiches. He was not sure what they consisted of, and didn't care. He was hungry. There were small bags of chips and soft drinks with familiar logos and colors, but the words on each in Portuguese.

Jason followed his brother's lead grabbing two sandwiches. Who knew when they would eat again? The men ate while Karla wrote on her notepad and drank bottled water.

Jason estimated they had been in the room about thirty minutes. Karla had cleaned up any wrappings from their meals that were on the table and disposed of them in a refuse can in the corner. The mystery of the President wanting to meet with them was beginning to make each of them more nervous.

Finally, the door opened and a tall man with dark hair and olive complexion entered the room. He was accompanied by the Counsel for the President they had met earlier.

The two military guards came to attention and saluted. Karla stood, glancing at the brothers and motioning for them to rise also. They both stood and waited for the President of Brazil to be seated at the head of the table at one end of the room. He motioned for everyone to sit. Karla sat at his right and the General Counsel sat at his left.

"Good afternoon everyone," he said in English."

"Good afternoon Mr. President," they replied.

"Which one of you is Dr. Jack Foster?" the President asked, looking at the two men.

Jack raised his hand, "I am, sir, um, Mr. President."

"Then that means you must be Jason," the President said, smiling.

Jason nodded affirmatively.

"Jason, no offense is meant, but I am really only interested in your brother. There are things I will need to discuss with him that are very sensitive in nature. Here is the situation, Jason. Today, you must make a decision. Your brother, Jack Foster, is needed by this government and the United States to work on something secretive that cannot go beyond a few individuals. If you stay with your brother, you will have to be with him the entire duration until the assignment is over. You will be held in areas where you will have very minimal contact with family. Do you understand what I am saying so far?"

Jason nodded, "Yes, Mr. President. How long would I be with Jack and away from my family?"

The President paused. "I cannot give you an exact time frame. It could be weeks or months, depending upon what happens. Your other alternative is for us to return your passport and belongings, fly you out of here to an international airport in Brazil, and get you on the next flight to the United States. If you choose that option, you may tell your close family only that your brother is working on a project and unable to have a public life or contact until it ends."

Jason was stunned. He had no idea he would be hit with such a hard decision. He came here to find Jack and he felt a responsibility to get him back home. He had promised his father. "What if Jack doesn't want to help and wants to go home?"

"He is free to choose, just as you are. However, at some point, Chadwell Pharmaceuticals will know he is alive. If Jack takes on this project, they will not be able to touch him physically. There is more to say that weighs positively for Jack to assist us, but I cannot share it at this time. Trust me, if he leaves here as things are, he has a big target on his back with Chadwell, and possibly other nefarious entities they are engaged with."

Jack reached out and wrapped his hand around Jason's arm. "Go, Jason. Whatever this is, I want to find out and help if I can. You would be miserable staying and being away from Sarah and the kids."

"Mr. President, can Jason let my family know I'm alive and okay?"

"Yes, and that is all that can be said of the situation except that you are working on a project for your country and will not be released until the assignment is over."

"I'm having trouble with my memory since the plane crash. For instance, I don't remember my wife or the house we live in. There could be other issues."

"Then, you are at the right place. You will have the best physicians and most advanced healing mechanisms available to you here."

Jason spoke up, "That's good. Mr. President, he has to remember his wife, Haley. His leg was injured also. He's limping as he walks."

"Jason, I give you my promise that your brother will receive world class care for his injuries." He looked at Jack. "How did you survive that plane crash?"

"I don't know. I've forgotten part of that as well, Mr. President."

"We will see what can be done to regain your memory and heal your leg should you decide to stay. You will be well fed, have ample opportunity to exercise and most of all be safe from those who want to kill you."

Jason looked at him as he said this and asked, "Why do they want to kill my brother?"

"Information, Jason. The entire world is in a war for controlling information and knowledge."

The room was quiet for a moment.

Jack looked at his brother, "Go home to Sarah. Tell mom and dad this was my decision and I sent you home. Tell my family I'll be back."

"Alright, I won't lie. I'm not crazy about being stuck here for some unknown length of time and having limited contact with Sarah."

Jack rose from his chair, "Then go and be safe and blessed, brother."

Jason rose and they embraced, holding each other for a long time.

"Karla, will you see that Jason is led back and provide whatever he needs to do so."

"Yes sir, Mr. President."

The President stood and reached out to shake Jason's hand. "We will take excellent care of your brother. You have my word."

"Thank you, I believe that you will. It was a pleasure to meet you Mr. President."

Chapter 12 ~ Separation

With mixed feelings, Jason left his brother behind.

He was escorted by two guards out of the underground mountain location back to the stone mansion. It was a black or white choice and he hoped the right decision had been made.

As they made their way down the stone steps of the mansion and back toward the helicopter, Jason took a deep breath of fresh air. His skin welcomed the warmth of the afternoon sun. Jason felt like he was being released from jail. But his brother was still imprisoned in a strange way.

One of the guards assisted him with headphones as he boarded the same helicopter he had arrived on … or at least he thought it was the same. He was given a bubble wrap envelope that contained his passport, wallet, watch and cell phone. There was a note suggesting he not turn on his cell phone until at the airport for safety precautions. He smiled. He was beginning to feel like a free human again just having his personal belongings.

Before takeoff, Karla came to the helicopter pad, climbed the steps, and peeked inside. Upon seeing her, he removed his headphones.

"Jason, many thanks for putting up with us today. I hope no one was too hard on you. I assure you Jack will be respected, protected, and given the best care with us. I have booked you a flight out of Rio back to the United States. Here is your itinerary." She handed a piece of paper to one guard who passed it to Jason.

Jason looked it over quickly. "Thank you, Karla. I don't totally understand what's going on. So far, no one has hurt me or my brother. I have no choice but to trust your word." She smiled and waved him goodbye.

The helicopter fired up, and moments later, they lifted into the sky. The view of the mountain and valley below was incredible. It gave him a bit of a rush. Now, he could appreciate the scenery, whereas before, he had no idea what was happening and why they were being held hostage.

By the time the chopper landed at another military base, the personnel on board were at ease and natural with Jason. Many of them gave him a thumbs up or high five as he departed the helicopter and was transferred to a sleek black government car. They traveled for approximately forty-five minutes before he was dropped at the Rio de Janeiro airport.

With no baggage, Jason checked in with the airline and received his boarding pass. During his wait in lines for security and customs, he kept unconsciously rubbing the stubble on his chin. A shower and clean clothes would have made him feel more comfortable sitting on a plane next to others. After passing through airport security, he entered a public restroom and cleaned himself as best he could, splashing water on his face.

He walked toward his boarding area with a final sense of dread about leaving Jack behind. In some ways, it was like a failed mission. His father would be upset, at least at first. The vast distance between here and home was overwhelming. Once Jason boarded the plane and took off, Jack would be so far from him and everyone else that loves him.

As suggested, he waited until now to contact anyone. He wanted to be careful with all communications. Jason sent a message to Sarah.

I'm coming home. Here is a pic of my flight info. Can you pick me up or have dad? I arrive in the middle of the night. I could also book a ride, but I'd rather not.

OMG, you're on your way. I'm so happy. Middle of the night. It would be hard with the kids. Let me see if

Sonya could come spend the night and stay with them. If so, yes, I will pick you up. Is Jack with you?

No

Why not?

He will come later. Keep communications with everyone minimal and by text message only. I love you and can't wait to see you and the kids.

Sarah had more questions than answers. She was going to assume this had something to do with the passport issue. Jack no longer had his and it would be risky for him to show up at the U.S. Embassy requesting a replacement. But she thought Jack would fly back first using Jason's passport. Whatever was going on, they must have worked out another plan.

Sarah wondered if she should let Haley know now or wait until there was more information. Haley would want answers right away, and she didn't have them. Her father-in-law would as well. She decided to lie low for now. She would wake the children, put them in the car, and pick Jason up. Tomorrow, they would have answers for everyone.

She glanced at the children in the family room from the kitchen. Allison was playing with Eli at the moment and they were adorable together. Sarah took some video with her phone of the two. It was moments like this that made the hard work of parenting absolutely worth it. She was eager to have Jason back home. Christmas was definitely different without him. Her heart felt pain for Haley. Her sister-in-law had been through so much. First, she thought Jack was dead to the point of attending his funeral. Next, she had to shift and believe he might be alive and thank the heavens above, he is. But now, he doesn't remember her.

She called Allison and Eli to come to the kitchen for a snack. "Guess what?" she asked.

"Tell us, mommy," Allison replied.

"Daddy is coming home from South America."

"Soon?" she asked.

"Yes, he will arrive at the airport tonight when we are sleeping."

"I want to see daddy as soon as he gets here," Allison whined.

"Yes, I do too. We could go in the car in the middle of the night in our pajamas."

"Does that mean we can stay up all night?"

"No, you both will go to bed at your usual time. But, I could wake you when it's time. We could get in the car and surprise him."

"Yes, I want to surprise him."

Eli, who was unsure exactly what all this meant joined his sister's excitement by banging on the table and saying, "Daddy, daddy."

"Okay, I want you to eat your snack. Once you two are finished, let's break out the new modeling clay that Santa left. Eli can have fun with that too at the table.

"He's going to try to eat it," Allison said.

Sarah laughed, "We will have to teach him not to, won't we big sister?"

Chapter 13 ~ Alice's Bar

Evan Lucky suddenly slammed on her brakes during her pursuit of Evan. She was not going to tempt fate and get pulled over running a red light. Her van was loaded up with just about everything besides paint. Waiting for the signal to change, she grabbed her phone and sent Ric a message while waiting for the light to change.

My lead is on his way to that bar and I'm trying to catch up with him. Just thought I'd give you a heads up.

Be careful. Stay in touch.

Will do

The light turned green and Lucky's foot hit the gas pedal. *C'mon you old clunker.* She was used to driving a sports car or motorcycle, not a big old box on wheels. During the drive, Lucky planned her next move once she arrived. There were several scenarios that could occur.

She would have to be ready to improvise. There was a reason Evan Mitchell was visiting this location. Hopefully, tonight would reveal why.

She took a mental inventory of what devices she had in the van. There was another tracker that she might be able to use on the vehicle of whomever Evan was meeting. She had some bionic ear buds but those would only work out if she were able to get the receiving device close to Evan.

Finally coming close, she drove by the bar at a normal speed, noticing the front door was closed instead of open as it was during the day. Lucky made a sharp turn onto a side street a block down from the bar. She ventured down the road until she could cross at an alley way. If she could come up behind the bar, she would be able to see where Evan was parked and anything else that might be noticeable.

There were several people walking down the alley. They appeared to be teens that were probably sneaking out of the house during Christmas break. She determined they were fairly harmless and continued driving, slowing only to make sure she didn't hit one of them.

As she made her way up the alley, Lucky came to the cross street where the bar sat. The Porsche was parked on the side of the building, almost right at the side door. Feeling brave, she decided to pull in the space right behind it.

Lucky quickly began setting up devices she might need for this late night venture. It felt too risky for her to go inside, but she needed eyes on who Evan was with, if anyone. Damn, if she had her ball cap painter's hat, it would help. Suddenly, she remembered a black hoody she kept in the back. She could use that to conceal herself a little more. But, wouldn't Alice recognize her and perhaps draw attention to her? She decided to take a chance and go inside. She wasn't breaking the law by doing so, at least not yet.

Sitting in the van with the engine turned off, she could hear music and laughter from the bar. It was probably pretty loud inside at night. It was imperative that Evan not recognize her. If he had even a suspicion, then that was the end of this part of the investigation. She wouldn't be able to teach at the club either.

Lucky adjusted her wig, making sure it was as secure as possible. She put the jacket on and raised the hood to conceal herself more. She grabbed her bionic ear buds and the receiver portion, along with the tape measure just in case she ran into Alice.

Okay, this is it. Hope this works out!

Her hand was shaking as she pulled on the handle of the bar's side door. The pool tables were to her right, and she decided to patrol that area, maybe going to the restroom if she had to in an emergency. She watched as four older men with potbellies, wearing biker t-shirts and jeans played the tables. Each seemed to have their wife or girlfriend along. The women sat at a table toward the back of the room, not far from where Lucky hugged the wall in her dark hooded jacket.

Hanging along the dark wall in the back of the establishment, she hoped to get a glimpse of Evan before she positioned herself closer. Scanning the patrons and tables, she spotted him — the back of him. Thank God. He was at a small table with another man, close to the bar area.

The men playing pool eyed her with suspicion, but said nothing. She was grateful they were leaving her alone. One in particular though watched her except for when he was shooting the ball. She needed to make a move or do something before he spoke to her. Out of nervousness, she went into the ladies' restroom. The place was probably in better shape than the men's but it was ready for a total makeover and thorough cleaning. However, the privacy of the room gave her a chance to gather her thoughts of what to do next.

If Lucky walked over toward the end of the bar where Alice's guy, Ben, was earlier, she could get a good view of the person Evan was talking to. She might even get a photo with her phone. So, that was plan one. She could approach that end of the bar, asking to speak with Alice. Lucky would tell her she was there to take a few measurements when she could take the time away from the bar. But how could she get the listening device at Evan's table? And then it occurred to her — the condiment holders. Each table had a metal condiment holder with salt, pepper and ketchup. Her device was tiny enough to slip into one. She had to find a way to get it to their table without seeming suspicious or drawing attention to herself. She couldn't keep walking around with the hood on either. It looked strange to wear it inside.

Lucky walked out of the restroom without the hood on and spotted two empty tables toward the back. They each had condiment holders. She sat at one of the tables and situated the device inside the holder. The pool players continued to watch her with suspicion. Suddenly, Evan stood up from the table. She quickly looked down to avoid his gaze if he felt her staring at him. Damn, was he leaving? She watched as he headed for the restroom.

This was the perfect time. Lucky grabbed the condiment holder. Acting like she was part of the staff instead of some strange wallflower in the back of the bar was her tactic. She did not hesitate to walk by the table Evan had been at. She greeted the man he had been speaking with. "Doing okay, need anything right now?"

"I'm okay for now, but check back in fifteen minutes if you like."

"I can do that." She lifted the condiment holder he had and replaced it with the one she was carrying.

There was loud laughter from the bar area close to the front. She could see Alice, Ben and others gathered around each other. They had not noticed her, at least not yet. *It won't take Evan long to take a piss. Time to get the hell out of here.*

Chapter 14 ~ The SCIF

Jack sat in the SCIF with the counsel for the President of Brazil. The attorney opened a file in front of him and pulled out several papers.

"Dr. Foster, in order for us to continue with bringing you into this project, we will need to grant you proper security clearance. In cooperation with the United States government, we have conducted a thorough investigation into your background, education, family, friends and more. This began as soon as it was suspected you might be alive."

He looked at Jack's surprised expression and continued. "With the preliminary investigation out of the way, we feel confident you are of an upstanding character. You will need to read this document which is provided in English to solidify your clearance with Brazil and there are a separate set of documents for the United States government. I'm here to answer any questions you have. Take your time and read through them before signing. Once signed, you will be briefed in detail by our President and one of his close advisers."

Unconsciously, Jack rubbed the malachite heart at his throat while reading through the documents which primarily spelled out the handling of classified documents and the keeping of information. It also went into detail citing applicable laws for the mishandling of top secret information or violation of the clearance. He signed the documents for the Brazilian government and then proceeded to read the papers from the United States. While similar, these documents included a separate section about clearance that is "above top secret". Jack understood that he would be handling information in that realm of secrecy. It made him nervous, but insanely curious about why him, and why now.

He signed the documents from the USA and handed them to the counsel.

"Questions?" he asked.

"Oh, yes. I have a lot of questions, but I'll remain patient and wait for answers.

"That's always a good idea, Dr. Foster. Not to mention that some information is best disseminated a little at a time," the counsel said, with a wry grin. "Let me notify Karla that we are ready to proceed."

He stepped outside the SCIF and asked for the guard to notify Karla they were ready to meet with the President.

Jack stood, stretching his legs a bit. His injured leg tended to go a bit numb if he sat too long. But it also hurt like the devil if he stood or walked too much. He knew he needed rest, but it was too late for that. Jason was probably boarding his plane soon and would go back to his normal life. Jack's life was anything but normal. Hell, he couldn't remember that he was married and had a house somewhere in Alpharetta, Georgia. People could tell him that, but it did not make it so in his mind. He began to worry about all the documents he had just signed. What if he ended up forgetting that something was top secret … or above top secret and let the information out? He would have to be cautious.

The President and another man entered the SCIF and Jack stood, remembering the drill. He liked the president so far and felt a sense of respect for him in his position.

"We meet again. I am glad you chose to stay." He pointed to the man beside him. "This is my former Minister of Health, Marcos Rosario. I have appointed someone else to that position and you will understand why shortly. Marcos, this is Dr. Jack Foster."

"Pleased to meet you, Dr. Foster. I have read many of your published papers during the last week."

"Nice to meet you as well. Please, call me Jack," he said, shaking Marco's hand.

The President adjusted his chair and sat down. "Thank you, please, everyone sit down. Let's get to work on this. Marcos, if you are ready, bring to us what we need to know."

"I will begin and please, Mr. President and Jack, interject where you need to with comments or questions."

Marcos opened a file and appeared to have a bulleted list of items he would speak of. He took a pen and put a check mark beside the first item.

"Now, Dr. Foster … Jack, what I am about to relate to you has some parts known by the public and some parts secret. What is public is that right now, in China, at least one city is shut down with citizens locked in their homes, sometimes literally barred in by the military. We also see there is a large portion of the population out of their homes, seeking medical care. Lines appear to be very long, often extending into hospital or clinic halls, and even overflowing onto sidewalks on the exterior. This is all due to what we believe is the intentional release of a lethal virus from a BSL-4 infectious disease laboratory in that same city. Any confirmation of that has not been revealed to the public, but I have heard that some alternative news outlets are reporting it."

"When did this happen?" Jack asked.

"It is estimated around September of this year. With it being a level four facility, nothing could escape very easily."

"Could it have been accidental?"

"We believe it is intentional but are gathering more evidence. A hacker group launched a cyber attack on the facility locking and disabling all of their computers. The climate control for the facility was accessible to the hackers who could then raise or lower the temperature to anything they wanted.

The facility was shut down and contractors were brought in to restore the air conditioning which had burned out some units of the building's mechanical systems. It is speculated the virus was released during the repair of the facilities. If so, the time frame would be late September or sometime in early October."

"Have you been able to trace the group that hacked the facility?"

"It was difficult, but with the assistance of your government, it appears to be a rogue group who may have a financial interest in spreading the virus. To make matters worse, they are now threatening each nation that does not cooperate with their plan."

Jack sat closer to the table listening. "I understand so far. You need something to keep people from succumbing to the virus."

"Yes, that's why we need your expertise and help."

"What can you tell me about the virus?"

"It has been weaponized with gain of function technology. This began at a research facility located at a university in the United States. It was then transported to the laboratory in China where further gain of function activities were performed. The virus falls into the SARS group so it attacks the respiratory systems of those infected."

"So, we're talking about not just a virus, but a bio-weapon?" Jack questioned.

"Yes, that is correct. We are hoping the spread will be limited, but as a precaution, we are assuming it could travel worldwide."

The President stood momentarily with his hands in his pockets. "This is why you are here, Jack. We heard rumors you might have survived the crash and that family and others were looking for you. When our eyes on the ground notified us you were alive, we tracked you and your brother. Our government, with the approval of yours, decided to intervene sooner, rather than later, with this virus threatening all countries."

The President now paced the room and continued, "Marcos was doing an excellent job in his cabinet position as the Minister of Health. In Brazil, we have two major political parties vying for power all the time. The opposite party had threatened not just Marcos, but his family too. I accepted his resignation, allowing someone that my opponents approved of to take his position. Now, Marcos works directly for me, but in a secret capacity."

The President sat down again and nodded his head for Marcos to continue speaking.

"We have word that you were working on something that is extremely effective against viruses. Is that true?"

"Yes, I've developed something that I believe is an excellent anti-viral agent. I've been working on it for three years now. It's only been through animal trials, not human."

"This is why we need you, Jack. It's a gamble, but if this new drug works for humans, it could save many lives."

"I've always felt this drug is a game changer. I can't make any promises. We do need the human trials. Often, a drug will behave differently once administered at the human level. Do you know if anyone has isolated the virus so we could get a better idea of what we're dealing with?"

Marcos looked at him and chuckled slightly. "Not yet. The Chinese have not been cooperative with that."

Jack looked puzzled. "Then, how do you know it's a bio-weapon and has been engineered?"

The President spoke up to answer this question. "We have information that is being shared between our government and yours. Your President wants to speak with you as well. We have a conference scheduled with him in about twenty minutes. Why don't we take a break and resume this just before the hour?"

The men left the room and Jack followed. He noticed the two familiar military guards outside the door. He smiled at each, relieved not to be handcuffed or have a gun pointed at him.

It had been quite a day. He thought he was making his way to the airport using Jason's passport. Instead, he found himself sitting in a SCIF with people of importance including the President of Brazil. It was surreal to think that next; he would communicate with the President of the United States.

Chapter 15 ~ Ears on Evan

Lucky pulled the hood over her head while simultaneously pushing the side door of the bar open. It was not a moment too soon with Evan Mitchell emerging from the men's room. She swiftly exited the building, finding a misty drizzle of rain outside. Her breath caught in her throat. It was a close call. But she was confident Alice and Ben had not seen her. Evan would not have recognized her unless she was face to face with him. And, then it would only be recognition of facial features.

Once inside her van, she let out a deep breath, feeling relief and some sense of safety. Lucky locked the door and left the driver's seat area, climbing backward into the center of the van where there were no windows. From here, she should be within range to pick up any conversation happening at Evan's table. She just wished she had a way to record it. *Damn, you can't think of everything on a moment's notice.*

She situated the ear buds. They were working, but the volume was a little low. She adjusted them and was now listening to the man Evan was sitting with having a beer.

"Here's what you need to realize, Evan. I may do work for you, but I don't take orders from you. If you want me to get my hands on those documents, thumb drives or whatever you're looking for, I'm going to have to get in there, hopefully when no one is at home."

"What's that going to involve? I don't want the woman living there alarmed in any way, much less physically hurt."

"Did you grow a heart-on for the bitch, Evan?" he asked, in his slimy accent.

There was silence for a moment.

"Look, I control the money and that means you actually do work for me, Ragland. It's the holidays and people stay home more. I'm sure she will be leaving to go somewhere soon. You're just going to have to stake out that side road frequently and watch for her to leave. If you place a tracker on their vehicles, it will help."

"I've got a tracker on the older car her roommate or friend drives."

"Good, that helps."

"With the lady who owns the house staying home and not going anywhere, it's been impossible to place a tracker with her car in the garage."

"They may both suspect the surveillance. In fact, we've already had systems interrupted or removed in the house. By the way, what is your cover? We don't want to make the neighbors suspicious."

"Just call me the cable guy, truck and all."

"Make this work. You need to pull this off. I need that information. Do it my way and I'll double the fee. Here's a deposit on that."

There was a brief silence again. Lucky imagined Evan passing an envelope of bills to the dude.

"That will help. Christmas was expensive."

"Look, I'm working tomorrow morning. I gotta go. Message me when you have the stuff."

Lucky's heart began pounding as she saw Evan leave through the side door of the bar and walk toward his Porsche parked right in front of her van. *Stay still and be cool. He has no reason to suspect anything about this vehicle.*

She exhaled deeply as she watched him slide into his beautiful ride and take off. Satisfied that she had gathered some intel, she now knew a little more about who Evan was meeting and possibly why. It was more knowledge than she had before this day began.

Today, she had found the bar, met the owner, and now there was someone named Ragland. Lucky wondered if that was his nickname or last name. What she really wanted to do was track him. He didn't leave the bar right away. She kept the ear buds in, but no conversation at the table was taking place.

Lucky imagined that he must have stayed to drink more. Ragland was after something, but not someone.

Evan sounded pretty solid about the fact that he did not want the woman involved spooked or hurt. *How noble!*

The rain had picked up with intensity. Lucky thought about going ahead and leaving now, but something inside told her to stay put and wait. The listening device was still in the napkin holder at the table. She would need to get it back if she could. It was one of her more expensive gadgets. But not tonight. She was not risking going inside, even though she was in her painter's disguise. It would definitely seem a little strange to Alice if she had any intuition at all.

She used her cell phone to make voice notes of everything that had transpired so far tonight. Then, she hit a couple of buttons and turned it into text sending the file to Ric with a message.

Productive night. Still more questions and I'm waiting for the guy he was talking with to leave the bar. Just want to figure out what he's driving and get some info on him.

Lucky I've been waiting to hear from you. Where are you now? Still in that bar?

No, I'm in my van. In the back monitoring things. It's raining heavy now.

Look, I'm going to stay up until I know you're safe. Don't forget about me now!

I won't. Thanks

Ric was and had been her rock on many investigative adventures. He was like the good guy, nerdy boyfriend you need, but don't want. Why was she always attracted to the more dangerous ones? Lucky knew Ric would be the kind of guy that was a good fit for any woman. He was the smart choice. The guy was a wizard at computers, plus emotionally stable and dependable.

The spark wasn't there for her though, even though he was attractive. Something about the chemistry was off. No doubt it was psychological on her part. She knew that stemmed from her past, but she couldn't change that easily. Besides, they worked well together. A relationship might totally screw that up. Still, she knew she could count on Ric anytime, anywhere.

The side door swung open and out popped the man she'd been waiting for. He took a few steps and was almost off the sidewalk getting ready to cross the side street when she heard a female call his name. She couldn't see her because whoever it was stood inside the bar with the side door propped open covering her. She also could not hear what she said to Ragland. But he had turned and was making his way back toward the bar. The rain was still coming down and he stepped inside once more. *Shit, I wish he'd make up his mind!*

Lucky continued to sit cross-legged in the floor of the van behind the front section. She kept the hood on her head to conceal any outline of a person that might show up with a stray bolt of lightning or car lights headed down the road flashing light inside the van.

She had to wait this out with the guy. He had to leave at some point. This was the hardest part for her. She was a fiery, impatient sort who was happiest when she was multitasking. Her ear buds provided no detailed conversations. In fact, she had taken one of them out, only leaving the other one in case Ragland sat at that table again and had some conversation going on. But all she heard was pool cues hitting balls, a television playing in the background, clinking of glasses or bottles and occasional laughter.

And then, something surprising happened. She couldn't believe her eyes. Ragland came out of the bar with Alice. They were touching and fondling each other like teenagers. Lucky watched as they headed up the steps to Alice's apartment. They were tipsy, but hurrying with the rain. They acted like giggling adolescents sneaking around. Was she doing him? Was he doing her? He was a lot younger than Alice. This was interesting. Now, she must paint Alice's bathroom and kitchen so she could learn more.

Chapter 16 ~ Commander in Chief

The President of Brazil, his counsel, and former Minister of Health sat waiting with Jack for the President of the United States to connect with them via a private satellite call. There was a signal on the screen of the wall indicating it would be momentarily, and to please stand by.

An announcer came on as the image of the U.S. President filled the screen, "The President is connected now."

"Hello my friend," the President of Brazil greeted him. "Can you hear me well?"

"Yes, I hear you very well. Thank you for finding Dr. Foster. Was his brother with him?"

"Yes, he was, and he has returned home."

The President addressed Jack now. "Dr. Jack Foster, I am so glad you are alive. I'm calling upon you to assist with what could turn into a worldwide pandemic. I understand you have some injuries from the plane crash. Are you up for this task?"

"My injuries should not hamper any work to be done, Mr. President. I do have a concern about some memory issues I am having."

"Yes, I was briefed a bit on that. I understand you do not remember your wife, is that correct?"

"Yes, Sir."

"Well, I hope we can help with that and I believe we can. Let me speak first to what's going on."

The President paused, looked down at his notes, and then continued.

"You have been briefed that we are potentially dealing with a virus that has been modified to be more lethal than it was originally using gain of function, correct?"

"Yes, Mr. President. And I understand no one has officially isolated the virus as of yet."

"That's right. Your task is to continue working on the drug that Chadwell Pharmaceuticals was trying to quash. You will remain in Brazil for two reasons while doing this work. Number one, we have good reason to believe your safety would be in jeopardy if you came back to the United States now. And, number two, we have an agreement off the books with our friends in Brazil to work ahead of the possible pandemic that could unfold. You see, Jack, we're dealing with some bad actors in other countries that would like to use this as an event to exert their political agenda worldwide. Those that would do this are monsters, in my opinion. But, we are ahead of them on this and hopefully will stay that way. Do you understand what I'm talking about?"

"Yes, Mr. President. Unfortunately, I do. I have not been privy to every piece of the puzzle, but I have known something was coming."

"Good, I thought a man of your intelligence and talent would recognize there were nefarious aspects lining up. You're going to be working against time, Jack. Each day, this virus will be spreading. I pray it is not as lethal as the people who engineered it wanted it to be. The United States, Brazil, and unknowingly, the entire world are counting on you, Jack. I understand you are excellent at team building and management of personnel. Every leader needs a loyal, dedicated team. I also understand you lost significant members in the crash. I'm very sorry. We need you to build a new team in Brazil, one that will work to counteract this potential plague."

Jack looked at the President on the screen and nodded in agreement. The President leaned forward slightly and continued. "We have highly skilled personnel in place from Brazil and the United States. More are arriving soon for you to work with. You'll be in charge of your project without hindrance. Simultaneously, I know that I and the President of Brazil will make sure you are tended to health wise and comfortable in every way. Is there anything you want to ask me?"

"Yes, Mr. President. It sounds like I could be here for a while. Is there some way to let my family know what is going on with me, especially my parents? I guess we better let my wife know too."

The President smiled, "Yes, we can give a personal limited briefing to them in private. Always good to let your wife know where you are, Jack."

Jack grinned. "Thank you, Mr. President."

The two Presidents exchanged goodbyes with plans to speak again soon.

Marcos caught Jack's attention, "Your day has been very trying." Jack nodded in agreement. "Karla and I will show you to your accommodations so you can clean up and rest before dinner. Once we dine together this evening, I would love to give you a tour of the facilities where you will be working."

"That sounds great, Marcos."

Jack was extremely fatigued, but his mind was nervously occupied with the situation he found himself in. His life was moving ahead fast and dragging him with it. He kept his mind open and curious most of the time, but the suspense of wondering what lie ahead made him tense inside.

Marcos led him out of the SCIF and back to the receiving area where the restrooms were located. He sat in a chair, waiting now for Karla to join them. "She should be here any moment. I bet you can't wait to relax a little."

He smiled, raising an eyebrow to Marcos. "It's been an interesting day. That's for sure."

Both men heard footsteps approaching the outer entrance door. Karla entered along with a young male carrying a piece of luggage. "See that this is delivered to Dr. Foster's new residence."

"Yes, right away," he said.

She turned to face both men. "I'm very sorry to make you wait, Dr. Foster. If you would like, we can see you to your accommodations now."

"I'm ready."

"This way, please"

Karla walked toward another set of steel doors to the right of the walled off reception area. She placed her hand on the biometric reader and the doors opened. They were again in another hall made of concrete and it descended further with a gradual slope. The same fluorescent lighting was present as in the tunnel leading from the mansion.

Another set of steel doors signaled they had maybe reached their destination. Jack wondered what kind of accommodations he would have. Perhaps it would resemble something you would find in a barracks or on a naval vessel. As they passed through the doors, they reached yet another walled off reception area. This time, the military officer greeted Karla and said something in the native tongue. Jack recognized the word "ready".

They stood momentarily while another employee came out of the back door of the walled off reception desk area. "Hello," he greeted them. "I have everything ready for Dr. Foster," he said, handing Jack a large envelope. "Inside, sir, you will find pertinent information regarding the entire facility, including our medical bay area, dining, exercise and entertainment areas. Your room has been assigned also. All I need from you is your hand print. Are you right-handed?"

"Yes."

He held out a thin glass tablet for Jack to place his right hand upon. "Please place your right hand flat here."

Jack placed his hand on the tablet making sure his fingers were apart and his hand was lying as flat as possible. The tablet gave off a beeping sound after a moment.

"That's it. Now, let's make sure it works," the man said.

He directed the party to walk toward another set of steel doors. "Go ahead, Dr. Foster, try your hand on the door's scanner."

Jack placed his hand on the scanner and the doors opened. "Wow, that made it into your system quickly."

"It's the best system we could devise, for now," he said, smiling.

"Welcome to Teju Jagu, also known as Underground Brazil, Dr. Foster."

Jack's eyes became enormous as he gazed at the space before him. The doors opened to reveal an expansive glass domed area with trees and a pond in the middle. Sounds of nature were heard in the space. He looked at Karla, "The trees -- are they real?"

"Walk over and touch one."

Jack looked down at his feet. No longer were they merely walking on concrete. He was on a path that resembled a brick road, but without differences in the level of the bricks. Obviously, it was a concrete finish made to emulate that, and it appeared to wind around the entire domed facility.

Butterflies, bees, and an occasional dragonfly passed by in the air, traveling from tree to shrubs. He walked up to what appeared to be a Japanese Maple tree growing close to the pond. It seemed real to him. To be sure, he brushed his fingers on the soft edges of the leaves. An azalea bush grew near it and numerous bees were engaged in gathering nectar. He glanced at the other side of the pond and could see a weeping willow bending its branches toward the water's edge.

"How are you managing to sustain this underground?" he asked, looking at both Karla and Marcos.

Marcos answered first, "It's a combination of technologies. One harvests sunlight outside the mountain, and then transfers that energy to the dome you see above you. But, there are other things involved too."

Jack noticed a man and a woman riding bicycles along a path toward the back of the domed area. Karla anticipated his next question. "You will be given a bicycle also. It's a preferred method for getting around. This place is even larger than you see now. It's also a great way to get some exercise in. Of course, this is up to you. We need to have that leg of yours examined in the medical bay by tomorrow at the latest."

Jack stayed silent feeling as if he had landed in a new world. He turned in a circle, marveling at everything around him.

Karla interrupted, "Let's go to your unit, Jack. Once there, I think you'll find a new toy or two that will assist you in answering many of your questions. I want to point out an area on our way. Follow me."

The men walked behind Karla as she led them to a massive indoor greenhouse. Inside, plants were being propagated alongside rows of vegetables and herbs.

"This area provides some of the food the full and part-time residents here enjoy," she said proudly. "We also have an area just to the right of the greenhouse that is more of a traditional gardening area, which you'll see when we exit."

"I'm intrigued with how healthy all the plants appear," Jack said. "Actually, I'm blown away with this entire facility."

"It's quite an engineering and technological achievement," Marcos said.

"Let's take a look at the garden, and then we will pass by the dining area on the way to what you will be calling home for a while."

Home, Jack thought. At this point, he was a nomad. But this was going to be an interesting place to call home, at least for a while.

Chapter 17 ~ Discovery Ride

Evening, December 26, 2019

Sonya and Haley had spent the entire afternoon and evening going through everything in the basement. So far, Jack's hiding place had not been discovered, only boxes full of memories. They had searched unusual places such as the box with extra kitchen items. Haley wondered why she had not donated those items. With a flashlight, they had carefully looked under each of the wooden shelves in the basement to see if Jack had attached something to the bottom of the shelving. Overall, each felt they had searched every inch of the basement and nothing was found.

"Could he have it buried in the backyard or something, like a time capsule?" Sonya asked.

Haley grinned, "You never know. Jack might have done something like that."

"Tomorrow, I'm going to walk down the hill and look around, see if any of the ground looks disturbed."

"Okay, I'll look with you. Right now, I'm hungry. Let's get some pizza, want to?" Haley asked.

"Sure, do you want to order in?"

"No, let's get out of here for a bit. Maybe leaving for a while will help us figure out where in the world Jack has hidden this information."

Haley bit into a slice of mushroom, olive and pepperoni pizza. "This is delicious. I can't believe how hungry I am. This is my third piece."

"Go for it," Sonya said, smiling. "I've wanted to ask you all day how you're feeling about last night — you know, seeing Jack again."

Haley took a sip of her soda and hesitated for a moment. "Extremely grateful that he's alive! I wanted to put my arms around him when he appeared on that screen."

"For sure," Sonya said, nodding her head. "What about the memory issue?"

"It matters. I sure hope it is temporary. If not, maybe I'll find a way to make him fall in love with me again," she said, smiling.

"There you go. That's a good angle."

"Last year, we visited with our neighbors, Alex and Jessie, the day after Christmas. This year, they flew to his parent's home in Minnesota and won't return until after New Year's Eve."

"I didn't realize they were out of town."

"I want to tell them Jack is alive, but I can't."

"What about that female investigator? Can she know?"

"Good question, we really need to talk with Papa Foster and Sharon. Want to see if they might be up for company? We could take them the rest of this pizza."

"Sure, give them a call."

"Pizza delivery," Sonya called out as Joe Foster answered the door. "Well, half a pizza actually." He grinned wide and Sharon stood just behind him.

"Come in you two out of the cold," he said.

"Where are your coats?" Sharon inquired in a loving, but motherly way.

"Oh, we kind of rushed out of the house. I was pretty hungry and pizza sounded good. Can we take this to your kitchen?"

"Absolutely," Sharon said.

Sonya sat the pizza box on the countertop and opened it, "You might want to heat it up first before eating."

Sharon bent down and pulled a stoneware slab from her cabinet. "Let's put it on this and stick it in the oven on low. Have your parents returned home, Sonya?"

"Yes, they left this morning. I was glad they could come for Christmas."

"Haley, you and Sonya did a wonderful job hosting. The food was fantastic and everything looked so festive and beautiful," Sharon said. Joe stood fooling with his cell phone on the other side of the kitchen.

"Thanks, we enjoyed hosting. Today, we have put away almost all the decor. We were actually killing two birds with one stone."

"What do you mean?" Sharon inquired.

"Is it safe to talk here?" Haley asked, looking at Joe and Sharon.

Joe spoke up, "Yes, it's been swept. I believe it to be safe."

"I began thinking of Jack not remembering me which made me wonder if he had any memory of our home we bought together. On our last night together before his trip, he told me there was information on the project he was working on hidden in our house somewhere. But he wouldn't tell me where. I'm wondering if he would have forgotten the hiding place. I also want to know what we might be able to learn from that information."

"Well, you may not remember, but you told us about this when we had our first big meeting after the fake funeral." Joe now referred to it as Jack's fake funeral. "However, we all forgot to make this part of our investigation to look for what Jack had hidden. I don't know why we didn't remember to take that into account, except we were so focused on locating him in Brazil."

"Yeah, you're right," Haley said. "We searched the entire basement today going through every container, box, nook and cranny. We found nothing. Maybe you could think of where he might have hidden something like that."

"Did you look in his office?" Joe asked.

"No, I thought that was such an obvious place. He would probably avoid hiding anything sensitive there."

"Yeah, you're probably right."

"I know we have to keep the fact that Jack is alive secret, but I was wondering if we should mention it to Lucky Adams."

Joe paused with his forehead wrinkling. "Honestly, I don't know. When I don't have a clear answer, I have learned to do nothing. To be on the safe side, we better keep it only within our family for now."

Sharon checked on the pizza and pulled it from the oven. "Perfect," she said, placing the stoneware on the counter.

Someone rang the doorbell and knocked on the door. Joe bolted toward the foyer. "Let me see who this is. Strange this time of night. Maybe it's Sarah with the kids."

Joe opened the door to find a man and woman dressed alike in dark suit coats. "Mr. Joe Foster?"

"Yes, that's me."

"I'm here on behalf of the federal government. We would like to speak with you and your wife regarding your son, Jack Foster."

"Okay, come in."

"Actually, we would like to make sure our conversation is secure. Would you mind taking a brief ride around the neighborhood area with us?" the woman asked him, motioning toward a long black vehicle parked out front.

Joe was feeling cautious. "Do you have any credentials you can show me? How do I know who you are?"

"We have credentials, and we're happy to show you."

The lady produced a letter with the seal of the President of the United States on it top center. Jack quickly skimmed the document. It appeared official and was addressed to the immediate family of Jack Foster.

It began with very gracious words stating that Jack was needed at this time to do something in service to his country. An envoy was being sent to explain the circumstances to prevent unnecessary worry for the family.

Joe looked at the two again. "Sure, we'll go with you. Jack's wife, Haley, is here with us now, along with her cousin, Sonya. Can they come as well?"

The two government employees looked at one another. "Yes, they can. We'll wait for you here outside and then go for a brief ride in our car to talk."

By this time, all three ladies had heard the tail end of the conversation. "Joe, what is it? What's going on?" Sharon asked.

"We're about to find out. We're going to take a ride around the neighborhood."

The long black vehicle turned out to be an older model limousine, but roomy enough for each to sit comfortably and have room for the two agents in the back with them. Two more government employees were in the front, the actual chauffeur and another one.

"First, thank you for coming with us. This will not take long, but we will drive to be certain nothing we say is being projected somewhere else for ears we don't want knowing. Let me introduce you to Chip and my name is Evelyn. We work directly for the President of the United States. We do not work for any of the three letter agencies you may be familiar with. Chip and I are part of the President's special envoy to carry information, messages, whatever we are entrusted with. So, what we tell you tonight is coming directly from the Commander-in-Chief. Do you understand?"

Everyone nodded in agreement.

"Chip, would you like to convey the message?"

"Sure. We are aware that you have discovered Jack is alive. The President was also extremely pleased to hear this."

"How did you find out?" Joe asked.

"I'm not allowed to speak of that," he said, with a serious face.

Chip cleared his throat, "Continuing, Jack is serving in a particular capacity for the government right now. His service is in line with his study and work. This was a special request by the President and Jack agreed to do so. At some point soon, we may be able to set up a secure line of communication for each of you with him. I cannot tell you the nature of the project. It is classified top secret. Evelyn and I are not privy to the details. Our job is simply to confidentially let you know that your loved one is alive, being well taken care of, and doing work to help his country right now. During this time, you will not know his exact location."

"What about Jason," Joe asked. "He was with Jack."

"We have been advised that Jason will be returning to the United States very soon."

"How long will he be performing this service?" Haley asked.

"The length of time is unknown right now. If we are able to ascertain a time frame, you will be notified."

The color in Haley's face turned pale and she looked as if she might be sick. *How much stranger and complicated could things get?*

The President's envoy messengers, Chip and Evelyn, returned to Sharon and Joe's home when there was nothing more they could say. The Fosters and Sonya understood detailed questions would go unanswered, either because Chip and Evelyn did not know the answer, or could not reveal it. As they entered the house, Joe Foster disarmed the security system and closed the front door, locking it.

"Well Sharon, I don't know how you feel. I'm shocked! If anyone would have told us this would happen with Jack, I wouldn't have believed it," he said, shaking his head.

Sharon sat down in the kitchen and stared for a moment at the pizza box saying nothing. She finally spoke, "Joe, he was always fooling around with things and experimenting. I'm sort of not surprised. He's a genius in his own way." She looked at Haley and Sonya. "Did I tell you that Jack did not speak until he was about four years old?"

"No, you didn't mention it, nor did he," Haley said, with surprise.

"Jason did the talking for him and Jack let him," she said, with a smirk on her face.

Haley and Sonya laughed.

Sharon reached out and took Haley's hand. "It's good to hear you laugh. I know this throws another monkey wrench in things, but maybe it's just the way it's going to play out. You know, I've learned in my life that sometimes you just have to surrender to what is and be patient."

"You're right. It's just so hard sometimes."

"Sure it is. You're doing great, Haley. We've all been through so much. Thank the Lord above that he's alive, and it sounds like in good hands."

Haley hugged Sharon. "Don't worry about me, I have tough moments, but I get through them."

Sharon took Haley by the hand, "I'm always there for you if you need me, okay?"

Haley hugged her, "Yes, you are. Thank you!"

"Well, I suppose this answers our questions we had. We must keep Jack's existence secret from everyone for now," Sonya said.

Chapter 18 ~ The Apartment

Jack left the greenery and wildlife splendor of the domed area with Marcos and Karla leading him into a wide corridor. The walls appeared to be aluminum or stainless steel. The ceiling was arched and high. It was like someone had taken a twenty-foot metal pipe and cut it in half to form the passageway. There were doors lining the hall which were numbered. Bicycles and adult-sized tricycles were parked outside many of the doors.

"This is one of our residence sections. I think you will be impressed with your accommodations," Karla said, with a proud expression and tone. She seemed to love her job and he wondered if she was required to live here.

Marcos and Karla stopped at number 449. "This is your apartment, Jack. Go ahead and put your hand on the scanner." As the scanner read Jack's hand print, steel pocket doors slid open horizontally. It reminded him of something you would see in a science fiction movie. The room was massive including a comfortable lounging type chair, and a very high tech looking desk area. A king sized bed dominated the center of the room. The bedding appeared very functional, but not beautiful or luxurious. A wall with four separate large screens affixed to it separated the bathroom from the living quarters.

"This is so surprising — in a good way," Jack said, still taking in all the details of the room.

"Let me show you some important features and then Marcos and I will leave so you can relax. Dinner is at seven."

"What time is it now?"

"It is almost five-thirty. So, not much time. First, we estimated your sizes for clothing. You will find most of what you need this first couple of days inside here," Karla said, pointing to luggage beside a closet door.

"You will have my contact information. Send me a list of anything you need and I will have it delivered. We want you to be comfortable, Jack. You will find initial toiletries in the bathroom. But again, let me know what you prefer. We can get just about anything in the world. We have a barber shop here by appointment also."

She reached into her large bag she had been carrying and handed Jack what looked like a piece of clear glass. "This is the first toy you will use for many communications. Think of it like an upgraded phone." Here is a cover for it also if you prefer that. Of course, due to its size, it can seem bulky, so there is a smaller version much like any cell phone that you can use interchangeably. To operate the glass pad, simply place your hand on it to begin."

Jack followed her instructions, and a screen lit up within the unit, turning the clear glass into a deep indigo blue.

"I see contacts here on the home screen. Is that how I send a message to you?"

"You got it. I am already listed there. I can tell you will have this device mastered in no time. The smaller phone unit works on the same principles. Marcos, do you want to show him anything?"

"Yes." Marcos walked toward the desk area and pointed to the three large wall monitors above the desk on the wall. "This is where you can keep real time tracking of your work, Jack. Later, you will see the laboratory and other facilities. But, if you wake in the middle of the night with a question or concern, you can check in with what's happening right here. On this project, we will run three shifts of personnel once the drug is at the production level."

"Awesome," Jack said. "I'm blown away by all the tech. What about the four screens on the wall over there? What do they do?"

Karla chuckled, "Low tech, Jack. These are ordinary basic televisions. Only programming coming in, nothing goes out on those screens. Some who have occupied this room like to watch more than one screen at a time, especially when it comes to news channels."

Jack looked puzzled, "Okay, so these two devices you gave me and the screens above the computers have information going both ways, right?"

"Yes, and if you are ever worried about your privacy, simply hit this button at the desk. This is like an airplane mode, cutting you off from the internal system."

Marcos added, "One more thing that will assist you greatly, at least it did me. There is an application on all the devices that is an internal instruction manual with explanations and videos that can answer just about any question. The name on the icon is InExpress."

"We'll get out of your way now. Your glass pad will remind you of dinner and give you directions to the dining room. One last question, would you like a bicycle or tricycle?" Karla asked.

Jack thought for a moment. "With my leg, I better go with the trike. If I want to change my mind later and switch, could I?"

"Yes, of course. That is no problem at all."

Marcos and Karla made their way toward the door. "You will need to let us out, Jack. You are now the only person who can access the door for this room."

Jack rushed over to place his hand on the scanner and the doors slid open for the two. "See you at dinner," he said.

The doors closed on their own seconds after they departed. Looking around the massive room once more, Jack wished he could just stay here for a while and not be bothered with anything further. He was exhausted from the emotional ups and downs he had experienced. From being taken hostage on the roadside in the rain and flown to another location handcuffed and under armed guard, his heart rate had been through several exercises today.

The excitement of meeting the President of Brazil and then conferencing live with the President of the United States was nerve wracking. From now on, he supposed anything could happen. He would need to just stay calm and steady.

Jack opened the piece of luggage and found a package of underwear his size along, with new socks. There were two pairs of sweatpants with various t-shirts. Karla had sent a jacket which was more like a windbreaker with the Brazilian flag on it. She also included a sweatshirt that matched the jacket.

Toward the bottom, he found three pairs of tennis shoes in three different sizes. This was sorely needed. His shoes had taken a hell of a beating, even though they were not that old. One pair out of the three looked like a size match. There were also three pairs of cargo type pants like the ones he wore now that belonged to Jason.

Jack reflected on his feeling of floating from one place to another, drifting without a real home. Supposedly, he had an actual home that held a beautiful wife he adored. But he couldn't remember it — couldn't even conjure any feelings about it.

He walked into the bathroom and relieved himself. The room was very functional and he couldn't wait to get clean. He turned the faucet of the shower on, shed his clothes and stepped in. Soap, shampoo, and body wash were within easy reach. This was his second time getting cleaned up in the last 48 hours and it felt good — real good.

At this underground facility, he had noticed small cameras along the corridor. He suspected every section of the subterranean space was under surveillance for security purposes. Hopefully, he had some privacy in his apartment area. He needed to ask Karla and Marcos about that.

Chapter 19 ~ Touchdown

Early Morning Hours, December 27, 2019

Jason slept off and on while flying home. Walking away from the plane departure area, he was craving food -- even fast food sounded great to him right now. He turned his phone on and saw a message from Sarah.

I will be there to pick you up. I may have to keep driving around the airport until I see you outside waiting.

Jason left his phone on for now, just in case he needed to call or text Sarah. He felt a sense of paranoia about being tracked. The entire last twenty-four hours had been traumatic. He was also weary of traveling and ready to see his beloved redheaded wife. He'd been in Brazil long enough. Thank God, Jack was alive. But things were complicated.

He took the elevator down to the baggage claim area, even though he had none. This would be the level where Sarah could easily pick him up. He walked outside to the sidewalk and watched for Sarah's vehicle. About ten minutes went by and then, she appeared. He grabbed the passenger door handle and jumped inside. She hugged him from the driver's seat, placing a kiss on his lips. "Strange meeting you here in the middle of the night, mister." He laughed and then heard Allison. "Daddy, you're here."

"Yes, I am. I missed everyone so much and I hope we never spend Christmas apart ever again."

"Me either, Daddy. Wait until you see what Santa brought us."

Sarah smiled, while navigating the vehicle onto the interstate. "At least the traffic isn't so bad in Atlanta this time of night."

She always found the good side of things and that's one thing Jason loved about her. Now, he had to explain to her about Jack's situation. "I have a lot to tell you, but let's wait until we are home."

"Okay, I'm so glad you're here, honey."

"Me too," he said, with a big sense of relief. "Hey, I'm starving. Can we go through a drive-through?"

"Sure, pick your poison."

Jason laughed, "Somehow, I feel like I've already tasted some of it while I've been gone."

Sarah pulled her vehicle into the garage next to Jason's. "Home sweet home, honey."

"It's so good to be here, Sarah. You would not believe the last twenty-four hours." She could see in his face how exhausted he was. Something was unusual about him. Sarah had the feeling Jason couldn't talk about it now, especially with the children present.

"Okay, you two. Let's get you out of your car seats and inside. We have milkshakes."

Allison and Eli were both excited, even though it was four o'clock in the morning now. They ran into the kitchen just off the garage. Allison removed her jacket and Sarah assisted Eli with his while Jason brought in the fast food bags. He sat the food and drinks on the table and reached out to both of his children. "I'm so glad to see you both. I missed not being here, especially for Christmas morning." They hugged him back and Eli wanted his father to hold him for a while.

"Okay, let's get our hands washed and we'll eat our middle of the night fast food dinner."

Allison followed her mother to the kitchen sink, while Jason carried little Eli.

All were quiet as they consumed their food and milkshakes, except for the slurping sound the children made with their straws as they reached the bottom of the shakes.

Sarah touched Jason on the shoulder as she rose from the table. "Honey, I'm going to get the kids tucked in for sleep again."

"I want to kiss them goodnight too. But then, I'm headed for the shower."

In the shower, Jason wondered how he would relay everything that happened in Brazil to Sarah, much less his parents and Haley. It was very late, or early, depending how you looked at it. He knew she was curious for answers. How could he condense the story without going into too much detail?

He toweled off in the bath and skipped shaving for now. He brushed his teeth and entered the bedroom area where Sarah had the sound of soft ocean waves playing and an aromatherapy dispenser misting the air with a clean, pleasant scent. She was reclining on the bed, smiling at him. "Don't worry. I know you're tired. Nothing is expected of you. I just thought this might help relax you."

"It's very thoughtful, babe."

Sarah rose from the bed and headed for the bathroom. "Go ahead and get comfy. I'll be back after I brush my teeth and we'll cuddle."

Sarah was cuddly. Sexy as she was, there was also a comforting motherly side of her that made him just want to snuggle and bury his head in her bosom. Jason looked forward to that. He would keep what he had to say brief about the situation with Jack. He wondered if it would create more questions for Sarah and make it hard for her to sleep.

She emerged with her long red hair loose now, falling past her shoulders. "Your hair is getting long," he commented.

"I'm trying to grow it out like it was when we met," she said, sliding under the covers with him.

"I'm so glad I have you, Sarah." And, he was. She was like the solid earth that made him feel real and grounded.

She hugged him tight. "Can you tell me anything about the last twenty-four hours that seem to have dragged you down so much?"

Jason let out a long sigh. Sarah rested her head on his chest without seeing his facial expressions.

"Jack has been commandeered to work for the government of Brazil and the United States on something secret that I don't know about. They gave me the choice of staying with him or coming home. I didn't want to leave him alone, but if I stayed, I would have had very limited contact with you and my family."

"Oh my gosh," Sarah said sitting up now in the bed. "How did this come to happen?"

"Well, that gets into the last 24 hours. It's crazy! I thought we were going to take gifts to the tribe that helped Jack heal from the crash. He changed his mind, saying he felt like he needed to get home and would thank them on a future trip. We left the hotel with my guide, Lucas, driving us in his jeep. We were traveling toward the closest city where we could book Jack on a flight to another Brazilian city with an international airport."

"The rain was so heavy at one point Lucas had to pull off the road. We were then ambushed by the military who took Jack and I into their custody. They drove us to a base where we were put on a helicopter and flown to a location I cannot tell you about. I cannot speak of it at all, Sarah. It might jeopardize things."

"Okay, I'm not going to ask. Damn, this sounds like a movie."

"Looking back, it doesn't feel real, but I know it was. Sarah, we were handcuffed a good part of the day. We had rifles pointed at us at times. Don't get me wrong. The military personnel were not cruel, but it was stressful and threatening."

"So, let me try to understand this. Is Jack working for the Brazilian military?"

"No, it's higher than that. Jack is working for the President of Brazil and our President as well."

"Wow, what about his memory failing him in certain areas?"

"They assured me they had the best care in the world and would help Jack in any way they could. They'll be seeing to his leg that he's limping on as well."

"That's good. Jason. How in the world is Haley going to handle this?"

"I've been wondering the same thing. Are you going to be able to sleep after I told you this?"

Sarah looked up at him and smiled. "Probably not. I'm so glad you are here and safe with us, Jason."

"Me too, honey. You don't know how good it feels to lie here with you in our bed."

Chapter 20 ~ Ric & Lucky

Ric cracked a smile as he noticed Lucky entering the restaurant in her painter's disguise. She made her way to the table and sat down. "Well, hello Picasso. Did you sleep in that outfit?"

"What if I did?"

"Easy girl, just wondering. Thanks for letting me know you got home okay."

"Thanks for being there for me to reach out to," she said, smiling.

"The smells coming from the open kitchen in this place are killing me. Hungry?"

"Sure. Yeah, I am hungrier than I realized," she said.

"Good! I'm going to try the cha yen with my meal."

"Isn't that the Thai version of iced tea?"

"Sure is, want to try it as well?"

"I'll stick with cream soda if they have it. If not, just regular iced tea."

"You and your cream soda! Okay, they serve family style here. Look over the menu and let me know what you'd like to try. I'm making the bigger bucks at Chadwell right now, so I'll buy."

Lucky scanned the menu. "I'm a fan of brown rice over white. Don't get me wrong, I love soft jasmine rice, but I know the brown rice is healthier."

"Okay, I'm in agreement. How spicy can you stand?"

"Ugh, not too much. This is like my breakfast. But, I can do a little spice. I know they're big on it."

"How about the Pad Thai with chicken."

"Perfect, I've had it before and it's not too spicy."

"Let's get some spring rolls too," Ric suggested.

"Go for it."

The server approached the table. He was dressed in a black shirt and pants with an oversized white apron. A black scarf was tied neatly on his head, covering his hair. "Would you like to order now?"

Ric spoke up, "Do you have red cream soda?"

The server looked behind him momentarily, searching. "Actually, we do. No one has ordered it yet. We've only been open ten days now."

"Great, because this lady loves her cream soda. We're going to begin with a plate of the brown rice and sautéed vegetables in sweet sauce. We would also like the Pad Thai with chicken. And, I'll have the cha yen to drink."

"Alright, thank you. I'll get on this now," he replied.

Lucky called after him, "Oh, and some vegetable spring rolls, please."

"Certainly."

"So, what's on your agenda for today?" Ric asked.

"Tonight, I have the Pilates class to teach. Last night was yoga. It was a small turnout. What can you expect the day after Christmas? Before that, I'm going by that bar again."

"Why?"

"I'm going to give the lady who owns it an estimate to paint her kitchen and bathroom in her apartment upstairs. Plus, I need to try to retrieve my little black listening device I left in one of her condiment holders."

Ric smirked. "The old napkin holder trick, eh?"

"Hey, I was improvising the best I could. It worked pretty well. But, that's only act one of my crazy night. After Evan left, this guy named Ragland that he had been talking to went upstairs and got cozy with Alice. He's probably twenty years younger than her. She's living it up like she's Cher. More power to her."

Ric rolled his eyes and laughed. "So, you want to paint her apartment to find out what's going on between her and this guy called Ragland? What kind of name is that?"

"Pretty much. I wondered about his name too. I'm assuming people call him by his last name."

"You're probably right."

"There's something strange about that bar, Ric. I've got a feeling about it. Also, Evan is meeting with the guy to get him to break into someone's house and steal documents or something. I have a good feeling that it might be the Fosters."

"Interesting. Do you think you should give Haley Foster a heads up?"

"You know, I do think I should tell her. I don't want to frighten her. But she needs to know."

"Well then, by all means follow your nose. Just be safe."

"Always — always trying to stay safe. You said you found some information, right?"

"Yes, I was able to retrieve some emails Chadwell believes are deeply deleted. They were encrypted."

"And, did you decipher them?"

"Yes, along with a lengthy pdf attached to one. So far, I've cracked two emails. I'm still working on another one. I brought a print-out so you could see for yourself."

He handed a file to Lucky and she read the first email which was from the head of the CDC to many different parties, some at the National Institutes of Health. She recognized Tellinger and Jack Foster at Chadwell. But there were more interesting parties. Lucky quickly skimmed the email and document referred to that Ric had printed. Much of it was technical, and somewhat veiled.

"What in the hell is P-2019 they keep referring to?" she asked.

"I have come to the conclusion that the P might stand for pandemic."

"Really? If so, that gives a whole different meaning to the substance in these emails."

"Doesn't it?"

"Ric, if the "p" stands for pandemic and we were to have one soon, that means these people either are privy to special knowledge, or planning it themselves. I mean, think of it. The people in this communication are the top echelon of government and big pharma. Here they are, discussing a pandemic coming?"

"Well, you and I both know that many of these government agencies are just extensions of the pharma companies. A choice employee leaves a pharmaceutical corporation and then they end up in a decision-making role at one of these agencies. Really, they are all part of one enormous group. They've done this for far too long."

Lucky became energized and a bit animated. "Yes, they have. You know, much of the public is aware this goes on. They just don't know what to do about it. We've got big pharma in bed with all the major news media networks too. Over half of their advertising dollars are paid by them. They're lining the pockets of senators and congressman at state and federal levels. Who knows about the judiciary?"

Ric nodded in agreement. "Yes, but that's just in the United States. This is going on worldwide now."

"Which is why I say they are going to ruin our entire world if someone doesn't get a handle on them."

"Damn straight!" Ric agreed.

The server arrived with their steaming hot dishes, placing dinner plates in front of Lucky and Ric. He then turned to another employee following him with the drinks. "How does everything look?" he asked.

Ric sighed, "This is beautiful. I can't wait to taste it."

"I'll be back in a moment to check on you again."

"Thank you," Lucky said.

The two were temporarily quiet as they served the various dishes onto their plates. Lucky took a long drink of her red cream soda. "Ric, you've done great work here. But you've found nothing about the targeting of Dr. Foster and his team?"

"No, I wish I could find the smoking gun on that and quick."

"There's a lot to unpack in that document, Ric. Can I keep this file?"

"Um, I don't know. It seems like if it fell into the wrong hands it could put you in serious danger."

"Tell you what, I just want to read through it at home, slowly. I skimmed it quickly and I probably missed things. I promise to shred it as soon as I'm done."

"Promise me that you will, Lucky. It could truly compromise you."

"I know and yes, I promise. I will shred it immediately after reading it once more."

"Okay then."

"Here's what I don't get," she whispered. "There is no pandemic and 2019 is over in a few days."

"Haven't you heard what's going on in China?"

"No, what?" she asked.

"They've completely locked down an entire major city, claiming a virus is on the loose. All businesses are closed and the military is guarding the streets. The only people outside are those waiting in lines to get in the hospitals. It's complete craziness there right now. I can't believe you didn't know about this."

"Jeez, no. Well, I've been preoccupied with this investigation. Is this in the mainstream media?"

"A little, just what they have wanted to leak out. Most of the news is coming from residents in that city posting videos on social media. But, I also hear that China is insisting the videos be taken down by those same social media giants. If you view a video, download it because it's probably going to disappear. They may have an Internet black out instituted in China for a while."

"Wow, I'm going to have to get online today and see what I can find. First, I need to try and get my little black box back from that bar. I've worked up a painting estimate for Alice before coming today. I hope she bites on it."

"Lucky, I'm serious. If we are onto some type of scheme here between these entities, you need to shred that document quickly. Go home, commit it to memory and get rid of it."

"Hey, you be easy now. I told you I will and my word is good. Thanks for lunch. This is absolutely delicious."

"You're very welcome," he said, smiling at her. *God she was beautiful even in that crazy wig and painter get-up.*

"I'm assuming that once I've destroyed what's in the file, you will still be able to access the same information for an investigative authority?"

"I have everything archived somewhere safe for possible future use. I just want to find more."

Lucky blotted her mouth with her napkin, "Keep searching and I'm going to be working things on my end."

Chapter 21 ~ The Box

Two days after Christmas, Haley and Sonya were renewing their effort to find whatever Jack had hidden at the property.

"Haley, do you think Jack would have put this information in a box, maybe one made of metal?"

"It's possible, but it could be wooden or plastic as well."

"I was just thinking we could try using one of those metal detectors in the yard."

"Metal could leak and rust with the rain."

"That's true."

"I'm thinking he would avoid a metal box due to possible deterioration, at least in the elements."

Sonya was very determined. "Alright, we'll stick to our plan of looking for any signs of disturbed ground outside."

"I've got an idea, Sonya. We searched everywhere in the basement and found nothing. What's another place people hide things in their house? Where did your mom and dad hide Christmas gifts?"

Sonya looked at her and smiled, "The attic."

"Let's try there first and, if no luck, we'll search outside. Right now, it's pretty chilly out there."

Haley brought in a ladder from the garage and climbed into the attic access located in the hallway leading to the bedrooms. "Hand me that flashlight, Sonya." Standing on one of the top rungs of the ladder, she shone the light around and could see there were areas where it wasn't safe to walk, with only a small section covered in plywood on top of the insulation.

"Unless it's right here within our reach, Jack would not have put it up here. It's too risky to walk on all the rafters." Haley said. "I'm leaving the flashlight here and coming down. I want you to get a look at this and see what you think."

Sonya climbed up and held the flashlight, shining it around every area of the attic walls, revealing the beams that held the roof in place and the insulation lining the rafters. "I see something," she said.

"What?"

"There's a small area where the insulation looks disturbed. It looks piled up there compared to a more even distribution everywhere else."

"Maybe it's buried there. Let me get you something long to check it out. That insulation will make you itch for days."

Haley left and retrieved some tongs for grilling that were about two feet long. "Do you think these will work?" she asked Sonya upon her return to the ladder.

"Let me give it a try."

The ends reached through the fluffy insulation and then touched something solid. "Is it the wood rafter, or something else?" Sonya said, thinking out loud. She jostled the item a little and found a plastic box with a handle. "This has to be it, Haley," she said excitedly.

Sonya grabbed the box and dragged it toward her with the grill tongs. There was something rattling inside it. Overall, the box seemed very lightweight.

"Oh my gosh, I know this has to be it, Haley."

"I'm bringing it down so you can look inside," Sonya said, once she had both hands on the box.

She climbed down the ladder after shutting the door in the ceiling to the attic and making sure it was secure. She followed Haley to the kitchen table where she sat anxious to open the box, but waiting for her cousin.

"Ready?" she asked, as Sonya sat down with her.

"More than ready, let's see what this is."

The plastic box popped open easily. Inside were two flash drives, one red and one blue, plus an envelope.

"Let's see what's in the envelope," Haley said.

She opened it to find a letter, handwritten by Jack, along with several clippings of news articles and a small journal. Haley read the letter silently and then handed it to Sonya to read.

If you found this information, that means something happened to me. The information in this box is sensitive. Here is a synopsis:

The blue flash drive contains all of the formulations we tried from the initial to final phases. It also includes spreadsheets and conclusions of studies performed to date. Overall, all critical components for recreating the anti-viral drug I am currently working on are located within the drive. I believe this drug may significantly eliminate suffering or death with many different viral infections that often lead to complications such as, but not limited to, pneumonia.

The red flash drive contains various pieces of correspondence, emails, charts, spreadsheets and other data that make up part of a puzzle I have been putting together regarding Chadwell's insistence that we halt the drug I'm working on and, instead, put finishing touches on something else they want to manufacture for a potential world pandemic level outbreak.

The journal in this box contains personal notes I have recorded throughout my work on the drug development. It also includes notes I made after conversations with some board members at Chadwell, J.D. Tellinger, and conversations with the CDC, FDA and NIH.

If you have found this information, it should not be shared openly, but only with those who have a genuine need to know. All of it should be treated as highly confidential.

"Wow!" Sonya said, handing the letter back to Haley.

"This letter imparts a sense of heaviness or gravity, don't you think?" Sonya asked.

Haley took a deep sigh. "Yes, it does feel heavy. There is something big here or Jack would not have hidden it. The way he begins the letter: "that means something happened to me." It's like he had a fear that something was going to happen."

"Yes, I agree. Perhaps this is where we can discover who wanted to kill Jack and his co-workers."

"Perhaps. Or it could just lead to more mysterious things. It seems Jack has become involved in a lot of secretive projects, more than I realized."

"I'm really glad we found the box," Sonya said, placing the letter back inside.

Haley thumbed through the small journal. "Yes, but the question is what to do with it now?"

"Maybe we should put it back in the attic," Sonya suggested.

Curiosity was pulling at Haley. This might contain things that would reveal the mystery of who poisoned the pilot and passengers. She sat silent, just thinking. "I don't think this will tell us with certainty who is behind the plane crash. If that was known, Jack could have prevented it from happening or would not have boarded the plane."

"That's true," Sonya agreed.

"I'm concerned about plugging the thumb drives into any random computer. It needs to be one that is not accessing the Internet and never will. "

Haley was learning that Chadwell had eyes, ears and long arms everywhere — almost like the government. It was becoming obvious they were in cahoots with at least parts of the government.

Both of the women startled a bit as Haley's phone sounded, indicating she had a new message.

Sonya looked at her and laughed, "Guess we're getting a little jumpy with these secrets we're discovering."

Haley pulled up the message. It was from Lucky Adams.

Coffee this afternoon? Important girl talk.

"Oh, she wants to meet today. I don't think I can do that. I'm afraid I won't be able to hide the fact that Jack is alive. At the very least, she may pick up on something unspoken from me. She's pretty sharp."

"Let me go with you. I can distract her a bit with my silliness."

"Okay, I knew that special trait of yours would come in handy," she said, nudging Sonya with her elbow. Haley messaged Lucky back.

What time and where?

Could you meet at The Coffee Roast at 4:00?

Sure, I'm bringing Sonya with me.

Sounds good. See you then.

Haley clicked off her phone and sat it on the table. She looked at the plastic box again, still trying to decide what to do with it. "I have an idea. Jack and I have a safe deposit box at the bank. These items are small enough to put in there and I feel no one would be able to get access."

"That's a great idea, Haley. Did you want to read that journal or check out the information prior to putting it there?"

"No, not right now. I can go back to the bank anytime and retrieve it. We'll let the family know we found it and what the letter said. That's all. Jack is alive and I don't know if he wants me to meddle in this. Then again, he might. I wish I could just see him again soon."

"Hopefully, they will let us know something more in a few days."

"Living on hope all the time, aren't we?" Haley said, smiling.

"Only way to roll around here!" Sonya replied, smiling back.

"Well, I suppose we should make ourselves a little more presentable for coffee today, huh? We'll stop by the bank on the way and get this taken care of."

"Yeah, I need a quick shower, but I'm going to put this ladder back in the garage for you first."

"Thanks, I'll hold the door for you while you carry it."

Chapter 22 ~ Evan & Tellinger

Evan woke thinking about Chelsea, the yoga instructor. He rubbed his hand over his throbbing shaft and then quickly whisked his hand away. He needed to focus on more important things. Last night, he increased the pay to demonstrate a sense of urgency to Ragland. He needed that information Jack left in his house and soon.

An hour later, he drove into Chadwell's parking area and quickly got out, locking his vehicle. The holidays, when the majority of employees had taken off, were a good excuse and perfect time to nosy around and see if there were other bread crumbs Jack may have left in various places.

Other than the low level hum of some of the machinery that stayed on in an energy saving mode, the laboratory was quiet. He flipped on some of the lights, but not all. Jack was smart, a genius really. If he left information at his house, he probably duplicated it elsewhere to be on the safe side.

Information didn't have to be physical, but it could be. Most information now was digital and possibly in a cloud system. Nevertheless, Evan decided to begin with Jack's file cabinet. He had made a quick search before, but Kendra was there and it was difficult to not appear to be "looking for something". Instead, he had quickly skimmed the file names and did not see anything that stuck out. This time he would go through it slowly and actually glance at what was contained in each file. *If I was hiding anything in a file, I would give it a common, unsuspecting file name.* He grabbed a cup of coffee and sat down to begin examining the files. It was going to take some time.

Evan glanced at his watch. Over two hours had passed. He knew this might be a real scavenger hunt. So far, he had examined all of the files in one drawer and turned up nothing. He rose and stretched, feeling as if he needed to go to the bathroom. He headed toward the front of the office area and used the restroom. As he emerged, the elevator dinged. Someone was arriving on this floor.

The doors opened and Tellinger emerged wearing a thick wool winter coat. "Ah, I saw your vehicle, Evan. I'm glad you're here. I want to speak with you. Privately, of course." Evan led as the two men walked back toward his office.

"How was your Christmas holiday, sir?"

"Oh, it was fine. Ate too much though. How about you?"

"I stayed in the area this year and didn't travel home. Too much work to do right now."

"I appreciate your dedication."

Evan ushered Tellinger inside his office which was formerly Jack's and sat down in a chair adjoining his boss, rather than taking a seat behind the desk. "You the only one here today?" he asked.

"So far, in this department anyway."

"Well, I guess it's just as well. I need to ask you what the status is of getting the information from Jack's residence."

"Don't have it yet, but I met with the operator last night. I doubled the money for him to make it happen swiftly."

Tellinger's expression was sour. "Why doesn't he already have it?"

"The risk has been higher. With the holidays, it seems his wife has been there and another person every day. He's waiting for them to leave so he can get in."

Tellinger stood, removing his coat. "It's getting warm in here. I tell you, Evan. This is not working. Whether or not she's there, he must get the information."

"I understand, sir. We were just trying to make sure we don't draw more attention to the Foster residence. If something were to happen to Jack's wife, it would really begin to look suspicious."

"Agreed, but whatever the cost, we must get it. We have public relations people who can deal with fallout."

"I understand. Here is something else I've been thinking about. Jack may have made copies of that information, placing it in various locations. I've been slowly going through his file cabinet here for over two hours."

"That's true. It would not hurt to search for other places he could have the same information. Good thinking, Evan."

"Yes, but I was also thinking about the fact that so much is now digital. It could be on a device or even stored on a cloud. Are you aware of a particular cloud storage Jack might have?"

"No, but we all have it now. Hell, sometimes I forget where things are stored. Cloud storage is everywhere including our cell phones."

"True."

"Why don't you talk to someone in IT.? Tell them you're searching for a report or study that Jack performed and you can't find."

"Okay, good idea."

"I'll leave now and allow your search to continue."

He walked the older executive to the elevator and they shook hands.

"Let me know as soon as the operator gets in that house."

"I will, sir. Hopefully, it will be very soon."

As soon as the elevator doors closed, Evan let out a deep breath. He watched as the elevator went up, instead of down, with Tellinger traveling to his own office floor. He walked back and looked up the general number for the IT Department. The phone rang several times and Evan was just about to hang up when a male voice answered.

"Chadwell IT department," he said.

"Hello, this is Evan Mitchell. I need some assistance from someone in IT with a question I have."

"I'll be glad to help, Mr. Mitchell."

"I have taken over Jack Foster's position since his tragic accident."

"I heard about that, sir. I'm sorry."

"Yes, me too. The reason I'm calling is that Jack had a report he was working on that needs to be presented to the Board of Directors at the first of the year. I've tried to locate it on his computer and his assistant, Kendra, does not have it. I was wondering if there is any other place Jack may have stored the document, perhaps on a cloud or another device. Do you have any way of looking at his activity say from November of this year?"

"Probably, but I don't want to say that for sure yet. Can you give me some time to research this?"

"Yes, of course. How long do you need?"

"I would say a couple of days, maybe less."

"That's fine. And, what is your name?"

"Ric — Ric Hartford."

"I don't think I've met you before."

"No, we haven't had the pleasure, sir."

"Okay, well perhaps we can do lunch once you find this out."

"Sounds good, sir."

Evan hung up, feeling like something might be possible with this guy from the IT department. He then grabbed his burner phone and placed a call to Ragland.

"Yeah, it's me."

"Ragland, just making sure you're on this and getting into that residence soon."

"Don't worry. I'm not going to let you down. I'm actually climbing into my cable truck right now."

"Good. By the way, do you have any eyes or ears you can place inside the house? It would be nice to monitor things?"

"No, I don't have any devices on me now."

"I should have mentioned it to you earlier. If you don't get in today, get some. And, call me as soon as something happens. "

"Will do, over and out."

Evan hung up the phone and placed it back in his jacket pocket. He needed something to bust open in his favor, and soon.

Chapter 23 ~ Brazil Underground

$\mathbf{D}$ing, ding, ding rang from the glass pad on the desk. It sounded like a reminder or alarm. It woke Jack and initially made him feel unsure of his surroundings. It was a common feeling now, waking up and wondering where he was. His room was very comfortable, but nothing felt like home. And, where was his home?

Jack's eyes opened slightly as he turned on his side. He closed them again, thinking how much he needed a day to just recover from everything that had happened. His leg ached and this bed would be a comfortable place to do that.

He opened his eyes wider, noticing the soft blue light emanating from the baseboard area of the walls. Jack turned on his back again, deliberately making himself find out what time it was. He grabbed his watch on the table beside the bed. Six-thirty in the morning. Placing his arms behind his head, he thought about his dinner with Marcos the night before. The food was very good, delicious really. Marcos said they had highly trained kitchen personnel, but he did not go so far as to use the word chef.

Afterward, he rode his trike, an abbreviated word he preferred over tricycle. He had followed Marcos, taking a tour of the facilities where he would work. The laboratory was outstanding. It was outfitted with the latest equipment with ample room for individual or group projects. Today, he would see it in action and meet the staff who manned that area. He hoped many spoke English. He really needed to rapidly learn more Portuguese.

The highlight of his tour with Marcos was the smaller, second domed area just off the lab. It was utilized as a greenhouse and it served a dual purpose. There were plants propagated for medicinal use, along with trees and plants for transplanting later to the larger domed area he was first introduced to. He walked through the smaller domed area on foot with Marcos. While it was remarkable in its design and all the plant inhabitants it contained, nothing could compare to real nature.

True nature held surprises. Something you didn't see before or expect that would appear in front of you. Sometimes, those surprises could be dangerous, even fatal. Often, they peaked your curiosity. Here, the duplication of nature was amazing, but contained within a zone of safety.

In the rain forest or the woods back home in Georgia, the ground had a certain feel as your shoes crunched leaves or pine needles under your feet. Whether the wind was gentle or strong, it was full of movement. Here, it was generated by fans located a select intervals.

Still, Jack had marveled at all of it yesterday. When in the domed areas, he definitely didn't feel he was inside a mountain. This room he would reside in did feel different, almost as if he were on a spaceship. The engineering and design of the facility were remarkable.

Marcos had informed Jack he had a morning appointment with the medical staff at eight-thirty. Normally, he wasn't excited about going to the doctor. But he was hopeful they could tell him something about his leg which was a constant source of dull pain. He also hoped they could help him regain his full memory.

Most of all, he remembered his response to the concern about sharing the formulation and Chadwell finding out. Marcos had said, once you share the formulation and process with the world, there is no need for anyone to target you. It's too late at that point. Jack agreed somewhat, but he wondered if he could also be hunted for slivers of knowledge he held about plans for the pandemic that was evidently unfolding right now.

The pandemic, if it truly was that, made him jump out of bed. *If this is a virus that has been engineered to be more lethal, my work is ahead of me right now.*

After dressing for the day, Jack picked up the glass pad and phone he had been given. The glass pad seemed a little bulky to carry around, especially with the trike, even though it had a large basket to carry items. Instead, he opted to take the phone only with him. Jack knew it was not like a regular cell phone. He could message people, like Karla or Marcos, but there was no communication going from that phone outside this mountain. He could ask questions and find out answers to at least some things utilizing it.

He lifted his sore leg, swinging it over the seat and straddled the trike. Jack rode to the area where he had dined with Marcos last night. He parked outside the enormous dining hall and entered using his handprint on the door scanner. Jack knew they had to be keeping track of where everyone was at any given time with this system. He wondered again how much visual surveillance was in place. He had nothing to hide, but he still would like to know when he was possibly being watched.

Grabbing coffee first, he perused the tempting row of bakery items. He selected a cinnamon roll and sat by himself at the closest table.

"Hello, are you Dr. Foster?" a female voice asked, walking up to him from the side.

He turned, looking at a woman with dark hair and hazel eyes that almost matched his in color. "Yes, how did you know?" he asked her.

"We were briefed yesterday that you were coming. I'm Eleanora. I will be working with you, hopefully, on this new project."

Jack stopped eating the cinnamon roll with all its stickiness now on his fingers. She was a tiny thing, and she made him a little self-conscious. "Wonderful, I look forward to meeting everyone as soon as possible. I would shake your hand, but …" He held his fingers up showing the residue from the cinnamon roll.

She gave him a nod. "Those are good, but a little messy. Do you think that you will be in the lab with us today?" she asked, twirling a strand of her long hair with her index finger.

"I don't know. I hope so. Right now, I'm following orders from others."

Jack didn't tell her about his appointment for the medical bay. That would complicate things as she might ask questions, wondering what's wrong with him. She spoke English very well, but still had an accent. Turning the questions on her, he asked, "Are you from Brazil?"

She had just taken a sip of her orange juice. "Yes, lived here all my life, but I have traveled a few places. I served in our military. That's where I was able to finish my education and learn biology and pharmacology."

"Interesting! How long have you been here, underground that is?"

"Not long. I was recently hired. This is my first official job in my field."

"Well, perhaps that's better," Jack said, smiling. "Sometimes those that have worked other places learn to do things only one way. Unfortunately, it can make them a bit difficult to work with. Do you consider yourself a hard worker?"

"Oh, yes! I want to learn as much as I can and help others."

"That's the right attitude to have. It was nice to meet you, Eleanora," Jack said, rising from his chair. "I'm sure we will see each other again soon."

She smiled, "I look forward to it." She swung her hair behind her shoulders as she turned.

Jack straightened the collar on his shirt and felt in his pocket for his phone. Eleanora was very pretty, and he felt she might be flirting a little with him. The ring he wore on his finger should let her know he was married. It was the only thing that made him believe he was. He had to figure out what was going on inside his head. With that thought, he climbed on his trike and began pedaling toward the medical bay that Marcos had pointed out last night.

Chapter 24 ~ Lucky or Not

Lucky had a carefree philosophy surrounding the way she approached life. Things were either going in her favor, which was tremendously lucky, or they were not -- in which case it was often tragically unlucky. So far, today was shaping up well for her. The bar was not crowded for lunch and that was good. She was able to sit at the same table Evan and Ragland were at the previous night. Her little black device was nestled nicely in the condiment holder and she retrieved it easily, placing it in her pocket.

Alice spotted her and walked from behind the bar, coming over to the table. "I didn't know you would come back so soon," she said.

"Well, I told you I would prepare an estimate, and I was able to do that last night." Lucky handed her the paper with her fake painting company name on it.

"Not too bad," Alice said, looking it over. "Not going to break the bank. How soon do you want to start?"

"I'm finishing today on the project I'm on. I could start as early as tomorrow with the drywall repairs and prepping the walls. Of course, that price is labor only. You buy the paint."

"Okay, yeah I can handle that. So what time tomorrow are you thinking?"

"Would around ten o'clock be an okay time to start or is that too early?"

"How about ten-thirty? I like to make myself breakfast upstairs and do a few extra things before I open the bar."

"Perfect, I'll see you tomorrow."

Lucky left the bar, heading back to her apartment as quickly as she could. She wanted to read those documents from Ric and make any cryptic notes needed for memory's sake. Then, the shredder. Haley had agreed to meet her at 4:00, so she had a small window of time to change out of her painting clothes and wig into her regular attire.

Fortunately, her apartment was located off the beaten path in an old carriage house at the rear of what was formerly a mansion in 1900's Atlanta. When she entered or exited, she was rarely seen. If she was, no one had questioned her different identities.

The man that owned the enormous three-story house was rich and had completely restored the Gothic Victorian. Her apartment in the separate carriage house had been completely updated as well. This was home to her, at least for now and she loved it.

Her landlord was also very good looking, but in a way that you figured he liked guys more than girls. Why else would he paint the massive Victorian pink? The color looked superb. With all the adornments such as crown and dentil molding on the exterior and the turret, it reminded her of Cinderella's castle.

He looked too perfect to be a regular guy that was into women. For one thing, he was always dressed impeccably — even when he was in a leisurely, at home mode. Lucky had observed him leaving for his business many days and wondered why he never brought anyone home with him, male or female. He was enticing. If she thought he might be into women, Lucky would have been borrowing cups of sugar and such from him a long time ago. He left her alone, and she did the same with him.

She had rented the carriage house since moving from Florida. The bottom portion held a garage where she kept her motorcycle and sports car. The van stayed in the small drive that was probably where a horse drawn carriage came and went in the early twentieth century. There was a newer, more modern garage that sat off to the other side of the house where the landlord parked his vehicles. He had beautiful taste in cars.

Stairs led from inside the carriage house garage to the upper apartment. She climbed the steps and unlocked her door. The wig she had been wearing for quite a while now was making her scalp sweat and itch. She ditched it right away. Next, she settled down at her desk with the file Ric had trusted her with.

Lucky began making notes of the names of those privy to the emails and the attached document that Ric had also printed. All of these individuals had some kind of knowledge about P-2019. As she read through the attached document that accompanied one of the emails, she could understand why Ric felt the "P" stood for pandemic.

There was a plan suggested of what their response would be to the event. This included lock downs and the shutting down of businesses. It involved mandatory testing and possibly the wearing of face masks. Lucky read the document with a sense of disbelief. She just could not see how such an event could happen. How could they shut down travel and transportation?

What kind of disease was it they knew about? Toward the end of the document, she noted they were involved in final development of a vaccine. *Well, that's good. Whatever this is, I don't want it and we can't shut down all of society over it.* Lucky wondered if the vaccine was something Jack Foster had been working on.

Grabbing her pen again, she made a few more notes and attempted to make them cryptic in nature with initials representing people and other things. She hated shredding the papers, but she promised Ric and he was right. This could be so potentially dangerous to have on her person. She turned the shredder on and fed the papers in about five at a time. She watched the last go through and then turned to get in the shower. It was time to meet Haley Foster and then teach Pilates tonight.

Chapter 25 ~ Medical Bay

Parking his trike outside the entrance, Jack noticed the medical bay did not have a locked door. It was open to everyone, just like the dining and exercise facilities. He wandered inside and noticed how calming the reception area felt. The decor was in soft hues of lavender and light blue, with an occasional hint of moss green. The lighting was very adequate, but low. Ambient music played quietly, but noticeably through speakers in the sky blue ceiling with white clouds painted above.

There was no reception desk manned by a person. Instead, a podium stood in the center of the room with a small sign instructing visitors to sign in with their hand print on the glass receptacle. Jack placed his hand on it and it made a soft dinging sound twice. The glass pad lit up and a computerized woman's voice said, "Your 8:30 a.m. appointment will proceed on time. Someone will be out to lead you into the medical bay. Thank you for being prompt for your appointment."

Jack looked at his phone for the time. Eight-twenty-eight. No sense in sitting down, even though the seating looked plush and comfortable. He stood, pacing a bit. While he was not excited about seeing a doctor, he knew that it was needed.

Momentarily, doors slid open and a man and woman dressed in scrubs emerged. "Dr. Foster, good to see you at the medical bay this morning. Welcome! I am Dr. Melo and this is Dr. Barbosa," he said, indicating the woman with him.

"Nice to meet you both," Jack replied.

"Follow us inside, please."

Both of the physicians noticed the slight limp Jack displayed and slowed their pace to the examining room. Once inside, Dr. Barbosa addressed Jack. "Please, sit in this chair and be comfortable."

She continued, "We received your complete file concerning the plane crash from your government and our Brazilian authorities. Please know that both of us carry the highest privileged information status and everything we discover about you or that you tell us is completely confidential and held as top secret. We also received your medical records from the United States and see that you've had a pretty normal, very healthy life so far."

"Yes, I have, but how did you get those records without consent?"

The two doctors looked at one another seriously. Dr. Melo answered, "It seems to be rather simple for your President to request any information and he receives it.

Your records were then passed to us so that we could make sure you had no allergies or conditions that we were unaware of."

"I see. There is no problem in you having the records. We have laws in the United States about such things and I wondered how you were able to obtain them."

Dr. Melo continued, "I will serve as your primary physician and Dr. Barbosa is a neuro-psychiatrist. It's probable that you will have other professionals weigh in on any conditions found that require treatment. We are wondering what happened to you after the plane crash?"

"I'm guessing some of the indigenous residents transported me to their village. I don't remember it, but that's where I woke up later and began putting the pieces together. They did treat me with their own brand of medicine," Jack said, smiling.

"What are your chief complaints right now?" Dr. Melo asked.

"I'm limping a bit on this leg and it does hurt throughout the day, especially if I stand or walk too long. I must have cracked my head pretty good too." Jack pointed toward the area of his head that was still tender. "Right here is where I think that occurred."

Dr. Barbosa used her hand to gently put a small amount of pressure on Jack's skull. "We will definitely want to have your head examined," she said to Jack, jokingly. They all laughed.

Dr. Melo commented, "If these two complaints are the only ones, you really are a very fortunate soul to have survived a plane crash."

Jack looked serious and gazed at the floor as he spoke, "Yes, I know I am. I lost three of my colleagues."

"That has to be hard. Were you the lone survivor of the crash?" Dr. Barbados asked.

"I was."

"Sometimes, that can make a person feel guilty. Have you experienced that?"

"Yes, I have."

"We'll talk about that more later. Anything else you want to mention to us?" she asked.

"My memory. I cannot remember some things like the details of the crash or my wife." Jack held up his left hand, bending his ring finger toward the doctors. "I'm married. But I don't feel like it and cannot remember her at all."

The two doctors looked at one another. Dr. Melo spoke first, "You are in good hands here. Dr. Barbados should be able to determine what is causing this."

"Can you help me fully regain my memory?"

Dr. Barbados shifted her weight from one leg to the other. "Hopefully, we will do all we can. First, let's figure out what's causing the situation. The brain has been studied for many years now, but we still do not fully know all of its intricacies. At this facility, we have the best staff and equipment we could hope for. You are in good hands. Let me ask you, do you remember your work that you performed in line with your career?"

"I believe that I do. It's strange. You don't know what you've forgotten until you go to do something and there's a blank spot there. Or, someone tells you something from your past, but you have no recall."

"I understand. Well, if you would change into the gown provided there. You will need to remove jewelry also. We will go ahead and begin collecting data on you by running some tests."

Jack had trouble removing the green heart stone necklace. Evidently, the clasp on one end was missing and the leather cords were tied in a tight knot at the back of his neck. The knot was so small; he couldn't get it with his large fingers. He left it on for now, but removed the wedding band on his finger.

There was a knock on the door and a nurse wearing bright blue scrubs entered. "Hello, Dr. Foster. I'm here to take you for some x-rays and a scan.

"I can't get the knot out of this necklace."

"Let me see," she said, walking toward the back of him. She worked on the knot for a few moments and the leather cord came loose. "There you go. Do you need some place to store this?"

"Yes, and this ring also."

She handed him a ziplock plastic bag and put his name and patient number on it by printing out a sticker on the counter by the exam sink.

"I've brought you a wheelchair. I know you can walk, but it's the way we do things here."

"I understand and hey, I'll enjoy the ride."

Jack sat in the chair and was wheeled away for testing. Hopefully, he would find out about his leg and memory soon.

Chapter 26 ~ Coffee Roast

Haley brushed her hair and pulled it back into a ponytail. She didn't have time or the inclination to do much more with it today. Going to the closet, she pulled on her jeans, topping it off with a cowl neck sweater. Haley spotted the boots Jack bought her and picked them up, carrying them with her to the kitchen.

Sonya was ready, waiting for her. She was dressed much warmer than she had seen her dress in recent days. "Is it pretty cold outside?" Haley asked.

"Yes, I was going to wear something else, but I stepped outside and it is freezing."

"In that case, I'm going to take my wool coat. I love your pea jacket. I have one more thing I want to do before we leave."

"What's that -- put your boots on?" Sonya asked, jokingly.

Haley laughed. "Well, yes, but I also want to put Jack's secret items in a sealed envelope, as in almost hermetically sealed."

Sonya watched as Haley lit a candle she grabbed from the dining room table. She placed the contents of Jack's information stash into a large manila envelope. "This shouldn't take long," she said.

Haley waited a few seconds until liquid wax was forming from the candle. She licked the adhesive end of the envelope and closed it tight. Holding the candle over the area, she carefully drizzled wax over the seam.

"Are we taking my car or yours?" Sonya asked.

"Let's take mine today, if that's okay with you?"

"Works for me."

The ladies grabbed their belongings, and Haley set the house alarm. They exited through the garage door, into her Honda, and backed out into the drive.

As they passed Alex and Jessie's home, Sarah asked how long the couple would be out of town.

"Awhile. I think they are coming back January 2nd."

As planned, Haley stopped by the bank on their way to meet Lucky. Before getting out of the car, she sent a group message to Jason, Sarah, Joe and Sharon:

Family dinner soon?

She wanted to let them know what she and Sonya had found. While they all enjoyed getting together for family dinners, they would also know that meant Haley had something to share with them. Just as she was aware that Lucky Adams had something important to tell her.

"You want to come in or wait in the car?" she asked Sonya.

"I'll wait if you don't think it will take too long."

"Okay, if I'm in there for a while, just lock the car and come inside."

The bank manager recognized Haley. She was very attentive and empathetic in an almost silent way. As Haley watched her unlock the vault area, she mentioned to Haley how sorry she was about Jack's passing. Haley said nothing, just smiled and nodded to her.

She followed the manager inside and used her key to access the safe deposit box. She pulled the box from the wall and placed it on the table in the center of the vault room. The bank manager waited at the door patiently. Removing the envelope from her bag, she placed it in the box. The bank manager assisted her with putting the safe deposit box back in its place, and then locking the vault door. Haley thanked her for her help and told her she might need to come and access the box again soon. She just wasn't sure.

Leaving the bank, she noticed the afternoon air was brisk and cold. She hurried to her car. "That was pretty quick, huh?"

"Yes, it was. Everything went well, I assume."

"Yes. I feel good about leaving that information there, at least for now. The bank manager was very nice. She thinks Jack is dead."

"Yeah, well, a lot of people are in for a future surprise."

Thirty minutes later, Haley pulled up in front of the Coffee Roast. The wind was picking up now, forcing the temperatures down further. "Feels like it could snow," Haley commented to Sonya.

"I've never seen real snow."

"Oh my gosh! We have to make that happen for you at some point. Let's get inside this cafe."

Lucky was there, waiting. Once again, she was sitting at a table near the back. Haley assumed she liked that position in a restaurant or cafe as this was the second time she had met her sitting like that. "Do you always like the back?" she asked approaching the table.

"I guess I do. Gives me a good view of all the people in the place. But I'm glad we are here alone. We don't need another set of ears listening."

"That's for sure. I am so tired of feeling like I'm looking over my shoulder. Changing the subject, can you believe how cold it's getting outside? The wind is wicked today," Haley commented as she removed her wool coat.

"I don't like it," Lucky replied. "I am so used to warm temperatures. I'm originally from south Florida."

Sonya spoke up, "Haley and I are from Valdosta, Georgia. Ever been there?"

"I've passed it on the interstate, going south. But no, I don't know much about that area. Let's get some coffee, want to?"

The ladies approached the elaborate counter area of the cafe. It was very ornate with a wood and marble bar that appeared to have been salvaged and refurbished. Haley ran her hand over the marble and wood. "This is so gorgeous!"

The barista turned out to be the owner of the cafe. "Thank you, my husband and I picked this up at an antique store. It had been carefully divided into three pieces, which we hauled here, refinished and then put in place."

"It's exquisite," Haley said.

The three ordered their drinks and made their way back to the table.

"How have things been going for you and your family, Haley? Any luck with finding Jack yet?"

Lucky's questioning made Haley a little nervous to the point of almost stuttering. Sonya spoke up quickly, "Yes, they found him living with a family of monkeys who claim they have adopted him," she said with a wry grin.

Lucky laughed. "Seriously, anything at all."

Sonya spoke again, this time more seriously. "Unfortunately, not yet."

Lucky sipped her coffee and then blotted her ruby red lipstick with a napkin. "That's a bummer. I hope something breaks on his whereabouts soon."

"Me too," Haley finally offered.

"The reason I wanted to meet you today is because I came across some information on Evan Mitchell."

Haley swallowed hard as Lucky told her she suspected Evan had hired a guy named Ragland to steal something either from her house or someone else connected with Jack.

"Really?" Haley responded. Always in concealment mode, she tried to appear that she had no idea what that might be, despite the fact that it was now in her safe deposit box.

"Is there anything Jack might have at home that someone would want to get their hands on?"

Haley wasn't going to lie about this part. Lucky needed to know some details. She decided to reveal this to her.

"There was something Jack left regarding his work at Chadwell. Sonya and I found it and it's no longer at the house. It's been moved to a safe location."

"Well, that's a relief! The only problem is they must think it's in your house. He's planning on breaking in when you're not home."

"How do you know this?" Sonya asked. Haley nodded, "Yes, how did you find this out?"

Lucky blotted her lips with the napkin once more. "Eavesdropping, spying. It's part of what I do."

The three were silent for a few seconds, but it felt like a lot longer. Haley was digesting this possibility of a break in.

"I would be notified by the alarm company if he broke in when I'm not there — or if we're there with the alarm set."

"If everything lined up correctly, that is what would happen. But I don't know this guy's capabilities. I would say he's done this kind of thing for a while. I don't want to frighten you, but you need to be on guard."

Haley nodded in agreement. "You called him Ragland, right?"

"Yes, that's what Evan addressed him as. I'm assuming it's his last name and I placed a request with a friend I have at the federal level to provide me a list of everyone by that last name in this area. I'm not sure what his regular transportation is, but he mentioned to Evan that he's driving what appears to be a cable company truck to stake out in the neighborhood."

"Holy crap, we passed a truck like that when we left, Haley!"

"I didn't notice it. Are you sure it was from the cable company?"

"Positive."

Haley checked her phone to make sure it was turned on and not silenced. "No calls from the security company." She noticed Papa Joe and Jason had messaged her back.

Lucky felt so bad for Haley. She was being thrown into all of this because of Jack. Obviously, he was also the love of her life. "I don't envy you, Haley. It's not good for you to have to live like this in fear."

"What choice do I have? I've got to get things back to normal with me and Jack, and no more of this bullshit we're experiencing because of big pharma."

Lucky could see the frustration was real in her expression and eyes. "You know how to contact me if anything pops or you need to talk. I will try to make myself available. There are times when I'm engaged in surveillance or something similar. So, if I don't answer right away, just wait. I will be in touch."

"I appreciate that, Lucky. You know, I can't even have an appointment with my therapist right now because I might say something I shouldn't. Thank goodness, Sonya decided to stay with me." She squeezed her cousin's arm.

"Do either of you have some protection other than the security system?"

"No, we don't."

"Let me give you the name of a lady who teaches how to handle firearms. I think you will like her a lot."

"Jack has a gun at the house."

"Perfect, if that gun is a good fit for you. Make an appointment with her and take it with you."

Sonya spoke up, "We are going to self-defense classes."

"Fantastic! I attended classes when I lived in Florida."

"Have you ever had to use your moves?" Sonya asked.

"Yes, but mostly with overly rambunctious love suitors."

With that, the three cracked up laughing.

"Seriously, I took someone down to the ground once and it gave me the time I needed to run away. It definitely saved me from being seriously hurt or even killed."

"Then it's worth it," Haley replied.

"Well ladies, I've got to get to my night job," Lucky said, shifting in her chair.

"Where is that?" Haley inquired.

"I'm teaching yoga and Pilates at Evan's clubhouse facility."

"You're joking?" Haley asked with an astonished look.

"Nope, it's for real. Already met him or should I say he met me."

"Be careful, Lucky," Sonya said, with her brows almost knitted together in concern.

"It's okay. Of course, I am careful — but no risks, no rewards. Now, get in touch with that friend of mine about learning to use a gun."

"We'll do it."

Haley and Sonya rushed to the Honda as the wind blew even colder now. "Where to now?" Sonya asked.

"Home. I've been feeling squirmy and concerned since you said you saw the cable company truck."

Chapter 27 ~ Mortality

Visiting the medical bay at the underground facility was nothing like going to a hospital at home. Everything was processed quickly with almost no waiting between tests. Personnel were also highly attentive, something he knew couldn't always happen in a busier setting. Out of curiosity, Jack asked the technician getting ready to perform a full body scan on him how many patients they saw per day.

"Right now, just a few. When we have new arrivals, we see many more. Everyone's health must be checked out prior to working here." This was more comprehensive than any physical Chadwell had required.

Jack finished testing within a couple of hours, dressed, and retrieved the malachite heart necklace and his ring. He mentally struggled with putting the ring back on. He could see from the tan line on his hand that he had worn it for awhile. While it seemed strange to wear this heart around his neck, somewhere inside him he knew this was what he was supposed to do. He tied it around his neck, but not as tight as before.

He exited the room and went to the desk outside as instructed. "All finished?" the attendant asked.

"Yes, I hope so."

"We have you scheduled back tomorrow morning at the same time. Dr. Melo will meet with you then to discuss test results with you."

"I'll see you then."

It was now going on eleven o'clock in the morning. Jack knew he needed to get to the laboratory area. He peddled quickly, passing others, smiling and nodding his head. He wondered who would ever know there was all this bustling activity going on under an immense mountain of granite.

As he came close to where he would work on the project, he remembered the vast array of scientific equipment it held. The latest and best centrifuges, spectrophotometers, and thermal cyclers would be available to him. He was feeling excited now. It would be good to be back in a lab after so long away.

Jack entered the dining hall a little late for dinner. There was hardly anyone there. He stopped at the restroom to wash his hands. He looked in the mirror and could see dark circles under his eyes. Inside, however, he felt good. He had put in a full day at the lab, working late.

Food was served almost cafeteria style, but not quite. There was no line to wait in. People simply gathered around tables with varieties of dishes available. There was a round table with nothing but salads and appetizers. Another table held various meats. There were vegetable, fruit and dessert tables.

He thought about his day at the lab. Marcos had popped in to say hello and inquire if he had everything he would need to begin the project. Jack let him know he thought so, but he was still getting acquainted and taking inventory of it all. He had been assigned a team of eight employees to assist with the formulation of the drug. He was also assessing the talents and abilities of each of the members. This had required a meeting with each one today, although brief. It gave him an opportunity to get to know each one and feel them out for their strengths and possible personality quirks. This worked in reverse as well. He hoped the team liked him. Often, being able to work together well in a cohesive manner made all the difference in a project.

He chose something lighter this evening for dinner and skipped dessert. After he made his way back to his apartment, he made notes and assigned each member's duties for the team. They would meet as a group tomorrow shortly after he arrived to the lab which would again be late with the doctor's appointment. They would define the exact goal of the project and break that down into individual goals for each to achieve.

Jack flipped on the television for one screen and reclined on the bed. He was tired. He scrolled through the viewing selections and settled on hearing world news in English, another thing he had been cut off from for quite a while. They were reporting about positive economic growth being expected for the last quarter of the year in the United States. Before the newscaster broke away to a commercial, she mentioned soon they would show events unfolding in China related to a viral outbreak.

Jack waited patiently for the commercials to end. Once they did, images were shown of people in tremendously long lines, some lying on the ground indoors and outside, waiting for medical care in China. The western reporter covering the story mentioned that many were locked inside their homes to keep the spread of the virus down. There were no details yet of the type of virus involved, but residents were said to be dying from it, including physicians who were treating patients and had succumbed to the disease.

Jack needed to know more about this virus. He wondered if the facility had an epidemiologist on staff. He sent Karla and Marcos a message inquiring about it. Within minutes, Jack's phone rang and he answered.

"Jack, what a coincidence. I have a video conference call with a very renowned epidemiologist at 9:00 this evening. I was getting ready to message you to find out if you'd like to be on the call."

"Yes, of course. I've been watching some of the news from China. It's very disturbing."

"I agree. Make sure your system is on at your desk in your apartment. I will send you a secure link to join the video call."

"Sounds great, Marcos. I'll be ready."

Jack continued to watch the news while waiting. More needed to be known in order to keep this invisible viral strain from reaching the shores of every country in the world. He felt pressured to produce the drug he was working on with the team. But he also didn't want to rush things and risk it failing. Everything had to be done with measured thought and action.

He heard a beep on the computer and went to the chair at the desk. Marcos had sent a message with the link to the call. He clicked on it. Marcos was present, waiting for the epidemiologist to join them. Momentarily, all three men were present, along with the President of Brazil.

"Good evening, Mr. President, gentlemen. I am Dr. Rugal and have a few things to share about the virus that have been ascertained as of now. First, it is clearly a virus that has been manipulated and made more lethal than it was in its original form. Let me share my screen while I speak."

The doctor showed a slide with two images. "First, we are not dealing with a rhinovirus, on the left, which is the cause of so many colds people experience. This is from the corona virus genotype combined with the SARS virus."

He went on to explain how SARS was first discovered around 2002 in China. Its symptoms include high fever, can include headache, but most notably acute respiratory illness. This SARS type virus is combined with the corona virus.

Jack asked him, "Dr. Rugal, do you know how lethal this virus is?"

He nodded his head, "I have some stats. In healthy individuals, especially children and young people, there is almost zero mortality if they have no serious co-morbidity. People age sixty and above are at more risk with a 98% survival rate from the disease."

Jack was astonished and skeptical of this man. So much so, that he lost the rest of what the doctor had to say. *How in the hell could he have those statistics of a virus that has just appeared and taken hold of a certain populace in China?*

His suggestions for preventing spread included distancing people, frequent hand washing, lock downs of businesses, schools, universities, and government buildings. If going out, a mask should be worn.

"Dr. Rugal, why would we go to all that trouble for a virus with such a low rate of mortality?"

The doctor seemed perturbed by Jack's question. "We need to try and save every life we can, right?"

"Certainly, we do. It's beyond my pay grade how world leaders handle this, but there will be a cost of such draconian measures on many different levels in society. Wouldn't you agree?" Jack asked.

"I can only recommend what I believe is in the best interest of keeping down the spread of the virus."

"Understood," Jack said. "Thank you for your answers."

The men thanked each other and said their cordial goodbyes. Jack was very curious about Dr. Rugal. How could he have mortality rate data on such a new virus that has not really taken hold yet except in one city? That would not be the best data to pull from. You need a cross section across various regions or countries. Perhaps, he was basing it only upon the data they had for corona virus alone — or only those with SARS. That is the only explanation that would make sense.

If he really believes the mortality rate is that low, why would he recommend the lock down and other measures? Why not allow it to spread and build natural immunity, having adequate treatment for those more at risk?

Jack knew what the doctor recommended was right out of the playbook of information he had been privy to at Chadwell. This was more than a virus which had undergone gain of function. This was some kind of deceptive   plan.

Chapter 28 ~ Breaking In

Ragland pulled the fake cable company repair truck off the road. He messaged a guy he partnered with at times on assignments. They had both served, side by side, in Afghanistan. While they were not tight friends now, as compared to their tour of duty days, Ragland could depend on him to work efficiently alongside him. He was good at keeping it all private too. Nowadays, they both found greater profit in working private assignments.

"Busy today? I could really use your help on something."

"How soon?"

"Like now. Don't worry, you don't need to get dressed up. Hell, you don't even have to brush your teeth."

"Tell me where"

Ragland gave his buddy an address of a gas station on the two-lane road that led to the entrance of the subdivision where the Foster house was located. He drove to a spot within the subdivision and parked his truck on the road as if he was there to perform work on the lines or equipment. From his vantage point, he would know if or when Mrs. Foster left the house. He would pay his partner for the extra eyes he was providing, even if she never left the house. But he had a feeling that she had to go somewhere soon.

A few minutes later, he heard from his friend.

I'm here, where are you?

I'm down the road in the cable truck, waiting for someone to leave their house. If they do, I'll send you a photo of their vehicle.

Then what?

I need you to sit at that station and immediately message me if you see them return on that road. It will be tight, but I should have just enough time to get back in the truck and take off.

What if they don't leave their house?

Be patient, go inside the station and get a drink and some snacks. I'll pay you whether or not they leave.

In Ragland's mind, this was not the ideal way to try to steal something hidden in a house. If this didn't work, he would go in there with several operators at night in dark masks. They would tie up Mrs. Foster, without harming her, and rummage the place until it was found.

He thumbed through a men's magazine he pulled out from under the front seat. Too bad Alice didn't look like these women. Her body wasn't bad for her age, but her face was nothing like the fresh youthful look of these chicks. He began to feel a bit heated and rolled down his window. That's when he heard a car approaching in the quiet neighborhood. Ragland picked up his phone and clicked the camera app.

Bingo! It was her and she had another woman with her. He quickly snapped a photo, only getting the car from its rear view. He sent it to his partner.

Here she is, just left. Look for her to pass you. Blue Honda.

Ragland quickly stuffed the magazine back under his seat, started the engine and drove toward the Foster residence. He stopped just before their street and pulled on a full face hood that only showed his eyes. As he entered the cul-de-sac, he didn't notice any signs of the neighbors. He was prepared with answers if they suddenly showed up like they did the night he was there. He parked close to the garage door and then walked around to the back deck. He had already calculated this would be the easiest door to pick the lock on. He felt his phone buzz. It was his partner.

She just went by.

You're about five minutes from me. Let me know the second she returns this way.

I got your back, buddy.

He pulled out his hand tools and got to work quickly. Trying to be quick, yet precise, he struggled at first, and then felt the mechanism move. He turned the knob and he was in.

Typically, a keypad to disarm the alarm would be close to exterior doors. The back door did not have one near it. He walked to the front door knowing he only had seconds before the alarm would possibly sound and send a signal to the alarm company. He found a keypad there. "Bingo!" he said to himself again. He used the code he had been given to disarm the system. It worked perfect. He was hitting all bases.

Ragland quickly thought where he should begin searching. Most people hid things in closets, basements and attics. He began with the coat closet nearest him. There was one box on the shelf, but it contained gloves. He made his way to the kitchen area and noticed the office to his left. For a few seconds, Ragland wondered if it would be hidden in an obvious place like this. He decided it wouldn't. If he didn't find it, this would be the last place he looked.

Ragland found the door to the basement and began his search there. He tried to look through things without making it obvious anyone had been there. But it was difficult because he also had to be fast about the search. He briefly looked in plastic totes of holiday decorations and felt that was a dead end. He looked more thoroughly through boxes of memorabilia and photos. But nothing was found. He searched the furnace area and places in the basement ceiling where things could be hidden.

Curious of how much time had passed he looked at his phone. Damn, it had to have been an hour now that he's been in the basement. He was hot and his skin itched under the mask but he would not take it off. Ragland had no idea where cameras might be hidden in the house. He had already spotted two upstairs. He made another walk around the perimeter of the basement, looking for any possible hiding locations and then started back upstairs.

Ragland began going to every bedroom, searching under beds, in drawers, and each closet. Obviously, there was someone else living here with her. Maybe Evan mentioned that to him, he wasn't sure.

He found a 9mm handgun and fought with himself on whether he should take it or not. It was probably registered and he didn't need it linked in any way to him. But what if he left it and needed to come back here as per his plan b? She could shoot him with it. He decided to take it.

He noticed the attic door in the ceiling of the hallway leading to the bedrooms. He would need a ladder to access it. Ragland almost ran toward the garage and spotted a ladder that would work. He carried it in and popped open the attic door. He ended up getting insulation on him and some fell down into the hallway on the wood flooring. And then, his phone buzzed. He pulled it out of his pocket.

Just passed. On way back.

Ragland cursed, "Holy shit!" and made way for the back door. He ran to the truck and started the engine, putting it into drive. Luckily, he had backed up and turned the vehicle when he parked. This made it easier to pull straight out of the drive quickly. Exiting the cul-de-sac, he realized he was still wearing the mask and pulled it off his head. His heart was beating so fast and he knew Mrs. Foster would be coming up on his truck any moment. He turned the opposite way and drove deeper into the subdivision so she would not see the truck. He waited for about seven minutes before leaving the subdivision so he did not possibly pass her. But he also needed to get the hell out of there. As soon as she saw that ladder he left in the hall, she would call the police.

After seven minutes had passed since his buddy texted him, Ragland drove out of the subdivision and to the gas station. He quickly paid his friend and headed out to hide the vehicle. Ragland decided to lie low for tonight. Tomorrow, he would set up a meeting with Evan and let him know they would need to kick things into high gear.

Chapter 29 ~ Moving Out

Haley pulled her Honda into the garage as soon as the automatic door opener made way for the car. She turned the vehicle off and pushed the remote button to close the garage door. As soon as they entered the kitchen, Sonya punched in her code to disarm the house alarm system. Instead, it began counting down as if she was leaving the house. 'What the ....?" she said, with Haley standing beside her now.

"Punch in your code again to make it stop," Haley said.

Sonya followed her instructions and looked at her. "I was sure you set the alarm when we left."

"Me too. Stay right here by the door, Sonya."

The hair on Haley's arms was raised. Her fear was climbing inside her but she was determined to face whatever situation was going on. In her mind, she questioned herself as she walked around the kitchen and peered into Jack's office. *Did I set the alarm?*

She looked at Sonya and whispered, "Get back in the car — quietly."

Haley tiptoed into the living area. She still felt spooked but maybe she didn't set the alarm. Creeping slowly, she knew there was one area of the wooden flooring that creaked and avoided it. As she stepped carefully, her eyes saw the ladder in the hall and insulation on the floor. *I know Sonya put that ladder back in the garage.*

Her spine began to seize up, and she felt like she couldn't move. She stood there frozen in one spot glaring at the ladder and the open attic door. If someone was up in the attic, she could move the ladder and that might prevent them from leaving, unless they jumped down. Finally, she decided she had to overcome what she was feeling and get out of the house. She quietly back tracked her steps, assuming someone was in the house or attic. She wondered if there was more than one person.

Walking backward and keeping her eyes on anything that might move in front of her, she suddenly heard a thumping sound behind her. It startled her. She bolted for the garage door and ran to the car. Even while her feet were on the run, she realized the noise was the ice maker in the refrigerator dropping cubes inside.

Simultaneously, she started the engine and hit the remote button to open the garage door. Sonya watched, but said nothing yet. By observing Haley's shaking hands and the terror on her face, she could tell that she could not talk right now.

Haley pulled out of the drive, shutting the garage door and peeled out of the cul-de-sac. Whoever was in the house was looking for what she had just dropped off at the bank. They had to be. No normal robber would climb into the attic. She pulled onto a side street in the subdivision, grabbed her cell phone, and dialed 911.

Three regular police vehicles arrived at the house and a detective driving an unmarked vehicle. Haley waited with Sonya in the car in front of Jessie and Alex's house. They had been advised to stay there out of harm's way in case the intruder was armed and still in the property. She sent a group message to Jason, Sarah and Papa Joe.

Sonya and I came home today to someone having broken in the house. The alarm did not go off but I know it was set. We are safe but if anyone wants to come over, please do. My nerves are rattled.

Jason messaged back immediately that he was on his way. Shortly thereafter, Joe Foster messaged to say he was getting in the car right now to meet them. Haley noticed the detective walking toward her car. She rolled her window down as he came to the driver's side. "Mrs.

Foster, I'm very sorry this has happened. We cannot tell if anything was taken or not, but we have searched every part of the house and attic. There is no one there. You have cameras in some locations. Do you know if they were working?"

"They only activate when the system is armed, whether I am leaving or in the stay at home mode."

"We've already reached out to your security company and their sending someone. They should be here any minute."

"What should I do?" she asked in a distraught tone. "My brother-in-law and father-in-law are on the way now."

"Wait for them here. Once they arrive, why don't you ladies considering coming back into the house with us. We'd like to see what you notice missing, if anything. We might have more information by then from the security company."

"Okay, thank you." She watched the detective walk back toward the house. Another vehicle pulled in and she assumed it was someone from the security company. Haley looked at Sonya as if to ask her if she could believe this.

"You know, Sonya. Your mom and dad would be so upset if something happened to you. I would too. I don't know if I feel good about putting you at risk like this."

"I'm not leaving you," Sonya said firmly. "We are going to find a way to catch these people. We have to fight this. It's wrong, completely sinister and wrong."

Haley sensed this was probably not the best time to talk about this with Sonya. They were both in a highly charged emotional situation. Just knowing someone had been in the house was such a violation to her, and probably Sonya as well.

Jason pulled in with Papa Joe right behind him. The cul-de-sac was filling up with vehicles. Neighbors from a street over were probably peering out their windows and wondering what was going on. Haley and Sonya got out of the Honda and walked over to both of them.

Papa Foster immediately hugged Haley and then turned to reach and hug Sonya as well. "I'm so glad you both are okay. Tell us what happened."

Haley began by revealing that she and Sonya had found the information Jack hid in the attic and took it to the bank, putting it in her safe deposit box today, probably only minutes before the house was broken into.

"Wow! That is incredible. Is that why you wanted to have a family dinner?"

"Yes, it is, but let me tell you more. After I went to the bank, Sonya and I met with Lucky Adams. She had information that Evan Mitchell hired someone to break in or something to that effect. She said that he drove a truck disguised as if it was from the cable company."

Joe and Jason looked at one another. "How did she find this out?"

"I'm not completely sure. She's been tracking Evan. I do know that."

"Let's all have dinner this evening so we can get up to speed on things. What about your neighbors? Did they see anyone?"

"They're out of town until after the new year."

"Can we go to the house and talk with the police?" Jason asked.

"Yes, they found no one inside and claim they've been everywhere to look, including the attic."

"Let's go then."

The four proceeded into Haley and Jack's house, entering by the front door. The person from the security company was speaking to the detective in the kitchen and they were looking at a laptop which was rigged straight into the system in the kitchen's keypad.

"Oh, Mrs. Foster," said the detective. "Let me introduce you to Wade Thornton. He's the owner of the security company."

He turned and bowed his head while holding his laptop in his arms. "Mrs. Foster, I'm sorry to meet you under these circumstances. I can tell you the person who broke in appeared to be alone. He wore a full face mask. Other than his build and other particular features the police are working on, we don't have facial recognition and probably won't."

"How did he get in and not set off the alarm? I know I set it when we left."

"Yes, I have the record here of where you punched in your code to set the system at 2:30 pm. I show someone entering another code that operates the system at 2:41. They entered through the back door off the deck. That would be him. Who has this code?" He held his laptop closer to her so she could see the entry and the code number.

"Well, that's Sonya's code. But she was with me."

"He knew her code. Could this be someone you know, Sonya?" he asked her.

"No, I don't really know anyone around here. I'm from Valdosta but I've been staying here with my cousin for a couple of weeks."

"Well, I don't know how he could lucky guess that code. Could you have possibly written the code somewhere and another person might have seen it?"

"No, I memorized it as soon as Haley assigned it to me."

"Okay, we'll move on from there right now. Let's get back to the suspect. The police department is working with the cable company to ascertain if it is one of their employees. The suspect was driving what appears to be a cable company vehicle. We'll see what they come back with. The vehicle could have been stolen or it might be a fake."

"As far as his identity, we only have him on camera when he pulls up into the drive and again when he gets out with the full mask hood on."

Haley turned to Sonya and spoke in a low voice. "I'm going to call that gun instructor that Lucky suggested today."

"Haley, where did Jack keep his gun?" she asked, out of concern.

She looked wide-eyed at Sonya and began walking toward the bedroom. Sonya followed. Haley pulled open the drawer where the handgun had always been kept except for when Jack had it on him. It was gone.

"Damn," she said. "We better tell the police about this."

Jason followed them and stood in the bedroom doorway. "What's wrong, Haley?"

"Jack's gun is gone."

"Wow, you know my father and I cannot allow you two to stay here tonight. I've already talked to Sarah and she's expecting you to come to our place."

"Thanks. I don't suppose we have a choice. We don't know if he's coming back to find what he was really here for."

"The security company wants to change all the pass code numbers. After that, grab whatever you ladies need and let's head out. It's getting late."

Chapter 30 ~ Attraction

Evan jogged a little faster than normal around the indoor track at the clubhouse facility. It was good to sweat a little of the poison he felt inside about the entire situation he had become embroiled in due to Jack Foster. All of it should have been clean and simple. He finished his last lap, breathing fast and feeling thirsty. Toweling off his neck and face, he walked toward the locker room to retrieve his belongings. He would shower at home.

Chelsea would be teaching a class tonight and he wanted to at least get a glimpse of her before he left. He sat in the reception area and put his backpack down between his legs. This was one way he could appear as if he was searching inside the pack for something should she glance his way. He didn't want to be obvious about watching, but he was intensely curious about her.

So, this is Pilates, he thought. Evan watched as Chelsea and five other women lifted their legs while lying on their backs. He wanted to know the difference between this and the yoga she taught. The yoga poses seemed to be slower in movement, even sustained at times. Pilates appeared to have more movement. All of it looked intense, at least for his body. Both exercise styles used mats. Chelsea glanced his way and smiled.

Well, she caught me watching. Evan smiled back and winked at her. *Might as well give her something to think about.*

He gathered up his things and headed toward the door. Evan looked directly at her as she simultaneously watched him leave. She kept up her movements the whole time. *Damn, she was hot!*

Lucky struggled to concentrate and keep up her instructive moves with the class. With Evan's eyes on her and the way he openly flirted by winking at her, it was messing with her ability to focus. He was showing himself to not be the shy type. Actually, the more she thought about it, he was kind of predatory. Evan was trying to figure her out, wanting to know the best way to score with her. Little did he know, she was the one tracking him. His game with her was simple, and Lucky was finding her game with him complex and potentially dangerous.

As the class ended and she said her goodbye's, she straightened the room, stacking the extra mats in one corner and turning off the lights. She exited the room and walked toward the front door. She was just about to grab the handle when she heard a male voice say, "Hey, can I ask you a question?"

She turned and was met with the hunky male Adonis she had admired her first day visiting the clubhouse. Lucky looked around for a few seconds and realized there was no one else around.

"Hi. I suppose you're talking to me?" she asked, almost sheepishly. Clearly, she knew this mild kitten voice that came out of her mouth was unusual. *Wow, this guy really affects me,* she thought.

"You're new here, right?"

Lucky nodded her head up and down and walked a little closer to him. He began walking closer to her. Each halted their steps when they were about two feet apart. It was close enough to check each other out, but not get in the other's body space.

"I'm Chelsea."

"I'm Dane."

"Nice to meet you. Did you want to know anything else?" she asked, tilting her head.

"Actually, there's a lot I would like to know," he said, smiling.

"Like?"

"Well, for starters. Do you have any men in the yoga class you teach?"

"No, not yet."

"I guess I will be the first."

"You're coming to yoga? That's great."

"Is this a class for beginners?" he asked.

Lucky questioned whether he was a beginner or not. She wanted to frame her answer appropriately. "I teach beginner and intermediate at this point."

"Good, because I've never done it before. What do I need to bring with me?"

Lucky wanted to say, nothing — just your body. She thought he was so gorgeous. He made her heart quiver and her palms sweat, but she tried her best to appear nonchalant.

"Just yourself and if you have a favorite yoga mat. If not, I have extra mats available."

"I'll see you tomorrow then, Chelsea."

"Sounds great, see you then," she said, turning and walking toward the exit.

Running to her car, the weather was nasty as she stepped out without a coat. The wind was intense, but still somehow, she felt heated internally. It had been a long time since any guy had affected her that way. She was so used to being the one who controlled the animal magnetism because she spent most of her time chasing down bad guys. Any therapist would tell her she was a workaholic trying to avoid intimacy with anyone. And, they would be right. After what occurred with her fiancé in Florida, she vowed to never let it happen again.

As she started the engine, Lucky wondered how in the world she would concentrate on teaching her class tomorrow night. The drive home was brutal. It was raining now, heavily. Occasionally, a gust of wind would be so strong she thought it might lift her little sports car off the pavement. Finally, she pulled into the alley that led to the carriage house garage. She hit the button on the garage door opener and pulled in.

Going upstairs to her apartment, she unlocked the door and collapsed on the couch. It had been a long day, having the Thai lunch with Ric, getting the painting estimate to Alice, reading and shredding the documents, and then the Pilates class. She was wiped out but had agreed to begin drywall repairs for Alice tomorrow morning. Thank goodness, the woman owned a bar and didn't expect her to begin work early. She would rather catch up on sleep. Her phone buzzed and she had two messages - she opened the one from Haley Foster first.

The cable guy came today while we were having coffee. Alarm didn't sound. He had code. Some video but he wore a full face hood. Sonya and I are with family but would like to meet with you soon.

Wow! So sorry to hear this. I want to meet also. My days and evenings are filling up with survey details on this. If it's on weekdays, can we squeeze a meeting in about the same time we did today? Like around 4 o'clock? More flexible this weekend. Let me know

She would wait to hear back from Haley on time and place. Lucky looked at the next message from Ric which included a photo of a small plug-in charging device.

Just now opened my Welcome Packet from Chadwell. This was the most interesting item in the box. Smirky face

Save it! We may be able to do something with that. Foster house broken into today. Happened while I was with her warning it might happen.

Wow! Anything taken?

Not sure. I'll be meeting with the family soon.

I have more news. Evan called my department and asked me to see if I could locate any files in the cloud servers for Jack. He said that he's looking for a report that Jack was working on to present to the shareholders at their next meeting.

Ric, it sounds like he's looking for anything that could be a smoking gun.

I'll let you know if I find one. Good night!

Good night. Stay in touch.

You stay in touch.

Lucky rose from the couch and went to the kitchen. It was small, but perfect for someone like her. She didn't need anything larger. That would be more to clean and take care of. She made a grilled cheese sandwich and warmed up some tomato soup. It was comforting food for a blustery cold night. Still, she could hear the wind howling at times outside. Wind chimes that were placed on the back porch of the mansion could be heard hitting each other wildly.

She turned on her laptop and searched for news or videos coming out of China where it was reported that a major city was locked down. She found dozens of videos made by actual residents of the city. Most did not speak English, but there were subtitles. Mostly, she saw tears and looks of despair with different individuals. They spoke of doors being sealed off by military guards so that no one could escape their home. There were reports of people dying trying to escape, presumably by falling or some other accidental tragedy.

One particular man making a long video indicated he was an investigative journalist from Hong Kong. His eyes were red from either lack of sleep or crying. He was in the city that was locked down and he couldn't get out.

He talked about a virus and said repeatedly throughout, "This is not right. This is deliberate."

Lucky logged off and closed the computer. She had to get some good sleep tonight, but it would be difficult after seeing those images and hearing the distress people were experiencing. What in the world was going on?

Chapter 31 ~ Unlucky Alice

Saturday, December 28, 2019

Lucky woke, stretching her arms and legs, trying to get her body to cooperate with her mind. She was sore from the Pilates class last night. But it was a good stiffness, the kind that told her she was working her body in ways it needed. Today, she would try to be as enthusiastic about drywall repair. It wasn't anything major with the walls, just filling in and sanding areas where something nicked the wall or small holes where an item had hung on the wall.

Her phone had been on silence all night. She grabbed it off the top of the chest of drawers. There was a message from Haley wanting to meet with the entire family at 4:00 tomorrow at a restaurant on Blevins Road. She messaged back that she could make it and asked if she could bring Ric.

Lucky leisurely sipped her coffee and was glad the rain and wind had ended. She gathered some wall repair tools she did not have in her van and set them beside the door. After a shower, she placed her wig over her wig cap and decided to go without makeup.

Today, it was cooler after the storm last night. Lucky slipped on a sweatshirt and leggings, then stepped into the paint splotched coveralls she wore each time. Performing odd jobs was one way to supplement income while she did her investigative work. It was the same for the classes she was teaching. People didn't know she was there to investigate, but she was. And, she intended to find out what went on with the deceased Chadwell employees and missing Jack Foster. The virus that was possibly on its way sounded like a pretty big deal. So far, from the documents she shredded, it appeared people had some sort of foreknowledge of it.

Once outside, she put the tools in her van and took off for Alice's bar. As she approached the rundown area, she noticed there were many people hanging around on street corners of most of the intersections. Police cruisers slowly drove by. Lucky was stuck behind one of them. She took a deep breath to calm any anxiety she was feeling. Why did she feel it? Was she doing anything wrong by beautifying Alice's apartment? No, but she did some unsavory things in her investigative work. She was thankful the police didn't know that. Finally, the cruiser made a turn onto a side street and she picked up speed in the van.

Lucky parked on the side of the building as usual, and gathered the small amount of tools she would need. It was just now ten-thirty, so she was on time. Climbing the steps to the apartment, she found Alice's door slightly ajar. She knocked anyway. "Hello, Alice … are you home?" There was no answer.

Lucky wasn't sure if she should enter the apartment. Perhaps the woman was in the bathroom. She waited outside on the deck for a few moments, leaving her drywall supplies sitting in a pile beside the door. Finally, she went down the steps to check and see if Alice was already in the bar working and had left the apartment door open for her. Both the side and front doors were locked. She peered through the windows seeing only a darkened tavern and no movement inside.

Lucky went back up the steps to Alice's apartment and knocked once more, entering this time. "Alice, you in there? I'm here to start on the drywall." There was still no answer.

She walked through the long hallway, noticing the kitchen appeared untouched this morning. No coffee made or dishes in the sink. The bathroom door was open, but Alice wasn't there.

The hair on her arms was standing up as she passed the small living room area with no sign of Alice. This was beginning to spook her, and she considered turning and getting out of the apartment. But she had always been the type that had to find out answers.

She went toward the bedroom at the end of the hall with its closed door. Stepping lightly with her shoes, she tried to be very quiet. Maybe Alice wasn't awake yet.

As she came to the doorway, she lightly knocked on it. "Alice, I'm here to work on the drywall. Are you awake?" There was no answer. Lucky held her breath for a moment, considering what to do next. With her hand slightly shaking, she touched the old-fashioned glass doorknob and grasped it, turning it toward the right. It clicked and opened.

She didn't even have to take three steps into the room before she found her. Alice was there, but she would not be waking up. Her eyes were wide open glaring at the ceiling and she had a long cord twisted several times around her neck. Lucky felt bile begin to rise in her esophagus — the kind of acidic taste that comes on right before you puke. She wanted to scream, but no sound would come out. What in the hell was she going to do. Here she was with a wig on and fake identification. But she had to notify the police. And she had to get out of this room with Alice lying there dead.

A myriad of thoughts ran through her mind. What had she touched while she was there? Should she get her prints cleaned off the doorknob or would cleaning them off look suspicious? Did she touch any of the doors? She could leave right now and let someone else find Alice. There was nothing she could do for her now. But what if someone saw her van or her? They could report her to the police. No, she had to call the police and see this through. She would have to show them her regular identification. As for the wig, any woman could want to wear a wig for a bad hair day. She could say she wore it to keep paint out of her real hair. She would deal with it.

She stepped backward down the hall for a few steps and then bolted toward the front door. Once out on the deck, she breathed easier. But she still felt sick and a bit lightheaded. Sitting on the upper deck bench, Lucky dialed 911.

In a way, time stood still as Lucky sat on the bench. She could not help but feel like she was part of something she didn't want to be involved in. Several police officers arrived. They asked her questions and told her to stay right there for more questions. Another officer sat with her for awhile.

An ambulance arrived. They went inside and a crime lab joined with more police. A detective traded places with the officer and now sat with Lucky asking her questions on the deck. Finally, someone from the coroner's office took the body of Alice out to their vehicle in a black body bag.

"Do you know what time it is?" she asked the detective.

"It's almost twelve-thirty. And you told me that you arrived here at what time?" he asked, for the umpteenth time.

"I was here right at ten-thirty, like Alice and I agreed upon."

"And you said the front door was slightly open, right?"

"Yes, that's correct."

"Stay here for a moment longer. I'll be right back."

The detective was probably in his forties. If she had met him on the street, she would never know he was with the police. He wore jeans and a pale yellow pullover sweater with a button-down shirt underneath. His shoes looked like they were made for hiking. He was heavyset and walked slowly down the steps to the sidewalk. She could hear him speaking to someone, but could only make out some of the words. Lucky heard search warrant, motive, and telling the truth. She was doomed to look guilty if they searched her van and found surveillance devices and different identification. Lucky strove to appear normal but the search warrant comment she overheard was eating at her soul now. *I can't let this happen*, she thought. She heard him coming back up the steps and she sat up straight. Lucky decided to go on the offense against him now.

"That poor woman's death was not caused by me. You've held me here a long time. I'm cold and more than a bit freaked out. Why would I kill someone and then hang around and call 911?" she asked the detective.

He looked at her and smiled. "You're right. You have been here too long. I was just about to tell you that you may leave. We have your address and contact information though. We may need to ask you more questions."

"I'm happy I get to go, but you need to understand. I've answered everything I know about this incident. Goodbye Detective."

"Goodbye Ms. Adams."

Lucky wasted no time in getting inside her van and leaving. She felt raked over like a pile of leaves or debris. She cranked up the heat inside the big boxy van. She was chilled to the bone. Warm soup would be nice right now and homemade bread. *I need to call Ric.*

She called Ric's burner phone from one of her burner phones. He answered just as she thought it might go to voice mail.

"Ric, I'm so glad you answered. It's been a bad morning."

"What's going on? Are you hurt?"

"No. I need to talk to you in person."

"Okay, I'm available. Where and when?"

"Someplace that has soup and homemade bread. Do you know of a restaurant like that?"

"Where are you now?"

"I'm just driving aimlessly right now through Atlanta."

"Meet me at 613 West Street in about thirty minutes."

"I'll be there."

Chapter 32 ~ Bread & Tea

Lucky met Ric at the address indicated, finding a small cafe with homemade bread, but no soup. Upon entering and inhaling the aroma of fresh baked bread, she didn't care. Ideally, she would like to just grab a loaf of bread and sit in a corner in the back with a blanket wrapped around her.

Ric arrived, just after her, and they ordered the homemade bread and hot herbal tea. Both spoke in hushed tones. Lucky told him about going to Alice's apartment and finding her dead. "The police held me so long I began to feel involved in the murder, but I'm not," she said, with whispered emphasis.

"Of course, you're not. This is crazy and unbelievable. Do you know anyone who would want to kill her?"

"I barely know her, so no. It appeared that she and the man she called Ben had a little tussle outside the bar the first day I met her. I saw them from the side mirror on the van as I was leaving. I also know the Ragland guy appears to have slept with her the night before last. But that's all I know."

Ric spread raspberry jam on a piece of hot bread. "Didn't you say you thought something else was going on at that bar?"

"Yes, it's the kind of place you see and wonder how they stay afloat. It's expensive just to pay the light bill on a building that size. I don't have any evidence of anything though."

"She could have been involved in a drug deal that went bad. Maybe she owed money and wouldn't pay up."

"Ric, I was so afraid that detective was going to search my van and find my surveillance stuff. I kind of feel like a fraud! Here I am going around doing all these investigative activities and I don't have the credentials behind it to be involved in spying operations."

"You are not a fraud. The murder of Alice has just shaken you. You're doing important work, Lucky. Think of what we've accomplished so far. There is a point where the police are brought into what we are uncovering, but we aren't there yet. And, we sure as hell would not be working with local cops that can be so easily bought off."

Lucky buttered another piece of the warm bread and took a bite. She chewed silently. "Something about homemade bread makes me feel better. And you, Ric. You make me feel better."

He smiled. "Good, I'm glad to know that."

Just then, her phone made its familiar tone and she glanced at it. "Evan's on the move again. Right now, I don't care. I just want to try and recover from this. Poor Alice!"

"You can check the app later to see where he went, right?"

"Yes, and I will. Tomorrow, I'm meeting the Foster family for dinner. I think you should come also."

"Was I invited?"

"Not officially, but I believe they would want you there. So much has happened in the last twenty-four hours. Is there a full moon or something? I forgot to tell you that Haley Foster's house was broken into yesterday while she was having coffee with me."

"You told me about that, last night when you messaged me."

"See, I'm losing my mind, Ric."

"You're almost in shock over this. It is a traumatic thing to walk in and find a dead body. Natural reaction."

The server came with more tea in a beautiful ceramic teapot. "Everything okay?" she inquired.

Ric nodded to her, "Yes, it's perfect. Thank you."

They both added a little honey to their tea and sipped, sitting quietly now. Finally, Ric broke the silence.

"What would you like to do now?"

Lucky closed her eyes and took a deep breath. "Curl up with a blanket and watch a movie."

"You could do that at my place," Ric offered. Lucky thought of how she had only been to Ric's apartment twice the entire time they had known each other. Right now, the police could be following her — maybe not right at this moment, but soon.

"Thanks, but it might be risky. Honestly, I need to think about each place I travel to right now. I'm really nervous about this, Ric."

"Lucky, you've not committed any crime. Well, maybe some small ones. I think you're going to be okay."

"I don't know. This time, I may not be so lucky."

Chapter 33 ~ Evan & Ragland

Evan lounged in his living room, listening to the Saturday morning news on television while having coffee. He had no plans for the weekend except to relax and hope that he received the information Jack stored away soon from Ragland. He still felt it was important for Haley not to be hurt. Tellinger would not care one way or another. Evan admitted to himself that he did have feelings for Haley, even if they had not yet been acted upon.

He understood that she and Jack's family were on a crusade to find Jack, alive or dead. Like any family would, he knew they had immense hope he would be alive. But how could he be after all this time? Finally, they would come to the conclusion that he was gone. Perhaps then, he and Haley might be able to be more than they were now.

In the meantime, he could see other women. They might not have the class of Haley, but he could still enjoy them. There was his old standby Becky who owned the bakery down the street. She put little demand on him, in fact none at all. But he was also drawn to the new instructor at the clubhouse, Chelsea. She was sexy as hell. In fact, she had him thinking of taking up yoga.

Suddenly, his gaze became fixated on the television. They were reporting the shutdown of a city in China with no travel in or out. He turned up the volume.

"Early reports indicate authorities believe a virus is the cause of so many hospital admissions. There are long waiting times for care. Many residents are camped out in the halls of the local hospitals and clinics. Some have overflow outside."

Evan sat his coffee cup down on the table. He wondered if this was what Tellinger had spoke of in the strictest of confidence. He wished he could contact him right now to know if it was or not. But it was the weekend and he still didn't have the information that Tellinger wanted. His burner phone vibrated on the kitchen countertop. He went to retrieve it, seeing a message from the number he knew belonged to Ragland.

Got in but there were problems. Can we meet at our usual spot today and talk?

Problems? Yes I can meet. How about 1 pm?

Works for me. See you then.

"Shit!" Evan exclaimed. Tellinger had passed the name of this stupid asshole operator to Evan. So far, he had been nothing but trouble to work with. Guy couldn't thread a needle if his life depended on it. Today, he needed to find someone who was capable since it didn't seem like Ragland could do the job. He would meet with him and hear him out first. After his shower and dressing, he made his way toward their usual meeting place.

While driving, he received a message from Ragland on his burner phone.

Change in meeting location Go east two blocks to Short Stop Tavern

Evan looked at the message and didn't respond. He drove and wondered why Ragland would change the location. He arrived and parked directly out front where he could see his car. This guy chose the worst places for meetings. Next time he dealt with another operator, meetings and things would be firmly on Evan's terms.

He stepped inside the tavern which was not unlike the one they usually met at. Ragland sat at a table not too far from the door. Evan sat down. "What the hell is going on?"

"I don't know. There were cops all over our usual meeting place. Did you see them?"

"I noticed a couple of cars out front. Paranoid?" Evan mused.

"There were several more on the side street."

Evan adopted a serious look. He deliberately wanted Ragland to know he was not happy that he had not obtained the material at the Foster's. Gazing at Ragland with a piercing stare he asked, "What happened?"

"Everything went well for me getting in. I was there for two hours and about fourteen minutes before I had to leave because she was on the way home. Seven minutes or less away from finding me there. I had to rush out."

"In all that time, you found nothing?"

"Nada, nothing. I searched the basement fully and that took some time. I searched every bedroom, under mattresses, in drawers, under the beds, shoe boxes in closets. Finally, I searched the attic. Didn't find anything, but that's also when my phone indicated she was on her way home. I had to run out of there, leaving a ladder I had retrieved from the garage in the hallway."

"Damn, so Haley knows someone was there and they were searching for something."

"That's right. She would also notice the system disarmed. I didn't take the time to arm it again. I just couldn't risk it with the limited seconds I had to get out of there."

Evan took a sip of his beer and then turned the bottle around with one hand repeatedly at the table. Ragland watched him, curious what his thoughts were.

"My mom used to hide money in the china cabinet. Did you look in the dining room?"

"No, I didn't look in the kitchen, dining room or an office I saw. The office would be too obvious a place to hide documents and such."

"Agreed, but who knows? You didn't find it and now, you've jeopardized your ability to get in there."

"You're right. I can't use the cable company truck and I'm sure she's going to beef up her security. I know I would."

"What did you do about the cameras? Will someone recognize you?"

"I don't think so. I wore a full face hood and covered my license plate before pulling into the drive."

"Here's the deal, Ragland. We know something is there and I've got to have it delivered to me soon. Have you figured out a plan b?"

"Maybe, but any ideas I have, you're not going to like."

"You're not as smart as I thought, Ragland. Think, think! How could you get in there quickly? You need to show up as someone reviewing the property for security issues. Or, you could impersonate a police detective. There has to be a way you can get in there now, rather than wait and miss the window of opportunity."

"Too bad you're not in my line of work, Evan," he said smirking. "Let me run some ideas and see what I can come up with."

"Do that ... and find the shit this time," Evan said, taking a final swig of his beer. He stood and looked at

Ragland seriously before walking out of the bar. "Don't let me down on this."

Chapter 34 ~ The New Team

Jack reported to the medical bay and was guided to a small room with a round table and chairs. The female doctor was seated, but stood as he entered.

"Good morning!" Dr. Barbados said. "Dr. Melo will be here in a moment. Please be comfortable."

"Thank you, good morning to you."

"Are you sleeping well at night?"

"Yes, I have been so tired. It takes me no time to fall asleep."

Dr. Melo came into the small conference room. He shook Jack's hand and sat down with a glass electronic pad in front of him.

"Dr. Foster, we have all the test results in and Dr. Barbados and I consulted late last night and again this morning on a suggested care plan for you. Allow me to begin with the situation with your leg. I'm showing a hairline fracture that is still healing with your tibia. This fracture could have happened with some kind of force on your leg or force as you landed on that leg. There's no need for a cast. No jumping or strenuous activity until it heals which could be another six weeks from now. I would reduce the amount of hours you are walking or standing each day for the next two to three weeks. You also have a ligament that was stretched or torn right here," he said, pointing to the image on the screen. This could be quite a bit of the source of your pain. Ligaments heal slower than fractures and often create more inflammation in the area, which in turn sends pain signals to your brain. I've scheduled you for some light physical therapy which will begin in two weeks. It will help you gain mobility with your leg."

"Okay, sounds good. Why two weeks from now?"

"Scheduling issues. Don't worry, you'll be working that leg on your trike and walking. This will be more pointed therapy for the leg."

"Do you think I'll be able to walk without limping?"

"Yes, I do. The physical therapy will help immensely."

Jack felt relieved that his injuries were not more serious. Did you get anything from my labs?"

"All of your lab results came back within normal ranges. Allow me to show you images of your brain. All of your scans show everything fairly normal."

He took a stylus and pointed on the glass tablet. "This does show some inflammation here in the occipital region, and again in the left temporal lobe, but just slight inflammation. Dr. Barbados, would you care to comment now on this?"

"Yes, Dr. Foster, I believe residual inflammation could be preventing you from having your full memory, but I cannot guarantee this is the situation. As I mentioned yesterday, the brain is something that despite so many years of study, it still eludes us at times. The inflammation will go away and we can treat that with some natural supplements for now and other therapies."

"What would you suggest for it?" Jack asked her.

"Something as simple as high-dose, pure grade turmeric may help, especially if combined with pepperine to assist with absorption. Have you ever taken that?"

"No, but I'm willing to try it."

"If it seems to have no effect, there are other things we can try. But that is to address the inflammation. Other causes of the memory loss could be a little more tricky. When someone has been through a traumatic event and there is no noticeable damage to the brain, sometimes it can be solved by approaching it from a psychological level."

She waited for his facial response before continuing. Jack did not waver in his expression.

Dr. Barbados went on. "As part of your proposed treatment plan, I would like to employ hypnosis, perhaps three or more times a week. Additionally, we would like to schedule you for hyperbaric oxygen treatment which assists in helping tissue to heal. Finally, we will do some psychoanalysis to see if there is something in your subconscious holding back your ability to remember. If so, we can then work on constructing a plan to reprogram your subconscious. How do you feel about those modalities I mentioned as part of your treatment plan?"

"I've never experienced any of those. I suppose I'm open to it."

"Well, they say there's always a first time, no?"

Jack rubbed the malachite stone around his neck. "Somebody gave me this and I know I'm not supposed to take it off. But I don't know who told me that or gave it to me. Isn't that crazy?"

Dr. Barbados shook her head from side to side. "No, it's not crazy at all. As I said, our brains can do some unusual things that may not make sense to us. Mostly likely, your brain is doing this because it is somehow trying to protect you. As we put your treatment plan in action, I believe we'll discover a lot more."

Jack was impressed with the medical team. He liked that they were not going to try and drug him up, and then send him on his way. Dr. Barbados had proposed some unconventional methods of treatment, and he was truly curious to try them. The most important thing he could do for himself was to be at one hundred percent. Right now, he wasn't there. If he was going to help his own

President and the people of Brazil, he needed everything on his side.

Entering the laboratory, he was greeted by a couple of members of the team he met the day before. He requested they call a meeting in one of the conference rooms to go over the duties and tasks that lie ahead of them. The team met in twenty minutes and Jack opened the glass pad he brought along with him today. He felt a little inept with it still, and wondered if there was a way to cast the information he was sharing onto a larger computer screen in the room.

"Hey, does anyone know how I can share my screen to that computer?"

Eleanora spoke up first. "Yes, let me show you. Simply touch this icon and it will ask where you want to share. Then, make the selection."

"Thank you, that's much easier than I thought."

She smiled at him.

"First, let me begin by thanking each of you for meeting with me individually yesterday. I enjoyed getting to know you. I feel assured that, as we work on this project, I will see even more of your strengths and abilities. I say this because if you're not satisfied with the position I have selected for you on the team, let's talk. If we can find a better spot, I am willing to entertain that. But more than anything, let's remember that each is away from family right now for a reason. We have been brought together because someone higher than us had an extreme amount of confidence that we could pull off something incredible together."

Jack paused, clicking on his first slide in his presentation. He took a sip of water before continuing.

"On the screen, you are seeing a photograph of a plant that I have used in the making of a new anti-viral drug. This drug has only been through animal trials. I believe the first trial was sabotaged. The drug had been working very effectively with no side effects. Suddenly, each of the subjects died -- all at the same time. Autopsy revealed something nefarious had taken place. I then took the drug to a second animal trial, this time to a contracted location where I felt it had less chance of mishandling or sabotage. It was highly successful. While I was traveling to Brazil with my team, my assistant at Chadwell was to begin setting up the human trial, which would hopefully be going on right now. But, the story didn't end that way, did it? I am what is left of that team. God rest their souls."

Jack paused and went to the next screen which was white with P-2019 on it. He sipped some more water and paced the room a little before speaking.

"Does anyone here know what that stands for?" No one acknowledged they did. Most shook their heads negatively from side to side.

"This stands for Pandemic 2019 and it has begun as of now in China. I can tell you that I know bits and pieces of this plan, but I do not know the entire genesis of it. This brings me back to why we are here. Basically, we have been charged with recreating this anti-viral drug with the hope it can be used to treat people during the spread of a virus that has probably been made more virulent with gain of function."

Jack continued through the visual presentation, explaining everything he knew about the drug he and his team had developed and its intricacies. He also spoke about the proposed medical device that was planned to be used on the populace. "It's not really a vaccine in the traditional sense as we know it — not at all. Technically, it could be classified as a medical device. Using nanotechnology and artificially created proteins, it changes the RNA in the body, including the way the cells respond in the future to foreign substances the immune system would normally attack. I see a lot of potential pitfalls with the use of it and I am in disagreement of its use unless it can be shown to be very harmless to the populace."

As he spoke, he explained that the drug they would be creating came from a more natural source and how effective it was in vitro and with animals in attacking viruses.

"So, if you don't like the position I have chosen for you, please know that I am doing my best. It is important that we work as cohesively together as possible. Always, I expect everyone to display respect for one another. Everyone here has something to contribute. Hopefully, each of you can tell your children or others in the future how you helped save many lives with this drug. I am going to teach you everything about it. If it is safe and has a high efficacy rate, it needs to be manufactured quickly. But we must not skip any important steps and safety precautions. Now, if you are with me in this endeavor, please accept your assigned positions, and let us begin to work together."

Each of the project participants stood, clapping their hands together, and some cheering vocally.

"Wow, what a great response from you all. I should have come to work here a lot sooner," Jack said, laughing.

Chapter 35 ~ Foster Dinner

Joe and Sharon Foster arrived at the restaurant first. They had reserved a private dining room and there was so much to talk about. Joe pulled the manager aside and requested that the servers give them plenty of private time to talk. He assured them they would.

Jason, Sarah, Haley and Sonya arrived soon thereafter. Sarah's mother watched their children so they could speak freely. The stakes were high. Once again, circumstances they were facing began to feel dangerous. Eli was too young to really understand what was going on. But Allison would possibly be upset with some of the conversations that would occur during the dinner meeting.

Lucky and Ric arrived next. She had cleared Ric attending with Haley the night before. The mood was friendly, but a bit stoic. Everyone was beginning to feel as if circumstances were taking a toll on them individually and collectively.

Joe and Sharon sat at opposite ends of the table. The group placed their drink orders and Joe asked the servers to bring a variety of appetizers to the table. "We might as well make this a feast, everyone," he said, smiling.

"Absolutely!" Sarah said.

The guests made a bit of small talk about the weather changing, along with winning and losing sports teams while they waited for the appetizers and drinks. Once it was delivered, Sharon Foster began the more pressing conversation.

"Everyone, thank you for coming. We want to make sure we talk about this situation only when the servers are out of the room. First, I want to address what is happening with Haley and Sonya. Since the break-in, they have been unable to live at the house. They're staying with Jason and Sarah. This cannot go on forever. We need a plan for the two of them long term. But, I don't know what that is yet."

Ideas were tossed around including trained guard dogs, hired bodyguards, and just simply leaving town for a while. Haley chimed in. "I thought about going on vacation with Sonya, maybe down to Valdosta and then on to Florida. The problem is, we still have to come back home. Plus, I don't want to miss ...." She realized suddenly that she almost revealed that Jack was alive as she was going to ask, what if Jack is able to call us. Sharon read her mind and interrupted her, "What if we find Jack?"

"Yes," Haley said, relieved her mother-in-law saved her. "What if we do and I'm not here?"

Lucky interjected. "What you need is leverage on whoever wants something in your house. More protection wouldn't hurt either. But you cannot let them control you like this. You should be able to live in your home without the threat of people breaking in."

Haley understood what she said, but didn't that only happen in a perfect world? Her life was anything but perfect right now. It had been turned upside down and many of the people she cared about were along for the roller coaster ride with her.

Sarah looked at Lucky and asked, "They didn't find what they wanted, and don't you think they'll be back?"

"Maybe, but now they're on the police's radar. It's going to be more complicated for them to break in."

Jason was curious about Lucky's first comment and asked, "What do you mean by leverage?"

"Have you heard of a dead man's switch?"

"Yeah, I have."

"This is what she needs. It would make the situation more transparent. She could let the guy that broke in know that she found what he's looking for. He would be informed that the information was moved to a safe location, and she has made copies that will be instantly released to the authorities and public should anything happen to her.

Jason nodded, "That would put an interesting spin on things."

Lucky continued, "Believe me, just the fact that she would know it was him who broke into the house will freak him out. He'll also wonder why she didn't sic the cops on him. That's another piece of leverage she has over him."

Joe Foster nodded, "Essentially, we would put them in checkmate, unable to do much about obtaining the information. I like that idea and letting them know it's not at the house any longer. But who do we notify and how?"

Lucky responded, "From what Ric and I have uncovered so far, we know that Evan Mitchell is the one who wants the information. That means his boss, Tellinger, probably wants it even more. The guy that broke into the house is just a hired hand. I would have Haley send a direct message to him, the thief."

Everyone at the table agreed. Ric added, "So, as you may or may not know, I am working in the IT department at Chadwell. Right after Christmas, I decided to come into the office, knowing many of the employees would be gone. This gave me a little more access to check things out. Two things occurred in the last three days. First, I was able to recover some high-level communications that possibly implicate Chadwell, two other pharmaceutical companies, the CDC, and the FDA in some type of plan. We should probably talk about that last. It's potentially huge."

"Okay, continuing as if my first discovery is not enough. My second is that Evan phoned the IT department and I answered. He requested that I find any digital place that Jack may have stored reports, notes or information, such as one of the cloud servers. I have not completed that search, but if I find anything, I will be locking it down for the authorities to look at possibly later. It won't go to Evan Mitchell."

The servers brought in the appetizers and refilled drinks. "Are you ready to order?" the head server asked.

Joe looked at Sharon and the others at the table.

"Honestly, we have not looked over the menu enough. Give us only five minutes and we will be ready."

They took a break to peruse the menu. The server returned in a few minutes and took their orders. Once they were alone again, Lucky spoke up. "Well, the last two days have been very eventful, in good and bad ways. I will try to condense things."

"As you know, I met with Haley and Sonya to warn them about a possible break-in. Little did we know, it was happening right then. Thank goodness, she found the items that morning and moved them someplace safe."

Jason asked her, "How did you know this was going to happen?"

"I had a listening device at a table in a bar where Evan was meeting the guy I believe did the break-in. He wanted more money from Evan which he gave him. Evan called him by the name Ragland. I'm going to assume that's his last name. If we can find out where he lives, that's where the dead man letter drop needs to happen.

Most likely, he will pull away from the situation and also let Evan know why."

"Sorry to interrupt," Haley said. "I like the idea, but I don't feel comfortable dropping off the letter to him."

"No, it will either be mailed, or we'll have someone else deliver it," Lucky said. "Okay, where was I? That same bar, I made arrangements to paint the upstairs apartment where the lady who owned it lived. I was doing this to gather more intel, not because I love wall painting. But hey, it was a little more money for me. Yesterday morning, I had the shock of my life. When I arrived, she was dead, murdered in her bed."

There were several gasps at the table.

"It was absolutely horrible. I feel so bad for her. I'm not sure what she got herself involved in that someone would want to strangle her. It seemed like whoever did it was very angry, like a crime of passion."

"Did you contact the police?" Jason asked.

"Yep, and they held me outside her apartment for a couple of hours questioning me. I'm afraid I'm now on their radar. I can't imagine why the detective who spent so much time with me would think I would have a reason to commit such a crime. I was very nervous they were going to search my van, finding surveillance equipment and other forms of identification. That would have really made me look suspicious. Here's the thing, I saw her and Ragland go up to that apartment together two nights prior to this."

"So, he might be the killer," Sarah said in a low tone.

"He could be, but it also might be this older man, Ben. He hangs out at her bar and I observed him manhandle her one day when I was driving away from the place. Honestly, it could be a drug deal she had going on that went bad."

Jason looked at Lucky with concern. "While you're on the police radar, you may need to hide your alternate id's and surveillance items in a place to keep safe. Once they find another suspect, you'll be fine."

"Yes, you're right. I shouldn't take any chances right now. Like I told Ric, I'm just investigating. I haven't committed any big crimes, but sometimes I do skirt the law with some small law breaking. I need to stay off the radar of the police."

"Agreed," said Joe Foster. "Both you and Ric are doing excellent work by the way."

Ric smiled and Lucky stood and took a tiny bow, "Thank you! We're trying. Oh, I forgot to tell you. Evan has taken an interest in me at the clubhouse where I'm teaching yoga classes. I may be able to get close enough to get more information soon."

Sharon chuckled, "Lucky, your life sounds like a movie."

"Pretty much, not too many dull moments."

The doors opened and the server and an assistant arrived to clear the appetizer plates and refill drinks. "Your entrees will be served momentarily."

The conversation broke until everyone's meal was delivered.

Chapter 36 ~ The Big News

Joe Foster asked his family and guests, "Is the food to your liking?"

Many were chewing and nodding their heads yes, simultaneously.

"I think this is an excellent restaurant," he added, and everyone at the table agreed, thanking he and Sharon for their hospitality.

Lucky looked at Ric, "Are you ready to share the more controversial news?"

Ric cleared his throat and looked upward for a few seconds. "Yes, I'm trying to understand what I found and make sure I'm not putting my own distorted interpretation on it. I don't want to panic anyone."

"Tell it the way you see it, Ric," Sarah encouraged.

"I was able to recover some deleted encrypted emails. They were addressed to a lot of key people. This includes Jack, so he had some kind of knowledge about it. There was also the CDC, FDA, NIH, and other high-level people from various pharmaceutical companies in the email chain. All of these people had some kind of knowledge about an event they referred to as P-19."

"What is it?" Haley asked.

"I believe the P stands for pandemic. When you read the document that was attached to one of those emails, you find they were planning what the world response would be to the event. This included locking down small towns, cities, and even entire countries where possible to prevent the spread. They acknowledged in the document that many businesses would not make it due to the closures and lock downs."

Sarah asked, "When is this going to happen?"

"It might be happening now if you've seen any of the limited coverage out of China."

"Will it only affect that area of the world?"

"Not the way the response is planned. In what they call the P-19 event, it sounds like it will be worldwide."

"Oh my gosh!" Sarah said. "Ric, my father died two years ago from the flu."

"I'm very sorry to hear that. Influenza can severely affect the very young and elderly. Did he have pneumonia complications?"

"Yes, he did. It happened quickly too."

Ric took a drink of his iced tea and continued. "They want mandatory testing of citizens and were also finalizing plans for a vaccine. Haley, do you know if Jack was working on a vaccine?"

"I'm not sure. His secret pet project was revealed in what I took out of the house. He had developed something he described as a game changer, a new anti-viral drug. From what I read in his documents I took out of the house, it's not a vaccine. He knew something about this plan, but indicated in his journal there were pieces missing he didn't know. He probably stood up to Tellinger about not participating in it. That's probably one reason they wanted him gone. He mentioned that the NIH, CDC and FDA were involved, along with others."

Everyone looked at one another and Sharon suddenly said, "China — I've heard about a city there locked down and they believe a really dangerous virus is infecting thousands." She looked grim for a moment. "Let's pray for them and also pray it's not coming to our country. I don't understand why there is so little coverage about this on the news."

Ric nodded. "I agree, but if we're speaking of the major news networks, they're very controlled on what they can report and even how that news is presented. They no longer have the journalistic standards set out in every journalism college in the world."

"Yes, I've noticed the same," Sonya said. "They will say this or that happened. But everything is framed a certain way."

"Exactly!" Ric said. "Whenever they're speaking of what's going on with the President or Congress, they try to make us believe that one particular party is the enemy.

They have already successfully turned many people in favor of the party they support with complete lies and propaganda. If you're watching what some people would consider a right wing news channel, their goal is to make you believe the left side is the root of all evil. They are behind all the problems in the world. It's the same if you're viewing a more left wing channel, they are intent on making you hate the right side. But even more than that, now they're pushing particular agendas. But I'll stop there, otherwise I may never stop."

Everyone at the table laughed. "At least your passionate about something and not apathetic," Haley said.

Jason knew there was much more involved with the virus affecting people in the eastern world right now. He couldn't speak of what Jack said in the hotel room in Brazil. Lucky and Ric had not been told Jack was alive, so this stifled the conversation. Ideally, he thought they should be told. But they seemed to be working well without that affecting their investigative abilities. He looked at his father and could tell he was thinking the same.

Joe Foster spoke to Ric and Lucky. "Each of you are contributing quite a bit to this secretive dilemma my family has found itself in. You may be uncovering information that is important to the entire world — secrets they don't want on the front page of any newspaper. Thank you to you both and I have something for you."

Joe had not paid them anything to date. He handed them each an envelope containing two thousand dollars in cash.

As Lucky opened the envelope, she was not sure how much money was there. She just thumbed through one hundred dollar bills. Ric opened it and fanned the money out.

"It's two thousand each — really not that much for the risk you've already put yourself in. But you've both been on this for a couple of weeks and I want to make sure you can keep the lights on at your place."

"Thank you so much," Ric said. "You know, I am on Chadwell's payroll right now."

"Yes, I realize you're both receiving other funds, but you must be compensated."

Lucky came over and hugged the elder man, "Thank you, but I want you to know I like your family so much, I would do this for free as long as I could."

"That's one of the things I really like about you, young lady," he said, smiling.

As the dinner concluded, Lucky and Ric thanked the Fosters for their gracious hospitality once again. Walking outside toward their vehicles, Ric stopped Lucky momentarily at her car. "We have stuff to work on. They need our help. Do you want to hide some of your things at my place for now?"

Lucky hesitated, wondering if it might be the best place. "I tell you what. Let me put my various pieces of identification someplace safe and hidden but that I can get to quickly if I need them. I will let you take the surveillance gear to your place for now, just in case they show up with a search warrant at my apartment."

"That works for me."

"Ric, I'll call my contact and see if she has that list of people who may go by the name Ragland in our area yet. She should be able to get it quickly, but maybe with the weekend, it got held up. I just feel that we need to get that dead man switch letter to him quickly before he tries another stupid stunt."

"I agree. I'm actually anxious to go to work on Monday morning. Wish me luck! I need to turn up more incriminating documents."

Lucky took Ric by the hand and squeezed his cold fingers. "May you have all the luck you need and then some."

Ric squeeze her hand back. *If only she knew how much I care for her.*

Chapter 37 ~ Hypnosis One

Jack invited all the team members to join him for dinner that evening. He never saw himself as the egocentric leader that needed to separate himself from those that worked under him. Rather, he liked to think they were technical creators working together.

Jack had given each of them their tasks and let them know he was receiving medical treatment for his leg. He didn't mention the memory issue. That could undermine any confidence they had in him. Instead, he let them know he had another appointment at the medical bay tomorrow morning, but would be in the lab as soon as he finished.

The team pulled four tables together, making it into one long unit. Marcos showed up, sat next to Jack, and gave words of confidence to the entire team. As the former Minister of Health of Brazil, it seemed to hold considerable weight with each of them.

Marcos turned to Jack, "So, did you find your plant?"

"I did, thank you. How did you get so much of it here and so quickly?"

"When you have a direct line to the country's President and he has the military at his disposal, it's bound to happen." They both laughed.

"For sure! I selected two of the team members to be fully trained on extraction and isolation. We did that today, in fact."

"Well, I'm not sure what that involves, but I trust you to train them well. You know Jack, if we can get the drug working in humans safely and the efficacy level is high, it can be manufactured here initially, and then other places. You could go home at that point."

Jack looked at Marcos with a look of amazement in his eyes. "Home, I'm not sure where it is right now, Marcos. I've been floating from one place to another. Don't get me wrong. I want to go back, but I have this awkward gap in my memory of where I will actually lay my head at night."

"Don't worry about that now. We are delighted you remember your work with this potential treatment. Give it some time. You are still healing from the accident."

Jack's phone vibrated in his pocket. He stood halfway to ease it out of his pocket where it was buried. Looking at the screen, he read a notification that the psychologist would like to visit with him this evening and to please call. He broke away from Marcos and the group at the table, dialing the number.

"Hello, this is Jack Foster. You wanted to speak with me."

"Dr. Foster, I am Dr. Andre Alonso. I am a psychologist and hypnotherapist. If you're available, I was wondering if we could begin with a session this evening?"

"Yes, I'm finishing dinner and then I planned on heading back to my room."

"Alright, I could come by your room if that's okay. My office was just painted and the smell is fairly strong."

"Sure, let's say 8:15. How long does this take?"

"Not very long. I'll explain more when we meet."

"Okay, see you then."

Dr. Alonso was on time and Jack invited him inside his apartment. He explained to Jack his procedure for hypnosis, how it worked, and that it did not work for everyone. It was something that just had to be experienced and tried. Jack agreed that he was up for trying it. He preferred to lie rather than sit for the session on his bed. Dr. Alonso pulled a chair beside the bed.

"Jack, I want to start off saying that today, we will not visit the aspect of the crash itself. We will focus on what happened afterward. In your medical notes, you believed yourself to be unconscious. However, did you know there is a part of us that may still be able to pick up things in our environment even while in that state?"

"No, I wasn't aware of that."

"Of course, there's no pressure if you cannot remember. I will begin by helping you induce a relaxed state. You will be awake, but very relaxed. We will spend most of our time getting you in that frame of mind. Once you have done it a few times, it's quicker each time thereafter. May I dim the lights?"

"Yes, go ahead."

The doctor left only the blue lights around the baseboard visible and the sound of trickling water he played from his phone. The fidelity was excellent and assisted him in feeling relaxed. Silently, Jack hoped he would not fall asleep during the session. He tried to lie still on his back, waiting for the man to begin.

He went through a long series of directing, by suggestion, the relaxation of each part of his body. This began with the feet and ended with his head and neck, where he held a great deal of tension. Finally, his mouth fell open naturally. Even his eyelids were light and did not hold tension.

As his body felt as if it was sinking into the bed and almost becoming one with it, he could hear the doctor's voice speaking, deep and almost monotone, but in a soothing way. Step by step, his words guided Jack down an old set of steps into a final area with a clearing. It was there that he allowed Jack's mind to stay.

"Talk about what is around you, Jack."

Jack let his mind stay in the cleared area of blankness. He felt his body lying on the ground. "I feel small twigs and the dampness of the ground under me."

"Good, what do you hear?"

"Birds, I hear the call of many birds. I feel like they are communicating in a distressed way about me being there."

"Excellent, do your eyes see anything around you?"

Jack hesitated, "I'm not sure. The light is dappled coming through the trees. They are very tall, ancient looking trees. The light is diffused but streams in making light shadows around me."

"Do you see anything else around you?"

"Palm leaves gently swaying. It's not from the wind. The air is still. I think it's from insects landing on the leaves and birds as they fly to and from."

Jack grabbed his throat area on the bed and touched the malachite stone. "I promised her I would wear it for the entire trip."

"Who is she?"

"I can't see her face, but I know I promised her."

Jack reaches for his mouth area while lying on the bed. "I feel like I have to vomit. Something is wrong with my leg. Oh damn, my leg."

"Okay, Jack. You're coming back now, climbing the stairs back. I want you to envision putting your foot on the first step. There's a handrail you can hold onto. Now, raise your foot to step two."

The doctor continued until Jack had reached the top of the staircase and felt relaxed, with no feeling of illness as he came out of the hypnotic state.

"Wow! That was strange. I really felt like I was going to heave up my dinner."

"It's part of the power of our minds. You revisited a time and place where you felt that way. Many people feel like vomiting when they break a bone."

"Yes, I've heard of that. But, it felt so real."

"You're fine now, right?"

Jack sat up on the edge of his bed. "Yes, I'm fine. It seems as if I was lying on the forest floor, injured."

"You did really well relaxing into a deep state. I have recorded the session for you and will send it to you on your phone if you want to listen to it again."

"Yes, I might want to."

"I will come by again tomorrow evening, if that works for you and we will have another session. Does the same time work well for you?"

"I think so. I'll message you if I need to change it."

Dr. Alonso stood from the chair and moved it back to the desk area. "I will plan on seeing you tomorrow."

Jack rose to activate the scanner and let him out of the room. "Same time, same place tomorrow, right?"

"Yes, you did well tonight."

"Only with your help. Goodnight."

Jack closed the door and sat again on the edge of the bed. The hypnosis experience had assisted him in uncovering moments he had forgotten on the jungle floor. The pain in his leg. The distressing sound of the birds in the forest, calling to one another. He wasn't sure how the process worked but it had definitely allowed him to regain even a few moments of lapsed time he couldn't recall before. It made him look forward to another session tomorrow night.

Chapter 38 ~ Helping Haley

Monday, December 30, 2019

Lucky had her entire day planned out with a checklist she began the night before after the long dinner with the Fosters. She added a few more items to the list this morning. First, she gathered the two sets of fake identification she used as covers. She needed a well-hidden place for safekeeping, but also rapid access should she need them.

She remembered there was an old trunk filled with antique carpentry tools in the carriage house garage downstairs. It was unlikely the police would search through the rusty tools. She placed the two sets of identification in a plastic bag that zipped shut and made her way down to the old trunk.

Just looking at it, you could tell the trunk was very heavy, probably made of oak. With the tools in it, only two sturdy men could move it. Obviously, it had been in this location under the workbench a long time. No one would move this trunk. It weighs too much. She found a crowbar and used it as a lever to lift the trunk slightly. She struggled with it for a few moments. She looked at her knees. Her pants were filthy from the dirty concrete floor. Just a little more leverage and there would be just enough space to slide the plastic bag under the trunk. With a final lift, she held the crowbar in place with her right arm and slid the plastic bag under the trunk with her left hand.

Part of her surveillance gear was outside in the van. Opening the side door, she gathered what items were there and took them into the carriage house garage. There were more things in her apartment and she made her way upstairs. Lucky had a gut feeling that she needed to hustle.

Making her way to her bedroom walk-in closet, she emptied a large plastic tote that held summer clothing and beachwear. *Won't be needing these for awhile.* Reaching on her tiptoes to the top shelf; she grabbed an oversized beach bag and placed the clothing in it.

One by one, she began gathering the gear for surveillance and placing it in the tote to drop off to Ric. That was another to do on today's list and she would meet him for lunch to take care of that. She showered quickly and dressed in jeans and a sweatshirt. Lucky then sent a message to Fran, her friend with access to the Federal databases.

You working today? I really need that list if you can help me, even though it's the holidays.

She messaged back quickly.

I did take the day off, but I have it completed. My parents are visiting. Sorry!

No problem. I hate to ask you, but can I get it now? I really do need it quickly.

Yes, I'm going to send it to you via a link on my cloud storage."

Perfect. I owe you big time!

We could settle up with a girl's night out soon?

For sure! I'll be in touch. Have a nice visit with your family.

Fran sent the link within moments. Lucky accessed it from her phone and then projected it to her printer. She then erased the message and cleared the phone's browser. Anyone could trace her on this. They would not even have to be talented like Ric. But, she couldn't cover all the bases, all the time. Risk was part of this, even though she wanted to minimize it.

The list her friend provided included any instance of someone using the first, surname, or nickname of Ragland in the area. It also gave their age, along with previous addresses. The list was broken down by zip code. She took a highlighter and only marked those that might match up. She excluded females with that last name, along with elderly men. Lucky folded the list and put it in her purse.

She carried the plastic tote down to the garage, locking the door behind her and added the items she had brought from the van. She lifted the hatchback on the z-car and it all fit perfect in the rear of the car. She opened the carriage garage door, and backed her car out. Her computer. They could find all kinds of things on it even though she was careful. She rushed out of the car, ran back upstairs, and grabbed her laptop. She hated to not have this for awhile, but she could not take any chances with the detective. Closing the garage door again, she sat back in the driver's seat and took off to have lunch with Ric.

"I have the list from my friend. It's massively long, but I narrowed it down by gender and age. Listen, I need your help. If we are going to get Haley's letter to Ragland fast, we have to narrow this down and find him. This evening, I have to teach the yoga class. That cuts into my time today. Can you help?"

"Hey, chill. I'll help. What are you going to do, drive to each address?"

"Pretty much. He's not going to show up at Alice's bar again, so I can't get his license plate or vehicle make. One thing to look for would be the fake cable company truck he uses. But if he were smart, he would have that parked in some random lot or in a garage, don't you think?"

"Yeah, probably. Just depends on how stupid he is. I think you should let me take the list and see if I can get into the motor vehicle bureau's system. That way, we'd narrow it more — possibly find that type of truck registered."

Lucky shoved the list over to Ric. "Sounds good to me. I've got the equipment in the back of my car in a big plastic box for you. At the last minute, I grabbed my laptop too. I hate to be without it, but I'll manage."

"You really think those cops suspect you?"

"Let's just say until they find her killer, I'm definitely on the suspect list. Yes, I think it's probable for now."

"Finish your lunch and let's get on this. We need to figure out which one of these is Ragland," he said.

"Agreed!" Lucky hoped they found Alice's killer soon and the detective would forget about her.

Chapter 39 ~ Letter Drafting

Sonya played with Eli and Allison in another room while Haley worked on figuring out the next steps to take. She made an appointment to meet with the firearms instructor that Lucky recommended. They would meet tomorrow on New Year's Eve at two o'clock.

She sat with her laptop, focused on constructing a rough draft letter to this Ragland character. Her main points were to let him know that she had a dead man switch in place and she wanted Jack's gun returned immediately. If so, she wouldn't turn him in for the break-in. If not, she would promise him that she and her family would make sure he did jail time. She finished the draft and then asked Jason to look it over.

"I think it's good, but if it were me, it would have a few more details and threats attached to it," he said.

"What do you mean? Give me an example."

"Right here, where you mention what will happen if you disappear, are hurt or murdered, the switch will turn on. I think you need that to include anyone in your family or inner circle. Anyone, you know?"

"Yes, I think you're right."

"Also, I would let him know how many switches there are, as in say seven. Then, give him some examples of where the information would be disseminated such as police authorities, news outlets, and such."

"Great idea, Jason. Thanks for your suggestions."

"No problem. It's kind of a blackmail situation really. But that's probably what this guy understands. He's not for law and order."

"You're right. Okay, I'll make these changes and have you and Sarah give it a final look before I print it."

Haley finished making the changes to the document. She read through it another time and felt like it fully conveyed everything. If this did not make Ragland sweat, nothing would. Her phone dinged and it was a message from Lucky.

There were hundreds of people with that last name. Narrowed it down by gender and age to a few. Checking them out now.

That's great. I've got the letter ready. Meeting with the woman you told me about tomorrow at two o'clock.

Fantastic, good to hear. Gotta run.

Sarah came in and looked at Haley. "You look kind of excited."

"I am. Lucky just messaged and is narrowing people down to find this guy. Jason critiqued the letter I've written and I'd like both of you to read through it before it's finalized."

"Okay, let me take a look."

Haley slid the laptop on the table toward Sarah who made several facial expressions as she read the document. "This sounds like you mean business and it's detailed. I love it and I believe it will work."

"Great, let's have Jason look at it and if it's a go, I'll print it today. Listen, I need a favor."

"What, anything!"

"If you and Jason are not going to your business today, I was wondering if you could go with Sonya and I to the house. I want to print the letter there and get some more clothing."

"No problem. We're staying home through the first of January. We'll go back on the second day of the new year. I think it would be better to take Jason with you. After all, I've only had one class in self-defense," she said, laughing.

"Yeah, me too. I know Sonya is anxious for the classes to begin next week."

"This situation has taught us it may be a necessary thing for us to know. What about the firearms lady?"

"I'm meeting her tomorrow afternoon. Want to go?"

"No, but I want to know what it's like. Tell us the details when you return. I've invited Joe and Sharon for tomorrow night. I'm planning some finger foods and non-alcoholic beverages for New Year's Eve. You're welcome to have wine or whatever you want. I just don't want to get tipsy around the kids."

"I'm not big on drinking. A little wine or a cocktail is alright from time to time. Right now, with the way things are, I need to keep my wits."

Sarah came over and hugged her tightly. "Oh Haley, I know everything is going to work out. I'm praying for you, Jack and all of us."

"Thank you. I don't know what I would do without this family. All of you are a steady rock for me to hold on to."

"It's what families should do."

"That's what I mean, Sarah. Most of my life, I grew up with no father and a mom who worked a lot. I had no siblings. It was pretty lonely at times. Once my mom became addicted to opiates, I really felt alone. Since I've been part of Jack's family, all of that has changed for me. You're truly like a sister to me."

"I feel the same way about you, Haley. Jack could not have married a better woman and someone to share life with."

They hugged again. "Keep the faith. I know things are going to work out."

"Thank you, I'm trying. No, let me rephrase that. I know he will remember me and come home."

Chapter 40 ~ Therapy

It was becoming a morning routine for Jack to go to the medical bay first each day. He parked his trike and went inside, going through the customary registration with his hand print at the podium in the center of the room. There were two other individuals sitting and waiting. Jack decided to take a seat also.

"Are you here for the hyperbaric therapy?" a gentleman asked. He appeared to be in his late fifties or early sixties.

"I'm not sure." Jack responded. "Probably. What's it like?"

"Oh, it's helped me tremendously. I am diabetic and have trouble with wounds healing. Somehow, breathing the high pressured oxygen ramps my body up to heal faster."

"How often do you have the treatment?" Jack asked.

"This week it will be every morning. Next week, I'll be off. The doctor has been alternating a week on and a week off."

"How long does it take?"

"I'm in there for a good two hours."

"Wow, if that's why I'm here, it's going to cut into my work time in the lab."

"Well, if you need the treatment, I don't think you can lessen the time."

A young man in light blue scrubs came out to the waiting room. "I see everyone has arrived. I'm going to have you stand, one at a time for me to scan for any illness present. If we have not met before, my name is Eduardo."

Holding a portable device, he took Jack's temperature and then held a separate device in his hand, scanning slowly up and down Jack's torso. "How do you feel today, Dr. Foster?"

"Good, absolutely fine."

"This is your first time in the chamber?" he asked, already knowing the answer.

"Uh, yes."

"You'll probably love it. Most people do." He pointed to a seat beside the entry door of the medical bay. "Sit in this seat, please. We'll get your blood pressure." He put the cuff on Jack's arm and started the machine. A moment later, he reported, "115 over 60. Your heart rate is at 75. Looking good, Dr. Foster."

Eduardo quickly finished scanning and testing everyone present and then asked them to follow him into the facility. Once inside, he gave each of them a pair of matching blue scrubs. "Please change into these and leave all personal items, including jewelry in your locker. I have a numbered key for your assigned locker, Dr. Foster."

Jack held out his hands, taking the scrubs and key. He was feeling like this was a big deal that he wasn't sure he liked. It definitely sounded time consuming.

Once dressed, he joined the others in the hall and Eduardo led them toward the hyperbaric oxygen chamber facility. They walked toward a door with a porthole window. It was made of metal. Jack wasn't sure if it was steel or aluminum. Eduardo opened the metal door. Inside, it appeared to be similar to a small airplane cabin.

Sweat began to break out on Jack's forehead. He knew it was from fear he held around the airplane crash. In his mind, he talked himself down. This was not a plane and it wasn't going anywhere. He noticed individual chairs inside along the walls on each side. The aisle was open in the middle. Tubes descended from the upper walls. It was strange and a little claustrophobic.

The older man looked at Jack and noticed his nervousness. "Once you get settled inside, you'll be fine. There will be a movie playing on that screen ahead to take your mind off things. Jack listened and nodded, following the man inside the cramped cabin.

Eduardo explained that each would wear an oxygen hood over their head for thirty minutes, and then have a ten-minute break. "Once the chamber is up to pressure, I'll have you put on the oxygen hood. I can assist you with that and make sure it's on correctly. First, we'll take a vote on the movie today since we have five of you. The first Jurassic Park or the first Star Wars movie?" he asked the group. The latter won and the movie began.

Jack found the seat to be larger than you would find on most airlines. They were nicely upholstered and comfortable. Relaxing into the chair, he took a deep breath and found the watching of the movie brought back memories of the first time he had seen it as a kid with Jason. He remembered the light sabers they had wished for from Santa that finally made their way under the tree, and other details he had not thought about in years. Why did he remember that and not other things that were very important?

Like yesterday, Jack grabbed a drink and fruit from the dining room since it was close to the medical bay. He jumped back on his trike and headed for the lab. He was late to work again. What would the team feel about him arriving late each day? He decided to offer them scheduling choices since he had just found out he would receive the oxygen treatment each morning until his doctor said otherwise.

He had to admit that the high pressured treatment must be doing something. He even felt a little giddy or extra happy afterward. As he entered the lab, he felt like he had more energy. He noticed it when he first got on the trike, riding it faster than he had before. It could have been the movie that put extra life force in his step. It wasn't a far stretch for him to feel like he was working to defend the dominion he lived in against dark forces.

"I apologize everyone!" he said arriving into the lab area where the team was gathered and busy working. "I was sent for a two hour treatment that began at eight-thirty this morning. I also found out that my doctor requires me to have the treatment each morning, for now at least. I was thinking that it might be fair for me to give each of you some scheduling options. I'll be working until seven-o'clock each night. If any of you would like to work from eleven in the morning until that time, please do so until this treatment ends. If you would rather work the hours you have been and leave at five o'clock, that is fine."

The team members seemed to appreciate that he was willing to bend and cooperate with them. For one or two, they planned to come in early and stay late. Others decided to use the personal time in the morning for other endeavors such as going to the gym or simply sleeping in longer.

Jack had shown two of the team members the best extraction process to use on the plant that Marcos had so graciously made available. This time, he hoped the drug would come to fruition. It simply had to.

Chapter 41 ~ Yoga with Dane

Time was tight with ten minutes to spare before her instruction time began with the yoga class. Generally, Lucky preferred to be there a little early to create a nice, calm atmosphere in the room. She quickly pulled on her favorite yoga pants which were a bright, electric blue. Lucky removed her sweatshirt and bra, pulling the matching tank bra on instead. She covered up a bit with a multi-colored loose tank over it.

Lucky stepped toward the sink, splashing cold water on her neck where she was already sweating. She touched up her underarms with some deodorant, topping it off with a spritz of her favorite yoga mist spray. It had undertones of patchouli and sweet orange, but a freshness of grapefruit extract also. The fragrance made her feel more in the mood for the long stretches and poses she would take the group through this evening.

Lucky breezed into the room and everyone was there, including someone new. She had seen him through the glass even before she entered the studio. Dressed in his usual tank top that fit like a glove and loose gym shorts, Dane was going to try yoga. "Hello everyone! Am I late or right on time?" she asked.

"Right on time," they answered.

"Good, it's not very cool for the instructor to be late."

She didn't want to make Dane feel singled out with all the women, but couldn't ignore his presence either. "Everyone, I don't know if you've met our new student. This is Dane. I was just speaking with him about the class a couple of evenings ago. Welcome Dane," Lucky said, trying to keep it polite and professional.

"Thanks," he said. "I'm just trying this out."

The other women seemed a bit shy around him. Obviously, his heart throb looks and hard as bricks body made many in the room a little tongue-tied.

"Oh, we need some equipment for you." Lucky strode to the corner and retrieved a mat, bolster pillow, and two smaller bolsters for Dane. He looked straight into her eyes and held his gaze there as she handed it to him.

"Thanks again," he said.

She rolled the mat out for him and then hustled back to the front of the room, hitting play on the music system. Sounds emanated into the room with a distinct eastern flavor. The instrumental included sitar, flute and soft percussion.

Lucky grabbed her own mat and supplies, placing them where everyone could have a good view of her.

"Namaste. Let's begin this evening by sitting on your bolster with your pelvis tilted slightly forward. Cross your legs so you are comfortable. If you cannot create a full lotus position, just be comfortable with your posture and cross those legs however it works for you. Close your eyes and place your palms on your upper thighs or knee area. Sit tall to lengthen your spine. Relax your facial muscles and take a deep breath. Allow each breath to be the vehicle that puts you in touch with your entire body. As you take slow, comfortable deep breaths, take notice of how your rib cage rises and falls. Use this moment in your practice to just be with no expectation — to sit with one's self. Feel the calm that comes over your being."

Lucky continued to take the class through approximately forty minutes of poses. Dane tried his best to emulate her and the rest of the class. Naturally with being new, he was a little clumsy at the beginning of each pose and some came easier than others. Lucky glanced at him frequently, trying not to be obvious. She noticed he hesitated to try the downward dog pose, watching the women raise their buttocks in the air. By the time they moved into half dog pose, Dane was willing to try it.

As they centered once again at the end from their practice, Lucky said, "I hope everyone is going to follow their new yoga practice into the new year. The next time we meet it will be 2020 and I wish you luck in the new year."

Many of the women gave her well wishes in return. Dane followed their lead, rolling his mat up and picking up the blocks and pillow. He carried them to Lucky who was rolling her mat also. She didn't see him coming up from behind.

"That was really something different. I have to say that it even hurt a little."

She turned and blushed as soon as she saw his massive body in front of her. Sometimes working out made her horny. She took a breath and smiled. "I'm glad you came. As you can see, this is a practice that works your mind, body and spirit."

"Yeah, I'm getting that. How long have you been doing yoga?"

"Honestly, I remember even as a child bending my body into yoga poses. But I didn't know they were associated with any particular practice. It just felt good to stretch and move my body in that way. When I came across yoga in my late teens, I knew it was for me."

Even as she spoke to Dane, she felt like someone was watching them. She turned for a moment to see Evan staring at her from the bench area outside. She put her focus back on Dane. He may not be the one she was there to spy on, but there was nothing wrong with getting a cherry on top of your sundae either.

"What about you, Dane? What's your favorite way to work out?" It was a loaded question she loved to ask men.

His golden locks were pulled back into a ponytail. She wanted to reach up and let them loose. Lucky glanced at his huge hands and imagined them grabbing her breasts, his fingers pinching her nipples. She wondered if the lust she felt for him showed. It had been a long time since she made wild love with anyone and she loved what she saw before her.

Dane held up his arm, showing her his biceps and triceps in a pose. "As you can see, I love pumping iron. But I can see how yoga could work my muscles in other ways."

Lucky openly flirted with him, "Oh, I think it could." She wanted to offer him private lessons, in the nude. This guy drove her crazy inside. She knew it from the first moment she saw him.

Dane broke her stare. "Do you live here?"

"No, I only teach the classes. Do you live here?"

"I do, Unit 1798."

Lucky wondered if he told her his unit number expecting her to show up. She stood still and his gaze was locked on her face, waiting for a reaction. She said nothing, but he noticed that she licked her lips.

"Come by anytime," he said. "I'd like to get to know you more."

"1798, huh? I might, or I might not," she responded. *Damn, does this guy drive you so nuts you would just turn yourself into a booty call?*

She looked over and while Evan tried to appear nonchalant while speaking to another person at the club, she knew he was watching them.

Dane sensed that he was being a little too forward with the yoga instructor. He thanked her and asked when the next class was. She gave him a one page calendar with the January schedule on one side, and February on the other. "See you next year," she said, letting him know she would not be following him home tonight like a lost puppy.

As soon as Dane departed, Lucky finished cleaning up the room and getting her belongings together. When she exited, Evan came up to her. "I see you have the first man in your yoga class."

"Yes, are you ready to be the second? It could be a new start for you in 2020."

"I don't know. Speaking of tomorrow night, do you have plans for New Year's Eve?"

"Not really. I thought I might stay home this year."

"The company I work for is having a large party at a hotel in town. They always go all out. Chelsea, you're the prettiest woman I've seen for a while and I would be really proud if you attended with me. No pressure, of course. We could go as friends."

"I haven't been to a big party in a long time. It sounds exciting. I'd love to go. Where should we meet and what time?"

Evan looked excited. It was obvious he thought she might reject him, especially after the interest he saw in the studio between her and Dane.

"Do you want me to pick you up?"

"How about I meet you here. You live here somewhere, right?"

"Fine, yes. Come by around seven and we'll ride to the event in my car."

"It's a date," she said smiling at him.

"Oh, let me give you my number just in case you …"

"Need to cancel? I won't do that, but yes, give me your number."

Chapter 42 ~ Hypnosis Two

After dinner, Jack hurried back to his room. He felt a strong pull to sink into his recent past again, guided by the hypnotic voice of the doctor. It was amazing to him that this process was helping him uncover at least part of what he had experienced. Jack was hopeful he could fully discover what he evidently had blocked out of his mind.

Entering the apartment room, he felt a peace and contentment in this space that helped soothe any stress he felt at the end of the day. His belly was full and it would be easy to just get ready for sleep. He used the restroom facilities and checked the laboratory task list on the computer system at his desk. Marcos was right. This was handy to have here in his room. He powered down the system just as he heard a melodic chime which meant someone was at the door. Dr. Alonso was right on time.

They began the same way as the previous evening. The doctor played the sounds of water trickling or falling softly in the background, helping him gradually relax his body beginning with his feet first. Once Dr. Alonso believed Jack had reached a very relaxed state, he asked him to place himself, once again, in the forested area.

"Tell me what you see, hear or smell," he coaxed him.

Jack was quiet for a few moments. His breathing was slow and easy. Finally, he must have felt himself in the scene and he slowly began speaking. "The trees — they are so tall. Old growth, ancient really. Some have beautiful palm leaf structures. Diffused light from the sky tries to break through their limbs and leaves. The trees saved me. They are like a friend."

This last statement peaked the psychologist's interest. "How did they save you?"

"The limbs. Strong limbs held me. But I fell."

"Tell me more, Jack. Go back to being on the tree limb."

Jack hesitated and the doctor worried he might have pulled Jack too far away from the scene. Then he began recounting more of his experience.

"The trees are holding the plane. A wing is down. I'm walking on the limb, tying a rope around a larger limb. I don't know if it will hold." Jack's breathing became intense instead of shallow. Lying there, he was now clenching both his fists. "It can't hold. I can't do it."

"Alright, let's breathe slowly now," Dr. Alonso suggested. He guided him, trying to get his breath and heart rate back down. He could bring him out now, but wanted to push Jack a little more to remember. "Let's go back to lying on the forest floor, remember that?"

"Yeah, I remember it."

"Do you feel safe on the forest floor with the trees above you?"

Again, Jack hesitated before recanting the memory.

"I do. They're quite beautiful. Very majestic." He paused again, creasing his forehead. "Something is out there. I hear rustling in the leaves. The movement's coming closer. It's not an animal. I hear voices."

"Can you see anyone?"

"No, I hear them though. They speak another language, one native to the area. Someone touched me. Oh, oh, that hurts bad. They took their hand away now. I hear them speaking, but I don't understand it. Someone is giving me water to drink. They're lifting me." Jack cries out, as if the pain is happening now.

"What is it Jack?"

"Searing pain in my leg especially, but my head too. They are carrying me away. It feels like such a long way down. They're putting me on a barge or some type of floating flatboat. We are moving now. It seems like we are floating down river."

"How long do you float on the river, Jack?"

"I'm not sure. I can barely open my eyes for just a few seconds to see anything. My eyes, it's like they want to stay closed, almost glued shut. Time, I'm not sure. The sun is still out. We come to a stop and they are tying up the flatboat. I can hear laughter — children laughing. This must be their home. I smell something cooking over an open fire. The scent of food is making my mouth water. In a way, I'm hungry. In another way, I'm not. I'm afraid to eat. Afraid to move. I hurt."

"We are going to return now, Jack. We are going to come back up the staircase and when you reach the top, you will be on your bed in your room. You will feel energized and have no trouble remembering each scene that your memory has just revealed to you. Ready? Put your foot on the first step up the staircase …."

Dr. Alonso gradually brought him back into his present awareness. As Jack came out of the second hypnosis session, he noticed his hands and forehead were sweaty. "That was even more intense, wasn't it?" He sat up on the edge of the bed.

"You did really well again. Have you had the hyperbaric oxygen treatment yet?"

"I had the first one this morning. The doctor has me receiving the treatment every morning until … well, I don't know when it will end."

Dr. Alonso rose from the chair. "Excellent! I know that particular treatment takes up a lot of time. It could be benefiting you in ways we can't easily measure or notice at all. Your memory opened up a lot this evening. How do you feel about it right now?

"I'm remembering more each time. The trees, the people who rescued me. I didn't remember them taking me to their village before. I just knew I woke up there. I have to tell you that I was skeptical of hypnosis, but it seems to be revealing things I've forgotten in bits and pieces."

Dr Alonso nodded in agreement. "You're doing really well. Not everyone takes to it as easily as you have. Tomorrow, same time, same place?"

Jack stood with him, walking toward the door. "You bet!"

Chapter 43 ~ NYE

Lucky finished applying her eye makeup, putting a little more color on than usual for tonight's celebration. This wasn't her dream date, but a necessary one. Evan would feel like he was her dream date. She would make sure of that. The hunt was on for any information she could get on the plane crash, break in at Haley's, and Chadwell Pharmaceuticals. Lucky wondered what Dane was doing on this last night of the year. Would he be celebrating with someone? Probably. She could not imagine he wouldn't be.

She slipped into the form fitting crimson dress, wondering if it wasn't too over the top. It cradled her breasts together, forming cleavage that looked more generous than it really was. The length was mid-thigh.

Remembering her cover, she reminded herself that tonight, she was Chelsea, the yoga and Pilates instructor. Fluffing her short platinum hair with her fingers, she gave a smile of approval in the mirror. One last thing, her signature red lipstick. *Go get 'em, Chelsea!* She sat and pulled on her black stiletto boots and decided to wear a knee-length black faux fur coat that hung in her closet with little use.

The last message she received on one of her burner phones from Evan asked what color she was wearing. She told him red. She found this curious until she parked her vehicle at the condominium's clubhouse where she met him waiting in his Porsche. He got out, walked toward her vehicle and opened the door. Looking him up and down, he wore a black wool suit that looked expensive. Ironically, he wore a crimson red shirt with it. The suit fit him well and appeared hand tailored for him. They matched.

Evan helped her out of her car and into his. He thought she looked stunning, but waited until they were inside the Porsche to say anything. "Chelsea, I didn't know I was going to this party with the most beautiful woman in the world."

She giggled and flashed her green eyes at him. They had a haunting effect on him.

"Nice touch with the shirt," she said. "You look very handsome."

"Thank you, just trying to keep up with you," he said, giving her a wink.

Lucky thought this might be more fun than she originally thought. As they rode toward downtown Atlanta, all thoughts of Dane receded from her mind. She needed to focus on Evan, allowing him to believe they were a potential mating match. He was very attractive and had a presence. She could tell that he was used to employing his aloof charm on women, but it wouldn't work tonight. He would be the puppy panting after her. That, she would bet her life on.

She had to remember that he was a dastardly dude — hiring someone to break into Haley's house. No matter what happened tonight or how charming he might be, she had to keep in mind who he really was.

Lucky thought about how most people don't show you who they really are. You have to find out the hard way. She'd been there and done that before. It's why she left Florida behind like a chapter of her life that didn't exist. Now, she spent most of her time pretending to be someone else, hoping to uncover other people's secrets.

Evan noticed she was quiet and somewhat serious. "Everything okay?"

She snapped out of her thoughts, "Yes, I was just wondering if I locked my car?"

"Do you want me to go back and check?"

"Oh no, if I didn't, I'm sure it will be fine parked there."

"I don't mind if you want me to turn around."

"It will be fine. Let's keep going and get this party started," she said, with a somewhat fake enthusiasm.

As they pulled up for valet parking, she noticed the hotel was grand in its design. A young valet came to the vehicle. He appeared anxious to park Evan's car.

Once inside, they were directed by signs to the Chadwell event that was held in a ballroom that sparkled like a case of expensive jewelry. Each of the numerous round tables were decorated with gold lamè tablecloths accented with white and gold floral arrangements. A tall, lit candle stood inside a hurricane glass in the center.

The room was crowned by a large stage where the band was already playing. Numerous couples filled the dance floor. The mood was loud and raucous. Evan spoke loudly into her ear, while holding her hand to guide her to a table.

"Have you ever seen this band, Midnight Rollers?"

"No, they sound really good."

"They play a lot of covers from the 70's, 80's and 90's. Some of the younger people at Chadwell like a lot of the music that has been produced since then. See that guy," he said, pointing toward the right side of the stage.

"Yeah, looks like a DJ."

"Exactly, he will be playing tunes the millennials like during the band's breaks."

"Sounds like Chadwell tries to keep everyone happy."

"Oh, they do. It's a fantastic company to work for."

They arrived where she assumed Evan wanted to sit. He introduced her to the people at the table.

"I'm going to get us a drink, what would you like?"

"White wine, please. A moscato if they have it."

During the evening, Lucky learned that Kendra at their table was now Evan's assistant and she used to be Jack Foster's. They spoke about the tragedy. Her gut said Kendra was in the dark, but who knew? She might be a potential contact for some type of information.

She also met Jared who worked in the lab with Evan. She didn't know if he had worked with Jack Foster or not, but she would assume he did as he said he had been there three years. It was a touchy subject and she could not ask everyone she met about Jack Foster. At the least, it would seem strange, and possibly suspicious.

The band played a slow tune and Evan asked if she would like to dance. She joined him on the dance floor and found his timing and leads to be very good. She was learning that Evan was well mannered and seemed to have come from a family that encouraged that in him. It was too bad he was who he was.

An older man with white hair tapped Evan and said, "May I cut in?"

Evan looked at Lucky and she nodded it was okay. The gentleman smelled of money in his high price suit and jeweled cuff links that flashed periodically. He carried a well-groomed persona an older rich man would have. My name is J.D. Tellinger," he said. Lucky's eyes almost bulged out of her head and her heart began racing. "My name is Chelsea Roberts."

"Thank you for dancing with me, Chelsea. I rarely get the pleasure with someone of such beauty."

Dipping her chin down slightly toward her chest, Lucky pretended to blush. He'd never know with the band's lighting providing multi-colored overflow onto the dance floor. But she was shaken. She had just touched J. D. Tellinger, and he had just touched her.

"Thank you, J.D. It was my pleasure," she said, politely as the song ended.

Evan came and rescued her from his boss. She was two glasses of wine into this shin dig and knew she better keep herself in check. A long table of food lined one wall of the ballroom. "Are you hungry, Evan?"

"No, not really, I could probably nibble on something."

"How about I make us a plate to share?" she suggested.

"Sounds good."

Lucky brought back a plate of finger food with cheese, crackers, olives, and small veggies. She also ordered a soft drink for herself to quench her thirst and keep her alcohol limit in check. Lucky noticed that Evan drank his scotch slow, but she had counted three so far. She didn't want him passing out, at least not yet.

"Eat some more, Evan."

"Alright, you're sounding like my mom, Chelsea."

She smiled, "Do I look like your mom?"

He reached over and placed his hand on her thigh. He moved his head close to her face and she could see his eyes were a little bloodshot. "You look nothing like my mom," he said, grinning.

The end of 2019 approached and, as the seconds counted down, Evan tightened his grip around Lucky's waist. They were standing now with the rest of the crowd. She was fairly certain he was going to kiss her at midnight. She was going to let him. Even more, she had decided to prolong the kiss when it happened.

The crowd counted along with the lead singer of the band. An energy of excitement surged in the air. With the final countdown to zero, balloons and glittery confetti dropped from the ceiling. He squeezed tightly and turned her toward him. It made her nervous at first. She had to make him think she just adored him. "Happy New Year, Evan." He pulled her body as tight to his as he could. Evan gazed into her eyes and then at her mouth. Slowly, he joined his lips to hers. She could feel his kiss deepen as he thrust his tongue into her mouth. She sucked on it for a moment and then thrust her tongue toward him. They stood, locked together in a tight embrace and an endless kiss. It broke when a colleague pulled on Evan's sleeve. "Happy New Year, Evan. Looks like you're starting out right," he said.

Chapter 44 ~ Evan's Domain

Evan was still maintaining a degree of sobriety, but he was definitely pliable and in what Lucky called a puppy dog mood. They walked arm in arm out of the hotel lobby.

"I'd love it if I could drive your Porsche," she said to him.

He hesitated, feeling very reluctant about allowing Lucky to drive his car. She put her arms around his neck and said, "C'mon, pretty please." He looked into those hypnotic eyes and watched her lips. He kissed her again, but not as long as the kiss at midnight. "Only if you come inside when we get to my condo."

"Deal."

When the valet brought the car, Evan gave her the keys. The valet watched with interest.

"I get to drive tonight," she told him. The valet smiled back at her. "Happy New Year!"

"Happy New Year," she replied.

Evan sat in the passenger seat and Lucky adjusted the driver's seat for maximum comfort and safety. She pulled out onto the freeway and kept her speed normal. This was a night the police were everywhere, just looking for a reason to pull people over.

"I've never sat in the passenger's seat before."

"Really? I'm the first person to drive your car?"

"Yes, well, actually no. One of the guys that used to work at Chadwell drove it one day with his wife in the car."

"Did he have fun?" she asked.

"Yeah, I think so. He was a real joker. Loved to cut up with everyone."

"Your company seems like a nice place to work. Why did he leave?"

"Unfortunately, he was in the small plane that our employees went down in."

"Wow. I heard a little about that, but what really happened?"

Evan retold the official version of the plane crash. Lucky listened to his every word for the slightest hint of foul play on his part or anyone else's. But it followed exactly what was reported in the news.

Pulling into the condominium complex, she feigned ignorance about where he lived or his assigned spot. Evan pointed the way, touching her forearm as she pulled into his parking space. His eyes were glassy and red. She smiled at him, but was silent. There was something he wanted to say. She could tell that he was tipsy, but he wasn't falling down drunk. Finally, Evan spoke. "You promised me you'd come inside."

"I know. Let's go, show me the way."

Evan felt in charge now. He had allowed her to drive the Porsche and she did a great job. He figured it was probably better she drove with the amount of scotch he had drank at the party. They stepped inside his condominium and he took her hand, guiding her toward the kitchen. "What can I get you?" he asked.

"What are my choices?"

"You're a wine drinker, right?"

"Most of the time."

"I have a wine refrigerator over beside the bar," he said, pointing toward the living room.

"Awesome, let me check it out."

No woman had turned him on so much. That body of hers made his cock start to harden just watching her move. She was bent overlooking the wine selection. Her ass looked so perfect. He wanted to come up behind her, but he made himself wait.

Lucky knew Evan was checking her out and she exaggerated the bend in her body, shifting her pelvis back, making her buttocks protrude more than normal. In a way, she was having fun with this game.

She chose a bottle of white. Evan assisted her with a wineglass and wine key. "I'll do it," she said, almost possessively of the bottle. He stepped back and waited.

She turned and looked at him. "How about you? Wine or another scotch?" He chose to stick with scotch and she grabbed a rocks glass and poured it about a third full of the amber liquid. Lucky quickly opened the hinge on a gold ring she wore and dropped the sedating crystals she had crushed earlier at home into his scotch. Nervous, she looked back at Evan and he was busy removing his tie.   Lucky swirled the glass around to blend the concoction quickly. She sat both drinks down on the small bar area.

"Hey, do you mind if I take my boots off? These heels are really bothering me."

"Not at all, make yourself comfortable, Chelsea."

She sat on his couch and tugged at the heel of one of her boots, looking a bit frustrated with the process.

"Do you want me to help?" he asked.

"Could you?" she asked, her voice sounding kittenish.

Evan grabbed hold of the back of one boot and pulled. Then, he removed the other one. For a short instant, he glimpsed the top of her black thigh-high stockings and panties. "Anything else you want to remove — anything bothering you?" he asked.

She laughed loudly and he loved hearing the sound of it in his living room. He wanted to make her laugh and scream with delight. Evan assumed that by her signaling the removal of clothing of any sort, they were definitely going to end up having sex. And he wanted to get up close to that body, inside of her all the way. He was feeling certain that's where he was headed, having sex with Chelsea Roberts, the yoga instructor tonight.

And, Lucky allowed him to believe it. Her boots removed, she moved seductively toward Evan who was now sitting in his recliner. She brought his drink to him and stood with her glass of wine. "Let's make a toast for 2020, Evan."

"What should we wish for, Chelsea?"

"Tell me, Evan. I want to know what you wish for."

He laughed, "No, you don't. I can't tell you that."

"Why?

"It might not come out of my mouth in a nice way."

"I see. Well, would you like me to make the 2020 toast?"

"Yes, please do."

"To 2020, may this be the year that we live our lives full of passion with no regrets."

He held out his glass and she touched her wineglass to it. She took a sip of wine and Evan took a large quantity of the scotch.

"That was fantastic. See, I knew you were better at making toasts."

"Still, I'd love to know what you wish for," she said, adopting her kitten voice again.

He grabbed her hand and guided her on his lap. She sat the wineglass on the coffee table. Evan was still holding his and she needed him to drink it all. Suddenly, she jumped off his lap. "Tell you what, Evan. If I guess what you wanted to toast to, you have to take a drink. If I'm wrong, I take a drink. Wanna play?"

"Sure."

"Let's see. I think your toast might have involved touching," she said. "Like this." Lucky took his hand and placed it on her upper thigh. "Am I correct?"

Evan rubbed his hand on her leg, inching upward. "Actually, you're partially correct."

"Close enough, that counts. Take a drink."

He dutifully complied.

"Okay, partially right. Let me keep going."

"Please do," he said, still rubbing her leg with his free hand.

"I'm going to guess that your toast has something to do with finding out what's under my dress," she said, moving his hand to her panties. "Am I correct?"

"Whoa, I think you're good at this game, Chelsea."

"Yeah, take a drink."

Evan looked at her with pure lust in his eyes. His lips were parted and she knew he wanted to devour her right then in that chair. "Aren't you going to take a drink, Evan?"

He tipped up the glass, finishing the scotch.

With his long arm, he sat it on the floor and then took both hands and grabbed her hips, situating her right over his lap.

"Kiss me," she purred.

Evan obliged and they kissed for a long time. His hands wandered her body, squeezing her in all the places he wanted to. They made out like kids in the back seat of a car, until Evan said he needed to come up for air. She pulled back and rubbed his shoulders. "You okay?" she asked.

"I just … I gotta breathe for a minute."

A few seconds later, he was passed out.

Lucky sat there for a moment with her hand on his pulse making sure he was okay. *He'll be fine. Now, get to work.*

Chapter 45 ~ Visiting Lucky

January 1, 2020 4:00 a.m.

Lucky arrived home and felt empty inside. Maybe she really wasn't cut out for spying. She went to all the trouble of drugging Evan and found nothing in his condo that could help with the investigation. She wasn't able to place any surveillance equipment there because Ric had all of it. Most of all, she felt angry with herself. Perhaps, she went too far tonight. She knew Evan was a bad dude in an expensive suit, but did she really have to stoop to his level?

Perhaps she would turn up something on the info she took from his call list on the two burner phones she found in his bedroom. She noticed he kept everything so tidy at his place. He was extremely organized. This made her extra careful to make sure nothing looked out of place.

She went to the bathroom and ran the water in the tub. While it was filling, she removed her makeup and then began to cry. Evan was going to be okay. She didn't hurt him, just knocked him out for a while. *If you're going to do this line of work, you can't be reacting like this!*

Turning the faucet off, she stepped into the tub and sank down into the hot water. She just needed to decompress. She didn't think she would be able to find out anything from Evan. He had things too concealed and probably carried most of his secrets in his mind or on the encrypted system at work. Ric would be better to work on Evan than her. Plus, if she kept seeing him, sex would almost be expected at a certain point. Sex — maybe getting close to him in that way would get him to open up and reveal something. She argued with herself, finally deciding only hitting him up with a truth drug could do that. And, she wouldn't go that far.

There were times when she wanted to talk to a girlfriend. Tonight was one of those occasions. Life was beginning to feel complicated in a way she wasn't sure was best for her. Without more normal interactions with people, her own sanity might suffer over time. But she had to find and expose what she could, especially surrounding the pharmaceutical companies.

Ric was a good friend she could count on, but she knew he had at least a minor romantic interest in her. It wouldn't be cool to call him up and start chatting about her date with Evan or the way Dane made the area between her thighs wet. No, only another woman would understand. She had to schedule a girl's night out with Fran.

9:00 a.m.

Lucky woke, hearing pounding and activity outside the carriage house. Grabbing her robe, she went to the window and saw the police cars outside. *I better let them in before they alert my landlord,* she thought.

She wasn't surprised that the bastard detective would show up on a holiday early in the morning. She felt like a zombie and knew she had not been asleep very long. But she would let them in if they had a warrant. She had nothing to hide now.

Lucky opened the garage door and stood with her heavy blue robe on and a pair of muck boots she kept at the bottom of the steps. The detective held a piece of paper in his hands. "Good morning, Miss Adams. I have a search warrant for the premises, including your vehicles."

"Be my guest. I told you I'm innocent. But don't mess this place up. You want to look, that's fine, but put shit back. Nothing out of place."

"We'll need you to wait outside while the search is conducted.

"I can't do that?"

"Why not?" he asked

"I'm naked under this robe."

"Oh, you're a smart girl. I'm sure you can grab something quick to put on. I've got a female officer that will accompany you."

She smiled at him, "I'm disappointed you won't be there to assist." She was going to give him hell all the way with this. He had to really be coming up short for suspects if he was chasing her down.

Silently, the female officer went with her upstairs and Lucky grabbed some sweatpants and a sweatshirt. "Do they really expect me to stand outside in the cold while they search?"

"Yes, Miss Adams," she replied curtly.

"I'd like to pee. It would probably be better for me to do that here, rather than outside," she said, being super snarky.

"Go ahead, I'll wait for you at the door, but do not flush the toilet."

Lucky took that to mean they thought she might flush something down the john. She did have to pee, but what she really wanted were the two burner phones sitting on the bathroom counter. She did her business, stuck them in her panties, and left the room following the officer down the steps and outside.

The search of her vehicles and the garage was already underway.

She couldn't pretend this didn't rattle her emotionally. It did. She wasn't a hard core criminal or a drug dealer. Lucky began to have concern that a couple of the officers might move the tool chest. Her mind was on overdrive with everything. *Calm down, find your center*, she told herself. She wasn't going to indulge in worry. Precautions had been taken because she knew this would happen. Now she needed to wait this out until they were finished and turned up nothing.

The search lasted a good hour and a half to two hours. She wasn't sure what time it was. No watch and she was glad both of those burner phones in her panties were turned off. They would find her regular phone in the kitchen, but it was pretty clean with nothing they could easily pull from, and it was in the name of Megan Adams.

Finally, the lady officer approached her. "You can go back to your apartment now."

Lucky said nothing. She walked into the garage, removed the muck boots and leaped up the steps like a gazelle. She looked around the living room, then the bedroom, closet, and bath to make sure they had not left her apartment a mess.

The detective stood in the small kitchen, leaning on the refrigerator, chewing on a toothpick he must have picked up from the holder on her counter. "I have a few questions for you, Miss Adams."

"Fine. Do I need an attorney?"

"You're not under arrest."

"Well, I shouldn't be. I haven't done anything."

"I noticed that you changed your hairstyle," the detective said, holding up her brown pageboy wig.

"No crime in that. Sometimes I like to wear a wig."

The detective raised his eyebrow and smiled. "Can you tell me why you have this handgun?"

Lucky gave the detective a blank stare and showed no emotion.

"For protection, silly. There are killers and maniacs everywhere."

"And you take this gun with you when you go places?"

"Have you been following me?" she asked, her eyes flaring at him.

"I'm the one asking questions, Miss Adams. By the way, I found it odd that you have a printer and no computer here. Care to comment about that?"

Again, Lucky stared at him, not answering his question.

"Well, I suppose you don't feel like talking this morning. I want you to know that you are a potential suspect in the murder of Alice Crandall."

"Crandall -- I never knew her last name. You're an idiot if you think I killed her. That was obviously a crime of passion, someone was very angry that strangled her like that. I would have no motive to commit that crime."

"You seem pretty angry today, Miss Adams. Don't leave town. I might have more questions. We could be seeing each other again very soon."

Lucky watched him descend the staircase. She followed the officers and locked the garage door behind them. Glancing at the old tool chest, it had not been moved. Her identification pieces were safe, but not her identity. She felt very violated having them come and go through all her things. She thought about what she did last night at Evan's condo. *Guess this is some instant karma.*

Chapter 46 ~ Good Secret

On the last day of the year, Haley and Sonya spent time with Vicki, the instructor, at the gun range. She supplied the weapons for them to use and suggested they purchase something similar. Both of the handguns had worked well for them in handling and loading.

Haley thanked her and paid for the time spent with them. "Be safe in the new year and always, ladies. Let me know when you find the gun you want and I'll make sure you feel comfortable using it. Once that happens, I suggest you come here or to another range for regular target practice."

Vicki was very serious and emphasized things to them, making sure they had an understanding of how important it was to know how to handle the firearms.

What stood out in Haley's mind was that she told them handguns were designed to kill other humans. "These are not hunting devices. They are killing devices to be used on other humans. They are what keep you from being the victim of a human predator."

During the drive, Haley asked Sonya her impressions.

"Well, she sure knows her stuff. It was kind of overwhelming at first. I was afraid to touch the gun. She made me feel a lot better about it. Honestly, I wish we didn't have a need for it."

"Yeah, I know. I felt the same, but really when she said handguns are specifically meant for killing other people … that stuck with me. Actually, it hit me in the pit of my stomach. I don't want to kill anyone and end their life."

There was silence for at least a half mile down the freeway. Sonya then asked, "Would you kill to keep someone from hurting Jack."

"Yes, I know I would."

"I know I'd kill someone if they tried to hurt you, Haley."

She looked over at her cousin. "And I for you."

"Shooting a handgun at someone is not something you want to do. It's what you must do if you're backed into a corner. You're a nurse and that means you are conditioned to save lives. I guess we just have to realize that sometimes someone might have to lose their life in order to save the lives of ourselves or someone we love."

"You're right. Jack has been through the training and I know he would have used his gun to protect those he loved. I want to get his gun back quickly from that creep."

On the way back to Sarah and Jason's house, they stopped at a local party supply store and grabbed a few hats, a pack of balloons, and noisemakers to use for tonight. The kids would love it and the grownups would get a kick out of it too.

New Year's Day, 2020

Haley felt a sense of urgency in the morning now when she had to urinate. She was also waking up many nights having to go. This only occurred one other time in her life — when she was pregnant. Her hand rested on her lower abdomen and she wondered? Her period had not come during the entire month of December. She didn't know whether to be happy or sad. Nothing was the way she expected, not even close. The man she loved with her entire being didn't even remember who she was. She had to pretend he was dead. And now, she might be having the baby they desperately wanted. She would need to get a test at the drugstore and check to see if it turned blue. Until then, she would assume she was not pregnant. With all she had been through in the last month, it would not be unusual to have a missed period due to the stress.

She thought back to the evening before. New Year's Eve had been a fun celebration with everyone. Allison and Eli stayed up, watching the huge glittering ball in Times Square countdown the last minute before midnight. Eli loved for Sonya and Haley to blow up the balloons without tying off the end and then letting them go flying around the room. He would chase after them and bring them back to be blown up again. He was so adorable. His sister, Allison, wore a princess crown with Happy New Year on it. She dressed up in last year's Halloween costume as well. Everyone had fun. *Jack would have liked being here,* she thought.

She went to the bathroom and then came back to the bed. She was safe here. That's all she really wanted in life. To have someone to love and be safe. Was that really so much to ask for? Deep down, she hated the idea of carrying a gun, or even keeping one in the house. But with the way things were now, her attitude would need to change. Sonya was right. What would she do if someone was going to hurt or kill her cousin or anyone she loved? Tomorrow, she and Sonya would shop for the right handguns when the stores opened again. Today, she might find a drugstore open and purchase a pregnancy test.

Wednesday Evening, New Year's Day, 2020

Haley spent most of the day making a big dinner with Sarah. Sonya played with Allison and Eli. At one point, she stepped out of the house, telling everyone she needed to run to the drugstore. No one asked why and she didn't volunteer the reason. Now that the day was done, she was ready to use the test kit in her purse. She went to the bathroom and pulled it out. Sitting on the toilet, she used the tester as instructed. She waited a few moments before looking at it.

She stared, tears welling up in her eyes, momentarily blurring her vision. Wiping her face, she strained her eyes looking at the tester again. Pregnant. She was pregnant.

Haley stood in front of the mirror and raised her shirt, looking at her body. All the signs were there — frequent urination, light nausea, changes in her breasts. It had to be that last night together when they had repeatedly made love until they were both completely spent. She had worn the fertility stone — well until it slipped off. Still, it would have been the right time for conception in her cycle. God had answered her prayers for a baby and her husband was alive.

This time, the baby was going to make it. Gesta had been right all along. Jack would be back, remembering her, and they were going to be a family. She was excited, yet it felt like another secret to keep. Everything seemed

like one giant secret and this was a happy occasion. She
would tell everyone soon.

Chapter 47 ~ Hangover

Evan gradually woke in his living room with throbbing in his head and pain in his neck. He looked around for any sign of Chelsea. She was gone. He raised his arm to his aching head and could smell her perfume on his shirt. Chelsea was unlike any woman Evan had gone out with before. She was flirtatious, but held back. He liked that. She was making this a game. He sensed that she did want to be more than friends. He wondered what really turned her on in bed.

They had kissed at midnight and it wasn't a peck on the cheek or a quick one on the lips. His lips had met hers and they were soft, warm and moist, the same way he imagined her pussy. When he put his tongue in her mouth, she had received him as if she was hungry, could not stop, like she wanted more, more, more.

Later, Chelsea sat on his lap in his favorite chair. They toasted once more and he was ready to nail her ass if she would let him. But he must have drank way more than he realized. He remembered the feeling of her sitting directly on his crotch. Kissing and feeling her body, he wanted to rip off that red dress and engulf her breasts with his mouth and hands. He had struggled to hold onto his sexual appetite.

She asked if she could take off her boots, as the heels were killing her. Struggling with them while sitting on the sofa, he remembered helping her slowly remove each boot. Did she show him her panties on purpose when he pulled off the last boot? Did she want him? God, she was gorgeous and just about everyone's eyes were on them at various points of the celebration last night. Tellinger had even asked to dance with her.

But sex didn't happen and now he had a hell of a hangover. What a dumb ass he had been for downing so much liquor. Evidently, she had let herself out and he wondered what in the hell she thought of him. Evan wanted to see Chelsea again and soon. He would contact her once he felt a little more together.

He popped some ibuprofen for his head and took a long hot shower. It seemed to help his head, or maybe not. Time would tell. Evan thought about the change in the calendar. It was now 2020 and no one had found Jack Foster alive or dead. This had to be the year Evan secured a position on the board at Chadwell. He took the risks involved and the plane had gone down, just as Tellinger wanted. He shouldn't hold Jack's hidden information over his head now in order to be on that board. They had an arrangement. And, while there may have been a few hiccups, he had made sure Jack and his team were removed.

Evan dressed and grabbed his stomach. He felt a bit nauseous and wondered if it was from hunger or hangover. With today being a holiday, he would rest, recuperate, and watch some television. Tomorrow, he was back in the lab and office. Hopefully, a few other employees would decide to come to work. If Ric in the IT department was there, he wanted to see if he had found anything.

Cleaning up the living room, he looked around to see if Chelsea left anything. He wished she had. Silly as that sounded, it would be like a souvenir. No scotch tonight, he told himself. Maybe not for a long time.

He turned on the television, finding a slew of different football games. He decided to watch a movie instead. Football reminded him of his brother, who he hated almost as much as his dad. He paused the movie before it began with his remote and reached for his phone.

Sorry I passed out on you. You were so beautiful and awesome last night. When can I see you again? Dinner this weekend?

Hopefully, Chelsea didn't think he was a total lightweight. He would wait to hear from her.

Evan had almost fallen asleep when he heard his phone buzz. He looked at it and it was Chelsea responding.

No problem about you snoozing on me. It was a little too hot to handle anyway. We both drank too much and yes, dinner is fine on Saturday night. What are you making?

Reading her message, he grinned. She was still interested. While he would have taken her out to dinner, she was indicating they should enjoy it together at his home. What could he tell her he would make? It should be something that went well with wine. He would pick up a meal from a decent restaurant. That was the only way to go with this. He messaged her back.

Saturday at seven then. Surf and turf sound good?

Surf and turf is one of my favorites. I'll be there. Let me know if I can bring anything.

Just your beautiful essence

Chapter 48 ~ Locating a Thief

Friday, January 3, 2020

Lucky and Ric rode in her van to the address he believed belonged to Ragland. Using the motor vehicle database, he narrowed the guy to this location. But, they had to be sure.

It was a normal middle class neighborhood in Atlanta. Nothing stood out when they passed the house.

"How can we get a visual on him, Lucky?" he asked. "It's winter, he's not going to be out cutting the grass."

"Let me think about it. There has to be a way. We could show up on his doorstep like he won some huge prize and we are delivering it?"

"You're braver than I am."

"No, I'm foolish sometimes."

"You've been down on yourself since the search warrant was deployed at your place."

"I guess. It's how a person feels when they may be arrested for a crime they didn't commit."

Ric looked at her and rolled his eyes. "They have no motive or evidence on you. Let's drive by the house once more."

"Okay. There's no cable truck there, but we knew he might keep it elsewhere."

Lucky turned the corner and began down the street again just as she saw a man emerging from the address.

"Quick, get a photo of him," she said to Ric.

Ric quickly snapped a picture as the van rolled by. Looking down at his phone, he could see that he managed to get a photo with a side profile of the guy.

Lucky continued driving down the neighborhood street. In her side mirror, she could see that he was getting into a silver Chevy truck. "He's going somewhere. Should we try to follow him?"

"Only if we stay way back … I mean way the hell back. We don't want to spook him."

"You're right."

The silver truck pulled out of the subdivision onto a four-lane road littered with stores and restaurants. With Lucky at the wheel, she had not yet been able to see the photo that Ric had taken. They watched as the truck pulled into a gas station. Lucky pulled into a fast-food restaurant next to the gas station.

"Can I see the picture you got of him?"

Ric handed her his phone and she looked at it, enlarging the image of him with her fingers.

"I'm pretty sure that's him."

"100% positive?"

"No. I wish I had some binoculars," she said, as she watched the man at the gas pump filling the truck.

"Let me see if I can get some better photos." Ric put the camera phone on zoom and took multiple photos of the man pumping gas. He pulled one up with a better view of the guy's face. "Take a look at this. Use your fingers to make it larger on the screen."

Lucky did as Ric suggested and looked closely. "That's definitely him. You did it, Ric. We've found him. Should we continue the chase and see where he goes? Maybe place a tracker on the truck?"

Ric thought for a moment. "No, remember our goal is to get the dead man switch letter to him. If we alert him, it could mess things up."

"You're right." Lucky sent Haley a message.

We have that address you need. It's confirmed.

Haley messaged her back quickly.

Great. My letter is ready. Meet up?

Can you meet at 3:00? You choose the spot.

Yes, how about the gun range?

I'll be there.

"By the way, Ric. I have some phone numbers I need you to run whenever you can. They might all be duds, but I retrieved these from two burner phones belonging to Evan Mitchell."

"How did you accomplish that?"

"Let's just say I have my ways."

"Did you sleep with him?" Ric said, trying not to sound possessive.

"No, no. I drugged him on New Year's Eve. But I didn't feel good about it. Never tell anyone, Ric."

He looked at her and understood. Lucky could seem vicious, but she really didn't want to hurt a fly. Obviously, her need to do what she felt was right made her break rules. He knew that her quest to discover the truth was greater sometimes than her moral conscience.

"I won't tell anyone," he said. "Did you discover anything else?

"No, but he's a pretty good kisser," she said, egging him on.

Chapter 49 ~ Affirmations

Each day at Underground Brazil was filled with non-stop activities for Jack. They either revolved around repair of his own health or testing and production of his new drug. He felt it was his drug even though he had produced it for Chadwell. They had rejected it. It was now his and he decided he would not patent it. The process was too time consuming for one thing. The other reason is that it would drive the cost up. Once production was underway, he hoped governments around the world could purchase it at a low, fair market price to distribute to their citizens for any viral outbreak.

Today he would not receive the hyperbaric oxygen treatment. Dr. Barbados and Dr. Melo wanted to meet with him first thing this morning. He showered, shaved and made his way to the medical bay. Placing his hand on the scanner attached to the podium, the artificial receptionist greeted him. "Good morning, Dr. Foster. Thank you for being prompt again. I'll notify the staff you are here. Please have a seat. Your wait will not be long."

A nurse came out relatively quickly and ushered Jack into the medical bay. "Let's get your vitals and then I'll let the doctors know you are ready to be seen." Jack weighed in and appeared to have gained a couple of pounds since his last visit. He looked at her and smiled, "Food's good here." She laughed.

Once settled into the conference room, Dr. Melo entered. "Dr. Barbados will be here shortly. How are you feeling since the treatments you've been receiving?"

"I'm feeling more energetic with the oxygen treatments, almost euphoric for a short time afterward. The hypnosis is revealing things I didn't know, parts of my memory, piece by piece. I have to admit I was skeptical about it at first."

Both doctors nodded their heads and smiled. "Most people believe it's not possible. Of course, I think you have to work with someone well trained and that you are able to fully relax around. It sounds like you have that with Dr. Alonso."

"Yes."

Dr. Melo looked at Jack, "Dr. Foster, we wanted you to have the oxygen treatments to assist with any tissue repair that perhaps our testing did not pick up. It is hard to measure if healing is occurring with regard to that treatment. Given that you are recovering some memories, Dr. Barbados and I want you to continue that treatment, starting up again tomorrow morning."

Dr. Barbados spoke next. "As I said at the onset of your treatment, you appear to have post-traumatic amnesia. For one reason or another, your brain has compartmentalized certain memories, like the actual crash. I understand you've had some recall on this. Is that correct?"

"Yes, I am remembering what happened right after the crash, even though prior to this I believed I was unconscious during that time."

"What about your wife? Anything there?"

"No." Jack replied, almost sullenly.

"Today, I would like to work with you creating affirmations that allow you to possibly open these locked sections of the brain. Essentially, we will be using your own voice to reprogram your subconscious. It's not your fault this is happening, Jack. Your brain did this because it believes it's protecting you. Would you like to create the affirmations with me this morning? It will take an hour or less."

"Sure, I've tried to remain open to everything you have proposed up to now. I'll try affirmations."

"Great, follow me and I'll show you our therapy room."

Jack followed the doctor to a room that had soft lighting and calm colors on the walls and furnishings. He noticed the traditional psychiatrist's couch in the form of a chaise lounge, along with several normal looking upholstered chairs situated in a circle. Dr. Barbados noticed him checking out the room. "The circle is for group therapy."

"Do you have much of that going on here?" Jack asked, truly wondering.

"No, but we had a couple of circumstances where information was compromised and it upset several employees. Talking things through and exploring how to prevent such occurrences was helpful for them."

"I see."

"We are going to be working over here today with the computer and microphone."

Jack noticed a long countertop along the left wall, locating the microphone. "Okay, show me what to do."

They both sat at the computer and the doctor typed out on the screen a series of statements which were contrary to Jack's present experience. She explained that the affirmations would be recorded in his voice and it was important he listened to them twice per day. Ideally, once in the morning and again in the evening before bed.

"I know you are very busy with your work and treatments, but I would really like you to do this. With each statement, you will be reprogramming your subconscious to believe a new story about yourself. In the story we are writing here together, you have perfect recall and memory of everything in your life. You know that your memories may evoke feelings, but they cannot harm you. Let's get this underway for you."

After writing and recording the affirmative statements, Jack watched as Dr. Barbados added calming music in the background of the recording. She handed him headphones and he listened to the beginning. His voice in the recording sounded far away, like it had a slight echo. It held a deeper resonance. Ocean waves and light piano played in the background.

Jack took off the earphones. "That's sounds incredible. You did those sound effects so quick," he said.

"Ah, I toy around with this a lot in my spare time. Affirmations helped me get through medical school. I would use them to train my brain that nothing could stop me from making the highest grades and that I would retain all the information I would need for my chosen specialty. It works, Dr. Foster."

"Hopefully, it works for me, Dr. Barbados. Thank you."

"You're welcome. Hold one moment while I turn this into a digital format I can send to you."

Jack watched as she clicked more commands in the program and the digital file was created.

"I'm sending this to you now. With someone as busy as you are, the best thing to do is put a morning and evening reminder on your phone. Use this, and let's see what happens."

Chapter 50 ~ The Letter

The day after Haley discovered she was pregnant, she purchased a gun. It felt like time to stop procrastinating about her safety. Somehow, she could not imagine performing many self-defense moves while pregnant. In fact, she might have to drop out of the class which would begin again next week. Haley didn't want to allow pregnancy to be a vulnerability for her. She would find a way to position herself to take on an attacker.

Sonya had accompanied her to the gun store and they purchased a handgun for her also. Today, they would see how comfortable their use was with target practice at the gun range. Lucky was meeting them there to see about delivering the dead man switch letter.

When Jason and Sarah looked over the new weapons, they both were supportive of the decision. Jason stressed learning to use them extremely well and following all safety precautions. Haley raved to them about their instructor that Lucky recommended. She assured them that she and Sonya would practice at the range regularly until they both felt quite natural with their weapons. She also mentioned that Lucky now had Ragland's address and it was time to get the dead man switch letter to him.

When Haley and Sonya arrived, Lucky was already at the gun range. They spotted her in one of the booths, shooting targets. "Look at her form, Haley. She looks professional or like someone in a movie."

Haley chuckled. "I'm not worried about how I look. I just want to feel confident and be able to hit the targets well."

Lucky finished a round of targets and glanced out the window. She waved to the ladies. Removing her headphones, she exited the booth. "Just thought I'd get a little practice in until you arrived."

"Sonya says you look so professional, like someone in a movie. I think she's right. Maybe you should be our instructor."

Lucky laughed. "Listen, I hope I don't have to shoot anyone — ever. Good to know I look professional. Maybe someone will believed I'm more skilled than I feel ... or at least look like I know what I'm doing."

"We just got new handguns. Vicki is meeting us here for more lessons. The gun shop we purchased from said if these don't feel comfortable for us to use, we can come back and exchange within three days."

"That's a nice policy. It's important that you feel smooth with your gun. You need to be able to load it with ease too."

Sonya spoke up, "Yeah, I could tell that was the case from the first lesson we had. Loading was kind of difficult for me the first couple of tries."

Lucky nodded, agreeing with her. "Well, ladies. Like I said, good news. We have his address. Ric made it easy with his computer skills and we rode out in person today to confirm it."

"Thank you so much. Do you really think this letter will work?" Haley asked.

"I do. He's going to freak when he knows you know. Not to mention, you're telling him the goods are not at your home. I think he'll leave you alone."

"Do you think it would be safe for Sonya and I to go back to the house after he gets the letter?"

"Yes, but with the caveat that I cannot vouch for what crazy thing could happen next. That's why you need it all - guns, self-defense, security system, and maybe a big dog with sharp teeth."

"My neighbors should be back home now. I always feel better just having them next door."

Lucky asked, "Did you bring the letter?"

"I did. Want to read it?"

"Yes."

Haley pulled the envelope out of her bag and handed it over to Lucky. She read through it, smiling at some points during her reading. "This is fantastic. I don't think you're going to have any more trouble with him.

There's one loose end here and that's a drop off point for him to return the gun. We'll have to work that out."

"Yes, I want that gun back. He could be out committing crimes with a gun registered to Jack."

"How do you want the letter delivered and when?" Lucky asked.

"If I mail it today, he might get it tomorrow or Monday. If it was delivered today, he's probably going to read it today."

"I agree. I just had an idea. Let's use a courier service that hand delivers items. That way, he's not going to see Ric or myself at his house. He already knows the letter is from you, so we don't need to hide that fact from the courier. I'll get it set up and have it delivered in a couple of hours if you want to try that approach."

"That's a great idea. Let's do it!"

Lucky tucked the letter back into the envelope. "No problem. I'll take care of it, ladies. Happy New Year, by the way."

"Happy New Year to you!" Sonya and Haley chimed in.

Chapter 51 ~ Back in the Lab

Jack parked his trike outside the lab again and surprised the team by arriving early. "My normal treatment was canceled today, so I'm a little earlier. According to my doctors, I will be back on it again tomorrow."

Eleanora spoke up, "Did you receive a prognosis, Dr. Foster?" She twirled the tip of an ink pen along her cheek while he answered.

"I did. I'm making some progress. It's all good," Jack said, offering nothing further. He had a hard time reading Eleanora. Was she displaying an innocent curiosity or was she flirting? The only thing that indicated the latter was her body language. He would have to let her know anything between them was out of the question. But how could he do that without seeming overt?

He turned his mind back to the team and the work they were there to accomplish. "Let's have a ten-minute meeting everyone. We can do it right here without the meeting room. Carlos, you are lead on this. Give us our current status."

Carlos, a tall man, with years of experience working for pharmaceutical companies, stepped forward. "I am pleased to report that examination and testing of the initial vials of the drug look pure and we are ready to begin testing. The human trials will be accomplished at one of our military bases. Dr. Foster, your government also wants to test at one of their bases. We will have two different populaces to monitor."

"Excellent!" Jack said. "Carlos, do you know what they intend to use as a base of infection for the participants?"

"No, not yet. Hopefully, I will know that today."

"Well, it sounds as if each of you have been doing your part and then some to make this happen quickly. As you know, our work is extremely important. It is my hope that you will each look back on this exciting moment and know you were involved in the making of a drug that hopefully has a high efficacy rate and hardly any side effects in humans. Let the trials begin!"

Jack visited the work stations and areas of the entire team, making sure he invited each one to join him this evening for dinner in the dining hall. The camaraderie of the group was excellent. His only problem team member might be Eleanora. He had experienced women coming on to him in the past during various internships and his job at Chadwell. He certainly didn't want to accuse her of anything, but he also didn't want to encourage her. Right now, he couldn't take the time to think about women, a wife, or anything like that. He wanted to focus solely on the human trials of this drug, analyzing the data as they received it.

He met with the team who had initiated propagation of the plant in the greenhouse facility. Because his former colleague, Sercy, had worked tirelessly on this at Chadwell, Jack was able to give the team members plenty of tips to make the progress a little smoother. The vine was finicky and required precise conditions to take off and begin to thrive. Luckily, Marcos said at dinner the night before he would have more shipments of it arriving soon from the rain forest.

Jack reflected for a few moments on his previous three team members lost in the crash. They were the real unseen heroes. Due to their dedication and prior work, this project was coming together at lightning speed. Each of them had been so unique and irreplaceable. Jack really felt that because of them, things were coming together here with the joint efforts of the team made up of Americans and Brazilians.

Eleanor sat directly across from Jack during dinner. It was easy to keep the conversation moving with everyone at the table. However, he noticed her staring at him a little too long a few times. If he was noticing it while he was conversing with others, they probably saw it too. That wasn't kosher. He wanted the respect of his team and they might suspect something was going on with Eleanora, when there was nothing. Her admiration was okay in a professional way. But the idolizing he saw in her eyes disturbed him.

As he finished eating and said goodbyes, he rode the trike back to his apartment. Dr. Alonso would arrive again soon. As he was about to enter his apartment, Eleanora pulled up on her bicycle.

"That was great conversation we had tonight at dinner. Very enjoyable."

"It was," he responded.

"I really admire you Dr. Foster. I hope your wife knows how fortunate she is. What does she think about you being away so long?"

Jack was taken aback by her directness. "I don't know what she thinks. Since I've been here, I haven't been able to communicate with her."

Eleanora stood on her bike, straddling the seat and asked him, "Do you love her?"

"I've heard I do very much, yes."

She looked at him perplexed and frowning. "That is the strangest response I've ever heard from a man."

Jack decided to put her on the spot. "How many men have you asked that question?"

She hesitated to answer for a few seconds. "Not that many."

"Well then, you would have no way of gathering enough data to know how a man would typically respond. Agreed?"

"I suppose you're right."

"I'll see you in the lab tomorrow. I have an appointment in a few minutes."

"Oh, I'm sorry. Yes, in the lab tomorrow. Have a good night."

He watched as she rode her bike away from him. Jack closed his eyes, sighing audibly before placing his hand on the scanner and going inside his apartment. Hopefully, Eleanora felt uncomfortable with his response and won't push her fantasy any further. He understood how anyone could become bored in an underground facility like this and seek out companionship, but it would have to be with someone other than him.

Chapter 52 ~ Breakthrough

Dr. Alonso arrived on time and Jack told himself to forget about the encounter with Eleanora. The lights were lowered and the calming water sounds played in the background. He was determined to revisit the past tonight without the intense emotions if he could. Mentally, he told himself he would remember more tonight. This was reiterated by Dr. Alonso as he took Jack down into a deeper state of relaxation than before.

"Jack, during this session, no matter what happens you will view it as a movie outside of yourself. It is not happening now, but a movie you are watching of something recorded in the past. Your mind will allow you to view this because you have requested it. Now, I want you to place your thoughts inside the small plane you were traveling in. Tell me what happened in the plane."

Jack was quiet for thirty seconds or more. Then he began to speak in a low tone. "The people on the radio at ground control. They were trying to help but were very slow finding someone who knew about that plane and could communicate with me. By the time we figured out the autopilot function needed to be disengaged, the plane was pretty high in altitude. I was trying to disengage the auto pilot. The plane shook inside the cockpit and I held onto the steering as they instructed. Hold the yoke steady, she said. It took everything I had strength-wise to keep the wheel from moving on its own, and then it snapped off the console. The plane was doomed at that point. But then I saw the other steering wheel in the co-pilot area where the pilot was. I moved over, practically sitting on top of the poor guy and tried my best to get the plane under control."

Jack hesitated and his breathing rate increased. Dr. Alonso guided him to regain composure. "You are safe, Jack. You're watching a movie of something that happened."

After a few seconds, Jack continued. "The plane is diving. It's headed toward the trees. I brought it up slightly right before one of the wings touched the treetops. The plane went into a fall, breaking treetop limbs."

"I grabbed my backpack and put it in front of me. We were going down. Dropping further, further until there was a huge boom and the ancient trees bent with the weight of the plane. The cockpit bounced and suddenly, we were tilted back, but the plane wasn't falling. It was still now."

"The plane was pointed downward tail first, kind of at a forty-five degree angle. The trees had both buffered the fall and damaged the plane's windows. Shards of glass were everywhere. I saw that all of us were cut on exposed areas of our skin. I don't think they felt anything — no pain. But I felt it all."

"I caught my breath. My heart was beating so fast. Faster than ever before. I heard a huge scraping and cracking sound and suddenly, we're in a fall again — tail first. I'm thinking we will not survive it. It's going to hurt. My eyes are closed and I'm seeing images from my life flash in my mind's eye. Haley, I have to survive for her. I was praying, dear God, and holding onto the backpack like it was my child. I looked at my hands and my knuckles were covered in blood. The plane is still falling and the trip down the tree line felt like an eternity. Boom! The right wing came off the plane. I heard the sound of the metal breaking upon larger limbs as it fell. The plane kept going and then there was a big thrusting stop."

"I looked around from my position. All I could see was the green of leaves and the black of bark surrounding us. The trees were cradling the fuselage. I could not determine if we were one hundred feet in the air or thirty. I wanted to see what elevation the plane was at. Most of the windows were broken. There was glass scattered everywhere. Crouching, I tried to move very carefully so as not to rock or move the plane. I didn't want to shift the weight inside much. The plane was literally perched on tree limbs. The trees seemed to be our friend, as if they were hugging and holding the fuselage."

'I began moving, slow as molasses, to keep my weight from shifting the plane. There is only one wing now. Staying center in the aisle, I moved toward Lance and tried to peer out a window near him. I could see nothing but green. There was no indication of how high or low we were. My eyes darted toward the plane's door further down the aisle. I knew I had to get out. I grabbed my backpack by its handle and squatted center in the plane making my way down the aisle toward the door area very slowly. The plane creaked loudly at one point. I wanted to shake my friends out of their drugged slumber. But I knew if the crash didn't wake them, I wouldn't be able to. They were all effectively tranquilized. I kept moving slowly down the carpeted aisle and could now see the door just to the right. I sat still for a few seconds wondering how I could move swiftly, yet smoothly, without causing a disturbance to the plane's balance. I didn't know. I moved like an inch worm toward the door. The plane creaked again loudly."

"I remembered I had a bundle of rope in my pack. I rationalized that I could use the rope to try to walk out on the left wing and wrap it around the most stable tree. If I could make it there, I would at least be out of the plane if it fell again. I felt inside the pack and wrapped my fingers around the rope. I tied it around my waist, making sure it was thoroughly in my pant belt loops. I wrapped it again around my right leg through my crotch, essentially making it into a harness. The rope was long enough that I should be able to wrap it around that tree if I could get on the wing without it breaking or moving."

"Suddenly, I realized that just opening the door of the plane might shift everything into a free fall again. It felt like a dangerous idea but I needed to get out of there. I moved the door latch slowly, praying the door would open easily. It opened as smooth as silk. I looked at my buddies. I felt remorse abandoning the plane. If the plan worked, I might survive. I'm not so sure about them. If the plane went into a free fall again, it could be horrific. I also knew that if I didn't make it onto the wing or if I caused the plane to shift with my weight, I would go down with it too. There was no easy answer. I had to go with my instincts to survive."

"With the plane's door open, I balanced myself in the doorway taking advantage of the short staircase that extended down when I opened it. I moved to the top step and leapt as lightly as possible onto the plane's wing. Immediately, I felt some movement and heard the sound of metal against the tree. I moved quickly up the wing until I could tie onto a large tree branch about forty degrees from the branches holding the plane."

"Standing out on the wing, I felt light rain. It began to make the blood on my hands streak. I noticed my hat was still on and I couldn't believe it. I laughed at the absurdity of it. And that's when I saw it, the crack in the wing I was standing on. Although the trees were holding everything well, the wing was breaking. I braced myself for what was about to occur. I rubbed my hands on my clothing to dry them and grasp the ropes tightly that were tied to the tree. Within seconds, I heard a huge metal cracking sound that was worse than someone's fingernails on a chalkboard. The wing split and the fuselage slipped shifting downward. Gravity took it down quickly as it fell all the way to the forest floor."

"I tied and looped the rope more, trying to make a repel system. It felt pretty secure so I began making an attempt to work my way down along the tree. Below, I could see the opening the plane's fuselage had made and estimated I was about a hundred feet in the air. I wouldn't be able to repel down the rope unless I could remove and retie it at intervals. For a moment, I felt defeated until I realized I was sitting on a strong branch that was holding me. I stood on the limb and was able to reach the other end of the rope and untie it. I worked like that, over and over. I would find a secure branch for my weight. Untie the rope and then retie it lower. It was working well and I wanted to get down to the ground to check on the crew. A fire had broken out toward the back of the fuselage. When I was about twenty feet above the ground, I took a misstep and begin falling before I had secured the other end of the rope. I landed on the forest floor, tangled in rope. It seemed like a few seconds went by before I actually felt the pain. My vision was fuzzy and I felt unsteady to move."

Dr. Alonso could not believe his ears. Jack's harrowing story of surviving the plane crash was like a movie he was retelling. But he must have experienced it, because he did survive. He spoke with Jack after bringing him out of the hypnotic state. "Jack, I am assuming you remember what you just recalled under hypnosis."

"Yes, I think so. I remember that I said something about Haley, the woman that is my wife. But, there was so much with the plane, that I forgot what I said."

"Would you like to listen to the recording? That may help you."

"Yes, I've been listening to each recording right before I go to sleep."

"You did an outstanding job of not getting emotional this time. I've never had a subject respond as well. Tonight, you've uncovered some mysteries that were lurking inside you."

"Thank you, Dr. Alonso. Thank you so much."

Chapter 53 ~ Dane

Crunched for time, Lucky skipped eating in order to get the letter delivered by courier to Ragland. She had to get to the yoga class on time. Lucky didn't want to run into Evan tonight. She still had the tracker on his Porsche and it currently showed him at Chadwell. Lucky noticed he was not afraid of work and spent some long hours there, even during the holidays. It was so good that Ric was there monitoring and digging the best he could. The guy did incredible work.

She arrived early enough to change in the locker room. Two of her female students were already dressed, hanging out there. One was pulling her hair back and the other filed her nails. "Hey ladies, glad to see you're back for more in 2020," Lucky said, smiling.

The lady filing her nails looked up at her. "Yes, I'm here for more of your torture," she said, with a giggle. "Seriously, I am beginning to feel some results with this. I love it!"

"I'm so glad to hear that. And, I'm glad you both are back for more torture," Lucky said. They all laughed.

Walking together toward the studio, Lucky went inside and they followed. One of the ladies asked, "So do you think our hot cover guy will be back tonight?"

Lucky looked at her and had a look of intrigue on her face. "Cover guy?"

"Yeah, that guy Dane. That's what he does for a living. He's a model here in Atlanta."

"I didn't know that. Got to admit, he has the looks," Lucky said.

"And the muscles!" the other woman chimed in. "Too bad I'm married."

The other woman agreed, "He's super hot. His hair is gorgeous."

"Well, I can't talk about him. He's one of my students now ... or at least he was for one evening. We'll see if he ...."

Just then, Dane opened the door and walked in. Lucky's face turned beet red. The two ladies acted like they were occupied speaking directly with one another."

"Hello. Happy New Year," Dane said, dropping a bag on the floor behind him.

Everyone stopped and looked at him. "Happy New Year."

Lucky regained her composure. "Dane, as I told these two a few minutes ago, I'm very happy you're back for yoga in 2020."

He looked at her and she could swear his eyes twinkled. She felt it again, the heat he caused throughout her body just being in the same room with him. Was she just terribly deprived and this is why she felt no control over herself? Dane didn't respond verbally — just offered that expression with the eye twinkle. Lucky paced a little, waiting to see if more students arrived.

She glanced over at him just as he began unzipping his pants. Embarrassingly mesmerized, she stood still staring at him. Sliding the pants down over his hips, he revealed compression yoga pants underneath. Lucky could not help but notice all the bulges he had. The pants accentuated his thigh and calf muscles tremendously. But it was the muscle in front between his legs that really made her feel the heat rising again.

She quickly turned her stare away and began the music, getting her mat laid out. Lucky couldn't imagine what the other women were thinking. She had the most exciting yoga class in Atlanta with a hot male cover model — especially in his compression yoga pants and matching tank top. With every pose, this was going to be another evening of fighting to focus on yoga instead of Dane.

Lucky felt emotional relief as she ended the yoga session. With every change in pose, the class tonight had been a workout. Dane had moved his mat closer to her, creating even more of a mind game for Lucky. She kept her eyes on the women there as much as possible, or on her own pose. Focus had been difficult. The guy had sexuality oozing out of him.

As they rolled up mats, she noticed he took his time. Once the ladies had departed and Lucky had everything put away, she grabbed her jacket and keys, hinting she needed to leave. At this point, it was probably not good for her to be alone in a room with him.

"That was a great session. I think I'm getting the hang of it," he said, pulling his pants on over the yoga compression tights. Lucky tried to look elsewhere as he zipped up.

"You're doing great, Dane. What is it that you want to accomplish with this discipline?"

"I've never heard it called that before, but it is a discipline. I always want to be more limber and have great posture. I model for a living and the poses in yoga might make for some good shots once I have them down. But, really ... I was attracted to taking the class because of you."

"Me?" Lucky asked, her eyes large.

"Yes, I was hoping I could get to know you. Maybe, we could have dinner. What kind of food do you like?"

Lucky hesitated. Should she pursue this with him? Would she kick herself if she didn't? She felt the fear she had inside and pushed it aside. Looking at him, the term Greek God came to mind again.

"Oh, I love exploring different cuisines. One I haven't had lately is Greek."

"Would you like to grab some Greek food with me soon?"

She could feel sweat forming on her forehead. "How soon?"

"As soon as you're available."

"I'm working days and evenings right now, but I have some time on Sunday."

"Perfect, Sunday is a slow day for me. Can I get your number, Chelsea?"

Lucky quickly thought of which number was Chelsea's. This guy had her tongue tied and her brain felt muddled. She pulled out her phone. Dane made her feel naked when he looked at her with those radiant blue eyes. She loved his mouth and the way his lip curled when he spoke. His voice was low and velvety.

"Actually, I just got a new phone and don't remember the number yet. Let me look." She glanced at her phone, finding the number and gave it to him.

"Great," he said. "I'll sure up the details with you tomorrow."

"Thanks," she said. "We'll talk then."

"Are you leaving now?" he asked.

"Yes."

"May I walk you out?"

"Sure."

She had parked in her usual spot, toward the back of the lot.

"You park way back here?" he asked.

"Yeah, I don't want to accidentally take up a resident's spot," she half-lied.

"If you're going to park this far away, it wouldn't hurt to have someone make sure you get to your car safely."

"This is a pretty nice, crime-free area though, don't you think?"

"Yes, but you're a very beautiful woman," he said.

Lucky blushed and looked down.

"Thanks, for walking me to my car, and the complement."

"You're welcome. I meant it," he said, with seriousness in his tone.

Her eyes were locked on him as she slid into her car. He closed the door and waved to her as she drove away. It felt a little overwhelming. She had this dreamy guy asking her out, telling her she's beautiful, wanting to see her safely to her vehicle. It made her feel something she had not felt in a long time, not since she met the guy who had been the only real love of her life. But that was a long time ago. She wanted to open her heart again, but that was more risky than opening her legs.

Chapter 54 ~ Special Delivery

Ragland startled awake when the doorbell rang.

He wasn't expecting anyone. He crept over to the window and saw a young woman at the door. He noticed a compact vehicle out front with a delivery service emblem on its side with a phone number. He relaxed a bit, and wondered if she had the wrong address.

Opening the door about six inches, he asked, "Can I help you?"

"Are you Mr. Ragland?"

"I am."

"I have a delivery for you," she said, holding an envelope.

Ragland opened the door a little more and took it from her. "Thanks," he said.

She turned and walked toward her vehicle.

Ragland looked at the front of the envelope. There was no indication of who it was from. He opened the seal on it and began reading the letter inside. *Holy shit!* He wondered how this woman knew it was him who broke in, but the police didn't know? He wasn't going to jail for anybody, especially not Evan. This woman was blackmailing him.

He flung the letter on the coffee table and sat back on the couch. He would need to find a secure place to drop the gun where she could pick it up without him being around. He wasn't going to jail for Evan. This mission had been screwed up from the beginning. He should have pulled out before he accepted more money. Picking up his burner phone, he sent a message to Evan.

Something even stranger has come up. We need to meet. Soon!

Evan received the message. He didn't want to drive all the way across town to that bar or another one. Not to mention that he didn't feel like drinking. He messaged Ragland back.

Meet me at the new fast food place that serves buffalo burgers on Watson at 8:30.

Will do.

He paced the floor a bit astonished this woman knew his name - Steve Ragland. She knew his address. He wondered now if she had someone following him. Before he met with Evan tonight, he would stop by the office supply store and make a copy of the letter for him.

Feeling exceptionally paranoid, Ragland kept glancing at the mirrors of his truck, checking for anyone who could be following him. It was Friday night, pretty dark out and hard to tell. Whatever the situation, this woman had him by the balls and he was going to do what she requested. What choice did he have?

Damn good thing I didn't try to show up at her house saying I was from the security company. What a disaster that would have been.

He went inside the office supply store and made a copy of the letter at a self-service machine. He slipped Evan's copy in an extra envelope he brought from his house.

Pulling up at the new restaurant, he parked toward the outer lot. The place was crowded inside. He stood in line and ordered a burger and drink. Once his order was filled, he carried his food toward the dining area. He saw Evan sitting in the back. As he approached, he could tell that he had finished his meal.

"Have a seat and tell me what's going on now," Evan said.

Ragland sat down and looked at him. He spoke in a low voice. "I had a big surprise this evening. I made you a copy of it." He handed the envelope across the table to Evan and took a bite out of his burger.

Opening the unsealed envelope, Evan pulled out the paper and began reading. As he finished, he looked at Ragland and said nothing. The silence was almost deafening. His stare at the failed operator said everything.

Ragland took a sip of his drink. "I can't work this anymore."

"Obviously! Your cover is blown. She has dirt on you. Worse, she knows what you were there for and very well knew this before you arrived. What's with the gun? You didn't mention that to me."

"I took a gun, a 9mm I found in the bedroom. My reasoning was that if I left it and had to come back, she could use it on me."

"How are you going to get it back to her?"

"I don't know, but not in person. I need a drop area that's safe where she can pick it up."

"I'll let you work that out."

"I'll be taking a trip out of town for a while as soon as I drop the gun."

"Can't say I blame you."

Ragland finished the last bite of his burger. "Pretty good food. You know, she must have some people working for her. How else could a woman who hardly goes anywhere know so much?"

"It's something I'm already thinking about."

"How do we know that she doesn't know you're involved?"

"We don't. Depending upon what is in the information she found and has now copied and put in various places, she could know things that will really put her in danger."

"Yes, but she's instructed seven separate parties to release the information if anything happens to her or anyone close to her."

"True, it's a real fucking dilemma now, isn't it? I gotta go. Good luck, Ragland."

"Good luck to you."

Chapter 55 ~ Ice Cold Water

Evan's emotions fumed driving away from the Buffalo burger restaurant. Haley Foster knew whatever Jack had hidden in their house. She had the foresight to make copies of it and place them at different locations to be released if anything happened to her or people she cared about. If she knew Evan had a connection to Ragland, she didn't indicate it in the letter. He would need to meet with Tellinger as soon as possible. He sent him a message requesting they meet before Monday. Within minutes, he messaged back.

My office tomorrow at 9am. I was just about to contact you. I have information you need to know.

I'll be there. Thank you, sir.

Evan arrived the next morning and took the elevator to the top floor. He walked to J.D.'s office and found him behind his desk with the door open. "I've come across some issues, Evan. Please, close the door so we can talk."

Evan closed it and made his way into a seat in front of the executive's desk. He felt a sense of doom inside, wondering what could be worse than the news he had for his boss.

J.D. seemed very calm as Evan told him the situation with their operator, Ragland. He listened intently, occasionally tapping a pen impatiently on a file sitting on his desk.

"Did you bring the letter he gave you?"

"Yes, I did." He handed it to the executive who read it and shook his head. She signed it so I will assume it's her signature. How do you know he didn't type this up himself to get out of this?"

"I never thought about that."

"Well, you paid him up front, plus gave him another monetary incentive right after Christmas. He botched the job and now has a hard time finishing the work. This would be a clever way for him to bow out of the situation."

"Evan, you're going to have to start using your brain and look at all possibilities. The way I see it, this is not really Ragland's fault. It's yours. You allowed some fantasy you had about being with Jack's wife to keep him from doing his job properly from the start, right?"

Evan looked at his boss, whose face was red and becoming enraged. "I did have some feelings for Haley Foster. I didn't want her to get hurt."

"Yes, but it's a time like this when you have to put that aside, Evan. Wasn't it enough that you were taking over Jack's position?" Evan noticed he was definitely raising his voice as he continued. "No, you had to have feelings for Mrs. Foster which prevented your operator from having full control over the situation to get the information no matter what he had to do."

"You're right, sir. I absolutely needed to put feelings aside. I'm seeing someone else I'm more interested in now anyway."

"Are you now? The young, beautiful lady I danced with, Chelsea Roberts?"

"Yes, sir."

"And do you believe she is equally interested in you?"

"Yes, I believe she is?"

"What if I told you that she is spying on you? Look!"

Tellinger handed the file on his desk to Evan. He opened it and it revealed a photograph of Chelsea with the name, Megan Adams. It had her birth date, drivers license, and social security number. Evan's face dropped at the realization Tellinger was probably right again.

"You see, you're not as smart as you think you are, Evan. But you could be if you would remove your emotions. On some level, everyone is crooked. Everyone makes deals. You better concoct a way to get that information utilizing your new love interest. She is now the key to making this happen."

Evan shook his head in disbelief. "I will, sir."

Tellinger was on a rant and kept going, "Otherwise, your new love interest, with your help, could sink this company and a lot of people will drown with it. Evan, like I said. It's not really the operator's total fault. You've fucked this up in a major way."

Hoping his boss was finished, he watched Tellinger put his hands together and lean forward across his desk. "Now, that problem I just told you about shocked you, didn't it?"

"Yes, it did." Evan felt like he had been splashed with ice cold water. Circumstances were trying to wake him up.

"There's a very serious rumor that's come my way. People are saying that Jack Foster is alive and being protected by the government."

"Do you know where?"

"No, somewhere in Brazil I believe. With Mrs. Foster having leverage over us with the information he left behind, it makes it hard to see a way through this maze right now. But, we'll find one."

"I have a lot to think about. I'm sorry I let you down."

"Learn from it, Evan. Trust hardly no one. Turn the tables on your beautiful spy and don't let your emotions rule you."

"Alright, sir. I'm having dinner with her tonight."

J.D. walked him to the door. "Keep me in the loop."

"Will do," he said, shaking his hand.

Back in his car, Evan couldn't believe he didn't see the signs. Chelsea, or whatever her name was, had appeared out of nowhere. She did not want him to pick her up at her place or stay there. He had no idea where she lived, only what she had told him.

Had she been spying on him for a while? He wondered why she was choosing him over that muscle bound model, Dane. Evan felt like an idiot.

He easily believed her lies because he was so busy making up his own. A victim of his ego, everything was crumbling around him. There was no real love or companionship you could count on in life. It was all a ruse.

Chapter 56 ~ Questions

Evening, January 4, 2020

Lucky sipped her coffee and wished she had her laptop at home to search for news from China. She flipped on her television and found a newscast with weekend Saturday morning hosts. It was just the usual bull crap being reported so she flipped it off. *Wait a minute, I can load an app on the television to watch videos.* She searched for the channel and downloaded it.

Immediately, video choices from the region affected popped up on the screen. She clicked on one and listened closely. The man making the video said that people were beginning to feel desperate with the situation. There were people locked into their homes with those that had the virus and they were not allowed out for medical care. Food shortages were an issue as nothing was being transported in or out of the city. He described how he was suffering mentally from being shut in so long.

Lucky watched several accounts, many corroborating the information in the first video. Ric had said to download them because they would disappear off the Internet. But she didn't have any way to do that with the television.

Tonight, she would have dinner with Evan. She needed to make him talk, tell her something of what he knew. Sleeping with him was out of the question. It probably wouldn't work to make him admit anything. She needed a truth serum, if one actually existed. She searched her browser on her phone for such a concoction, finding that there were really only three things that may make a person reveal secrets or tell the truth about things. One of them was barbiturates and she had a prescription of those in her medicine cabinet. It's the same thing she gave him the other night. But with so much scotch, it just knocked him out. If he drank less tonight, she could give him the same dosage and possibly be able to get him to tell her something. Pulling the bottle out of the cabinet, she ground up two pills in the kitchen and filled her ring with it.

According to the article she read, there is no real truth serum that exists. It seemed that certain chemical substances made a person more relaxed and willing to answer questions. However, it stressed that the questioner should plan this out. Open-ended questions did not work well. It would be better to have pointed questions that the subject could answer with yes or no. Immediately, she began forming questions in her mind.

Evan began to wonder how he could get some dirt on Chelsea Roberts, or whoever she was. He called another operator he used sometimes, asking him to tag her car while she was here with him tonight. Exposing that he knew she had a motive with him would not work. She would simply pull away, probably disappear. Instead, he needed to play along with her game, acting like he was totally in love with her. In the meantime, he would try to find out more about her. Like his boss said, "On some level, everyone's crooked."

He phoned in the food order that he would pick up about an hour before her arrival. He could keep everything warm in the oven until they ate. Evan thought about why she wanted to have dinner here. Was she planting surveillance in the condo? It was super risky for him to pass out on New Year's Eve. She would have had the opportunity to do anything while he was out cold. And, she probably did. He walked into his bedroom and looked around. Thankfully, he kept nothing here that could tie him to anyone or anything.

Lucky wore a tight sweater and pair of jeans that showed her curves. She threw on a jacket and scarf and made her way toward the condominium complex. This time, she parked next to Evan's Porsche. As soon as he opened the door, he hugged her and held her there for a moment. "God, I missed you," he said. "I can't believe I screwed up so bad on New Year's Eve."

"No worries, Evan. It's happened to almost everyone at some time or another." She handed him a gift bag. "Here, I brought you something."

Evan was surprised and suspicious of whatever was inside the bag. "Come in. Let's go to the dining area. Dinner is ready."

He set the bag on the counter and began to open it, revealing a book inside titled *Yoga for Tantric Sex*. He looked at her. "You really know how to get to a guy's uh ….. heart," he said, chuckling.

She laughed. "I thought it might motivate you to take up yoga."

Evan thumbed through the book, pausing at various photographs and diagrams. He smiled at her, "It very well might. Thanks, Chelsea. I have our surf and turf staying warm in the oven. You ready to eat?"

"Yes, I'm famished."

He poured her a glass of wine and told her he's on the wagon for this evening. She smiled and understood. That would work out better for her in the long run, but it might be a very long night.

The food tasted superb and they dined by candlelight. Evan had a lot of questions for her tonight, wanting to know about her family, childhood, and all kinds of things. Most of his questions she dodged by making silly remarks, but some she answered. Many of those answers were lies. This was Chelsea Roberts' background she was sharing with him.

But, it also gave her the opportunity to ask him a few. She learned that his brother was a pretty famous football player. He didn't care for him or his dad, but she wasn't completely sure why. He had attended prestigious schools and was an excellent student.

After dinner, Evan asked if she would like music or a movie. She thought for a few seconds. Music might create a more sensual mood, but she was trying to avoid that. A movie would be a good thing to cuddle and do together. "How about a movie?"

"Let's see what our choices are," he said, wielding the remote. "Tell me, Chelsea. Do you like films with a lot of suspense?"

"Usually, I do. I like a wide variety of movies including chick flicks and romantic comedies."

"I was kind of in the mood for some Bond. Have you seen *The Spy That Loved Me*?"

Chelsea almost choked on her wine.

"You okay?" he asked.

"Oh, yeah. Just went down the wrong way. That sounds like a great choice. Let's watch it."

Lucky cuddled up to Evan on the leather couch and he put his arm around her. Everything felt a little different and she wondered if there was something he knew, that she didn't. For now, she decided just watching the movie and acting completely normal was best. Evan wasn't drinking. Unless he was very tired and could believe that he just fell asleep during the movie, this wasn't going to work.

She felt like she needed to engage with him some, but she wasn't sure how. There was nothing of the touching and kissing he had displayed before. Either he was the kind of guy who needed alcohol to bring on that behavior or he had his guard up with her. Lucky ditched the idea of using the barbiturates.

After the movie, she thanked him for the amazing dinner and hugged him, pressing her body into his. She found him aloof with her. They ended the evening with Evan walking with Lucky to her car. The kiss goodbye was on the lips, but not real long and lusty. Something was different and he couldn't hide it. She knew what this meant. Her cover with him was probably blown.

When she returned to her apartment, she texted Ric even though it was late.

Had dinner date night at Evan's. He was very different. I'm feeling like he may know who I am.

If that's true, you could be in danger.

I know. Let's talk later. I may need a plan.

Lucky woke, finding a message from Ric again.

Couldn't sleep and I have info. Meet at the bread place 11am

Looking at the time, she could down some coffee, shower, and be at the cafe at 11:00. Whatever the situation was with Evan, it was bothering her. She wanted to talk to Ric to see if he had any ideas of how she could find out for sure, plus learn what new information he had.

Ric was waiting at the same table they sat at before. The cafe was more crowded on the weekend. She saw that he went ahead and ordered herbal tea and fresh bread.

"Hey, I'm glad we could meet up quickly," she said.

"Me too. I've got some not so lucky information to share."

Ric explained that he had downloaded communications through Chadwell's system for the past couple of days to a thumb drive that he brought home. After her message last night, he couldn't sleep. He stayed up for quite a few hours going through all of Evan's emails for the past two days, but found nothing that stood out. Then, he looked at Tellinger's communications. It was there that a Detective Monohan from the Atlanta Police department had forwarded to the executive a file containing her photograph from her driver's license with her real name, social security number, address, etc.

Lucky dropped the bread she was eating on the small plate and stared at Ric. "I knew it. He was so different last night. I tried to believe maybe it was because he wasn't drinking. Tellinger told him who I was."

"We don't know that, but from the way you describe his behavior, it could be. If he hasn't told him yet, I bet he will Monday morning."

"Ric, I need to leave town. Detective Monohan — I think he's the same cop investigating me for Alice's murder. He told me to stay in town."

"Shhh!" Ric said. "Listen, he has nothing on you. Here's what I think. You need to tell Haley Foster what's going on. She can then let the rest of the family know. You do need to pull off this case. I don't want you to end up like Alice or worse," he said, in a whispered voice.

She looked at Ric with tears forming in her eyes. "I don't know what could be worse than Alice."

"We'll figure something out."

Chapter 57 ~ Love Remembered

At first, Jack only listened with headphones to his own voice stating affirmations. After a couple of days, he would speak the affirmations at the same time. He didn't know if this helped, but he felt it might. The entire exercise seemed silly when he first began it. Yet, he had taken Dr. Barbados' request serious.

Something good was happening as he regained some of his memory. Was it the hypnosis only? Maybe the oxygen therapy was helping. He didn't know for sure and he knew his doctors didn't either. The important thing was the progress he was making.

Haley was now more than a person someone told him he was married to. She still felt invisible to him, but he knew she was real. During hypnosis, he had felt a deep pull to Haley. In his mind, he knew he had to return to her because she needed him.

He heard his doorbell buzz and he opened it to Dr. Alonso who he had been anxiously awaiting. The doctor came inside and pulled the chair he normally used over beside the bed. Jack sat on the edge. "Dr. Alonso, do you mind if we discuss things before we begin?"

"Yes, please do so. What's on your mind?"

"Haley is on my mind. I now feel there is a real love connection, but I need to remember us being together. Don't get me wrong. I think you're helping me make a lot of progress."

"Jack, here is my hypothesis on this situation. When your brain scans were examined, there was no injury noted. You had some inflammation. This has probably decreased significantly. Has the pain in your head gone away?"

"Almost completely."

"Good. Let me continue. I think it is possible you unknowingly blocked out anything to do with Haley or your friends on that plane and the crash. The reason you might do this is because those were circumstances you did not know how to reconcile if you lost them. If you died and lost Haley, there may have been a part of you that couldn't deal with that idea, so you compartmentalized anything to do with Haley just like you did with the actual crash. Does that make sense?"

"Sure, yes. I've sort of wondered about that myself. What can I do about it?"

"You're doing it. By discovering little pieces at first, they open up to much larger memories. When we started, you could only see yourself on the forest floor. Eventually, you could recall the entire crash. That's when you had some revelations also about your wife, Haley. I think these memories will break loose. Just knowing this is powerful and an impetus to allow those locked memories to be set free."

"Alright, let's get started. I want to know more about Haley and me."

The doctor took him through a deep relaxation exercise, eventually having Jack see himself in the United States at work in the laboratory there.

"Jack, it's time to go home now. Are you ready to leave work?"

"Yes, I can leave work now. Everyone has packed up and I want to leave too."

"Good, now I want you to begin your routine of leaving, telling what happens next."

"I'm walking to the elevators. An elevator car comes to my floor and I get on. I push G for the ground floor and wait. The doors open and I exit the building into the parking lot. I walk toward my jeep and unlock it. Once inside, I look at my phone. I send a message to Haley that says, *I'm coming home, baby.* She sends a message back. I read it and it says, *Can't wait. I have a great dinner planned for us.* I feel something in my chest, in my heart. I love her. She is sweet natured and loving. I begin driving the jeep, leaving the parking area and heading out on the road. Home is northeast in Alpharetta."

Jack begins to tighten his fists and his face reddens. His breathing is now fast.

"I can't find it. I know I live there, but I don't know the way. How can I get home to Haley?"

Jack was visibly upset and Dr. Alonso brought him out of the session. He'd never seen a man become so frustrated during hypnosis. Once he had calmed down, he asked, "How are you feeling, Jack?"

"I can't believe that I know something, but I don't know it. It's the most screwed up feeling in the world."

"I'm sorry you're frustrated. Let's try again tomorrow. Get a good rest tonight. You're still doing well."

Before sleep, Jack practiced the affirmations and fell into bed extremely tired. During the night, he dreamed about Haley. He could see her clearly, touch her hair and look into her eyes. He knew they were deeply in love. The next morning, he still felt frustrated. He wanted to remember how they met, when they married — all the stuff that people do together. He needed to know. It was a big part of what built a relationship, the memories you made together. How could he uncover it?

Looking at his messages, he saw that Karla and Marcos scheduled a meeting with both Presidents again. It would be today at 10:00 a.m. Jack confirmed his attendance and knew he would need to be taken to the SCIF where they had met his first day.

He needed to forget about Haley for now. No, no — he had to stop thinking that way. He was not going to forget about Haley. He needed to remember her, even though his work was important too. Today, he would ask if he could get a message to her. *I want her to know I love and care about her.*

Jack left the SCIF after the teleconference with Marcos and the Presidents of each country. Marcos walked back with him toward the domed area. "Marcos, I have been so busy since I came here. This is only the second time I've seen this part of Brazil Underground."

"Jack, you need to get out more," he said, jokingly. Jack laughed with him.

"I've been remembering Haley, my wife. Mostly, its intense feelings surrounding her. I want to let her know I love her, and I'm beginning to remember. Is there a way we can do this?"

Marcos looked at him seriously now. "Of course. This is not difficult, but we have to coordinate it. Let me see what I can do and I will send you a message."

"That would be great. What are you thinking? How would I communicate with her?"

"I'm going to see if we can get a secure phone call with her. Do you have her cell phone number?"

"Uh, no, I must have forgotten it."

Marcos laughed again. "I don't even know why I asked you that. We'll find out, Jack. Brazil Underground can find out almost anything."

"Thanks Marcos!"

Jack went about his day, still thinking of Haley periodically. Marcos messaged that a secure call would happen in the SCIF at 8:00 pm. He canceled his appointment for hypnosis tonight. This was more important. Making his way toward the secure room, he did not know exactly what he would say to her. Marcos was already waiting inside for him.

"You're here. Only important people like you get these extra perks, Jack. Keep it hush-hush or everyone will want to do this."

"I will keep it a secret. I'm nervous."

"Hey, my wife makes me nervous too," he said, chuckling. "Here's how this will work. You will see her, but she will only be able to hear you. It's too complicated to get into, but without her being at a secure location, we had to do it this way. I felt it would help though if you could actually see her."

"It's great."

"Okay, let me put the call through." Marcos made sure it was working and then left the room.

Jack could hear the phone ring and Haley answered, appearing on the screen quickly.

"Haley," he said.

"Jack, it's really you. I'm so glad we're talking."

He watched her facial expressions. This was his sweet woman. He did know her, even though he couldn't remember so many things.

"Haley, I asked to communicate with you because I have something important to say. I am remembering you, bits and pieces here and there. I hope everything, all the memories are coming back to me soon. I want you to know the first thing I remembered about you is the way I feel inside. I love you, baby. I promise you I'm trying to heal as fast as I can."

Tears streamed down Haley's face. She grabbed a tissue and laughed. "See, I have tissues nearby, Jack. I had a feeling I might need them tonight."

He laughed at her humor.

"Jack, they said the call cannot be very long. I love you with everything I have inside me. I am waiting for you, along with your family — our family. Jack, I'm pregnant. We're going to have a baby."

"Wow, that's amazing. When is the baby due?"

"Not for a while. I just found out. You probably don't remember the night you knocked me up, but I do. It was right before you left in early December."

"Haley, I love you and I'm coming home. I just don't know when yet."

Marcos came into the room and whispered, "One minute left."

"Jack, we have so much to talk about and catch up on. Honey, if you don't remember everything, it's okay. We'll have fun discovering each other all over again."

"There you go," he said. "I'll be thinking of you each day and night. I have to go. I love you, baby."

"I love you too!"

Marcos clicked off the call and Jack hung his head on the table and cried. "She's beautiful, Marcos. That's Haley, my wife. And, she's pregnant. I just found out we're having a baby."

"Congratulations, Jack. I am so happy for you. God has a plan for you. You survived that crash for many reasons."

THE END

Thank you for reading *A Dose of Discovery*, Book 2 of The Big Pharma Series. The author loves to hear your thoughts and accolades. Please leave a written review when you have a moment.

If you have not done so already, download the free prequel novella to this series, *A Dose of Danger*, at www.lotusjames.com

Nestled throughout the world are corporate and government entities with the power to control the populace through the delivery of their products. In this series, the Foster family and their investigative contacts strive to:

- Solve murder mysteries
- Avoid surveillance
- Thwart personal threats
- Experience love
- Reveal greed
- Expose to the world

The diabolical plans of Big Pharma

Read Book 3

Find out more at www.lotusjames.com

Lotus James

About The Author

Within every human life, there will be ecstatic, loving, joyous moments along with those we wish to avoid, such as peril, loss, betrayal and grief. Lotus James fills her stories with romance, danger, and threatening events. Her mission is to weave stories that allow the reader to experience emotional peaks and valleys through her characters instead of real life.

On a more serious note, she is a light social drinker, having celebrated with a glass of wine at the completion of her most recent book. She works too much and needs to schedule leisurely days of pampering here and there.

Lotus loves to travel and explore new locales where her mind is busy gathering ideas and information and constructing fictional scenarios in that setting.

She states writing is a necessary component in her life, much like breathing. Her mind inhales images, feelings, smells, sounds and history and must somehow exhale them into existence.

She views herself as fortunate to play at work. However, it is often difficult and mind-boggling, like an enormous puzzle with some pieces missing. When that occurs, Lotus takes a short pampering break or perhaps a nap. When she is feeling unfocused, naps can be a necessity, not a luxury. Sometimes, dreaming about the next move in the storyline is a creative option.

Follow Lotus as she breaks out exciting, fresh stories as frequently as she can dream them up. Make sure to stay informed of happenings by signing up at her website – www.lotusjames.com

Lotus James

414